# Revenge IS SWEET

FELICE STEVENS

**Revenge is Sweet**

felicestevens.com





Published by Good Man Press

ISBN: 979-8-88949-000-5 (Digital eBook)
ISBN: 979-8-88949-001-2 (Trade Paperback)

First Edition, March 2023
Printed in the United States of America

Cover Art by Reese Dante
Cover content is for illustrative purposes only. Any person depicted on the cover is a model.
Edited by Keren Reed
Copy Editing and Proofreading by Flat Earth Editing
Additional Proofreading by Lyrical Lines

# DEDICATION

To my friends. The ones who stick by me, in good times and bad.

# ACKNOWLEDGMENTS

Thanks always to Keren, whom I knew would be Team Miles the moment I started writing him. Thanks to Hope and Jess, for being the best of the best. Thank you to Dianne, for always being there, no matter what or when. And last but never least, thanks to Reese, for everything.

And as always, I'm most grateful to my readers who give me the chance to do what I love. Thank you for your reviews, which help keep my books alive. I appreciate each and every one—no matter how short or long.

Don't forget to click the link at the end of the book and read the steamy short!

# Chapter ONE

"Ready for this, Lyon?"

My brother stood by my side, and our eyes met in the full-length mirror. While we were similar in looks, Scott's good nature and lightheartedness were apparent in the easy smile he wore. Unlike me, the "angry Elliot brother" as I'd been called.

Unfairly, in my opinion. I wasn't angry *all* the time. I simply couldn't deal with people, and listening to their bullshit annoyed me. Some people hid it well. I did not.

"Sure am. But where's Dan? He's late." I checked my watch, the beginning of a migraine blossoming behind my eyes. "That dumbass better not make me wait on my wedding day."

"He'll be here, don't worry," Scott soothed. "He's probably caught in traffic."

"Bastard's always late, but you'd think on his best friend's wedding day he'd get his head out of his ass and be here on time."

Dan and I grew up together. Our mothers were best friends and had met our fathers at a college fraternity party. We went to the same private school in the city and used to spend almost all our holidays and summers with each other's families. Naturally, we decided to go to the same college as our fathers and room together. Dan might not be the sharpest tool in the woodshed, but he was fun-loving and up for anything, no matter how wild and crazy, and he was loyal. Most of all, I could trust him. I'd never let on to his girlfriends if he was seeing someone on the sly, and he'd never talked of any of my exploits with women…or men.

Yeah, I'd kept my bisexuality on the down-low, not because I cared what other people thought, but I could barely keep up with the women I was sleeping with. Adding guys into the equation, while double the fun, would also double my headaches, which would inevitably occur when people found out. Better to go a little undercover when I wanted to get some ass.

Literally.

Speaking of headaches, my brain throbbed as if my skull were being used as a punching bag, and I stomped across the living room to one of the three bathrooms to splash water on my face and swallow three extra-strength Tylenol. The presidential suite was palatial, but I had no time or desire to admire the stunning view of Central Park spread out before me nor the vast array of food and drinks provided.

There was no need to. I couldn't eat and had barely slept these past few nights. No, I wasn't nervous. It was simply the fact that tomorrow I'd wake up and Lindsey would be there… forever. Was I prepared for that? I wasn't sure. I had no idea what stability looked like. I'd never expected to marry—my parents divorced when Scott was one and I was three. Both remarried and promptly divorced again.

And again.

And again.

Leaving me to realize that marriage was for fools and suckers.

So why was I standing here, then, waiting to get married, when I didn't believe in the institution?

Lindsey.

We'd met at a benefit a few years earlier, and she'd become someone I actually liked. Lindsey possessed a razor-sharp business mind and could keep up with me. Not to mention, she had a gorgeous face and body. Even Dan wasn't mad that I didn't go out with him anymore. *"Can't blame you, bro. If I had that waiting for me at home, I wouldn't be out boozing it up either."*

Did I love her? *Hmm.* I mean, I liked her a lot. We had fun, and I trusted her—enough to agree to a partnership between my business and hers. She was the creator of Dorado, an upscale brand of tequila and had suggested a deal between her liquor company and my exclusive men's club, The Lyon's Den.

Like the boss babe she was, Lindsey proposed to me and suggested a merger in every way possible—both in our personal lives and our businesses. Once we were married, we could forge ahead and open up clubs all over the US and eventually, the world.

When it came to the business, Lindsey was ruthless. I'd seen her in action when she'd believed—rightly or wrongly—that she'd been cheated in a business transaction, and let me tell you, a six-foot rattlesnake was cuddlier.

I couldn't care less about getting married and wasn't that keen on going worldwide, but she did, and Lindsey Cunningham always got what she wanted. And she'd decided she wanted me, and I figured why not? I was going into the marriage with eyes wide open. She was my friend and business partner, and the fact that she was smoking hot didn't hurt, but even when we had sex it was like receiving directions from a CEO: *"Harder. Faster. Right there. Lick it. More, goddamn you. Yeah, that's it. Now fuck me."*

Lucky for me, she was a fast orgasmer—*Is that a word?*—and her tight inner muscles clenching my dick gave enough friction for me to come hard and quickly as well.

I wondered if she thought about anyone else when I put it in her.

Probably.

I definitely did.

Not anyone specific. I didn't cheat on her, not because I didn't find other people tempting or there wasn't opportunity—God knew I had enough cleavage shoved in my face, as well as the occasional squeeze of my ass from interested men. But I didn't cheat on Lindsey because it was wrong. I might be a bastard in business, but when it came to personal relationships, once you were my friend, you had me for life. I was a loyal fucking soldier and would die on your hill, at your side.

So while this wasn't a grand love match on either side, I would be faithful. I would be there for her. I trusted her—not in the way I did Dan, of course—but she and I had been together long enough that I allowed her into my tiny circle that consisted of my brother, our great-uncle Harry, and Dan.

Out in the living room again, I spied Dan's younger brother, Miles, hiding in a corner as usual. I still couldn't understand why Lindsey had asked him to be one of her bridesmen, but I didn't bother arguing with her. She loved him, and he, of course, couldn't refuse her. Miles was quiet, bookish, and not a partier—the complete opposite of Dan. I'd noticed his sweet smiles and hot body during the summers we'd all spent together, but he was on the no-no list. Dan's younger brother. Untouchable.

Miles stared out the window, silent and unobtrusive. Scott handed me a Scotch, and after gulping half the glass, I tipped my head toward the pensive figure.

"When did Miles the Mouse arrive?"

Scott's eyes danced with amusement. "He's been here the whole time."

I snorted. "Figures. Does he ever get out of the bookstore mindset? I think I've heard him speak above a whisper maybe four times in my life."

Scott shrugged. "I don't know why you've always looked down on him. He's a nice guy. Nothing wrong with that."

How Dan and Miles were brothers was a quirk of nature no one could explain. Where Dan was loud and boisterous, always up for a party, a six-pack with tequila shots and a woman or two in his bed, Miles cringed when meeting people, barely spoke, avoided crowds, and rarely drank more than a glass of wine. Dan was a quick-to-smile, dark-haired, hulking, six-foot-three, beefy football type. Miles was six foot, lean, with a swimmer's sculpted muscles, and possessed thick golden waves and big blue eyes you rarely saw, as he usually kept them focused on the ground.

I'd known him forever, and I didn't think we'd had one conversation that wasn't about the weather. I knew nothing about his personal life other than he was gay and liked to swim.

Oh, except that he'd once had a massive crush on me, which Dan had revealed when he'd been drunk off his ass. When I'd asked for details about how he knew, Dan refused to say anything further and had warned me with a fist to my nose to leave his little brother alone and never even think about having sex with him. Family was off-limits; plus he knew my MO—fuck them, then forget them.

*"If you even think of Miles like that, I'll fucking cut your nuts off. He's too nice for a dog like you. He deserves someone better. Miles has already been hurt enough by guys he thought he could trust. Stay away from him."*

I assured Dan that the thought had never crossed my mind. A blatant lie, because I'd spent plenty of summers at their family pool, admiring Miles's tight ass and the outline of a surprisingly healthy dick in his skimpy bathing suits. I'd pretend to be reading in my lounge chair while I'd watch him churn through the water in the pool, doing laps. I didn't look down on him, and I wouldn't mind *going* down on him.

The idea of fucking Miles the Mouse, as I'd dubbed him, brought a smile to my face. I thought he'd faint if I ever came within breathing distance of him. But all that shyness was damn sexy. I wondered if he'd brought a date today and made a mental note to check the guy out, to see his type.

As if sensing my thoughts, Miles glanced over his shoulder and met my eyes. His brows flew up, and he did an immediate about-face, but not before a blush crept up his neck to his cheeks and his teeth worried a plump bottom lip. I grew hard, desire slamming into me like a bolt of lightning.

It must've been the fact that Lindsey and I hadn't slept together in the months leading up to the wedding that made me horny as a damn goat. Since college, I hadn't been without sex for a week, and I was ready to explode, but all the wedding plans stressed Lindsey out to the max, and sex, she informed me, was the last thing on her mind. Right now, the fucking couch pillows looked good to me, and I contemplated locking myself in the bathroom and jerking off, simply to release the tension that had me coiled so tight.

I glanced at my watch. Dan was over an hour late, and I was pissed as shit. Where the hell was he? Lindsey must be losing her mind—the woman had her entire life scheduled to the minute. I was lucky she made time for sex when we were having it. If I wanted a morning quickie, I knew to wake her up early so as not to make her late for the rest of her day. If that happened, I was in big trouble. Her teeth were sharp. Ask me how I knew.

My phone vibrated, and when I saw Dan's name pop up, relief rushed through me. I hit the screen.

"Where the hell are you, man? I hope you have a good excuse, like you're in a hospital bed getting ready for surgery because nothing else will do for Lindsey. I'm surprised I haven't heard her screaming from the floor below. She's gonna chew you up and spit you out."

"Listen, Lyon."

"No, there's no time for excuses. Just get your sorry butt up to the suite, and you can kiss my ass later and beg Linds to be forgiven. She will. She's always liked you."

"Yeah, I know. Look, Lyon, I have to tell you something."

"What?" I paced the suite, my agitation growing by the second. "What's so important that it can't wait until you see me?"

"I'm not coming. And neither is Lindsey."

I laughed. "What the fuck are you talking about?"

"Lindsey and I…we're in love. We eloped to Vegas yesterday and got married."

I couldn't stop laughing. "You and Lindsey? Are you fucking kidding me? Tell me this is for one of those stupid reality shows you watch. I'm supposed to get mad and curse you out and then *surprise*! Someone pops out of a closet or a bedroom and says it's all a joke." I strode around the suite, throwing open the closed doors.

"It's not a joke, Lyon," Lindsey broke into the conversation with that no-nonsense voice I knew all too well. "I decided I couldn't marry someone I didn't love, who didn't love me or make me happy. I never laughed with you like I do with Dan."

"That's because he's a fucking idiot." I ran my hand through my hair and shouted into the phone, "So you made everyone come here and let me think we were having a wedding? Guests, the caterer, band…everything. Now I have to go and tell everyone the wedding is off and look like a goddamned fool!"

From the corner of my eye I saw Miles's jaw drop and his big blue eyes widen with shock. Scott, too, stood pale-faced and frozen.

"Oh, please. You can handle it. Don't pretend it's some big love affair and I broke your heart."

Maybe that was what turned the tables for me. Here I was, planning to give her the rest of my life…and she didn't give a damn. She was as cold-blooded as the snake I'd compared her to, and as it turned out, rightly so. "Hardly. You're just a business deal down the toilet, Lindsey."

"Don't talk to her like that. She's my wife."

It was Dan's betrayal that hurt me to my core, even more so than Lindsey's.

"How could you do this to me, Dan? Sleeping with the woman I was going to marry? You were my best friend since we were little kids, and you threw it all away for someone you've only known a few years. A nobody. A nothing."

"I said don't speak about her like that," Dan roared.

"I'll say whatever the fuck I want," I yelled. "You fucking traitor. How long have you two been screwing behind my back?"

I dropped to the couch, and Scott sat next to me and put a hand on my rigid shoulder. I barely felt his touch. I barely felt anything at all.

"It started three months ago. You went on a business trip to London, and you hardly called her. She was lonely, so I went over there to keep her company."

"And by company you mean fucking her."

"We didn't mean for it to happen. We both had too much to drink, and…I'll admit I made the first move. She's beautiful, and I couldn't help it."

"You couldn't help it? You couldn't help what? Kissing her? I could even forgive that. But sleeping with her? In my bed? That you couldn't help? News flash, yes, you fucking could have helped it. You're my best friend—*were* my best friend. We grew up together. I trusted you. I loved you almost as much as my own brother. When I asked you to watch out for her, I didn't mean for you to stick your dick in. When I said we shared everything, I didn't mean Lindsey. I would *never* have done that to you."

"Let's get this straight, Lyon. I didn't say no." Lindsey's nonchalance shouldn't have surprised me. After all, we weren't madly in love. "Dan felt bad in the morning, but I didn't. The night I spent with Dan woke something inside me, and I realized you and I were going through the motions. I didn't want to spend the next forty or fifty years like that. Unlike you, Dan tells me how much he wants and needs me. He has emotions, he's sensitive…"

I snorted. "Keep going. You make me sound like a robot. Like I'm not human."

"Sometimes you're not. You're a machine—wake up, exercise, eat, work, come home, have sex, and go to sleep. I could be anyone sharing your bed. Even a blow-up doll. Face it, Lyon. You don't love me. You just hate that I'm with Dan. I'll bet in a week you won't even miss me."

I opened my mouth to deny it, but nothing came out. I refused to ask her if she'd ever cared for me at all or if it was an act she'd put on. I didn't want to know. I'd already been humiliated enough.

The hurt that had tied knots around my heart didn't stem from the fact that she'd left me. Maybe deep down I'd expected it because it kept happening all my life with my parents. I thought I was smarter, but it turned out I was the stupid fool after all. It hadn't been a grand love with Lindsey, but I'd believed she was my friend and was angry with myself for giving her a part of me she didn't deserve.

But Dan was different. His deceit hurt so bad, I pressed my hand to my chest, the pain so intense, I thought I was having a heart attack.

Dan betrayed me and our friendship. He'd gone behind my back and violated the code of our brotherhood in the worst way. It was his hand I'd held when we went into our first day of kindergarten, not my mother's. We learned to swim side by side, rode our first roller coaster sitting next to each other, sneaked out and got drunk (and sick) together. I'd spent my whole life with him. He'd been there the night I'd met Lindsey, had helped me pick out the engagement ring from the pictures she'd given me. He knew how hard it was for me to take this step, and was always there to listen to my fears. Every single important moment of my life, I'd spent with him.

Now, with this one action, this violation of our friendship, he became a stranger. No longer the man I could count on and trust with my life. It was akin to cutting off a limb, and hot tears rushed to my eyes at the excruciating loss, because like that amputated arm or leg, I'd feel the phantom pain long after he was gone.

And just like that pain, it turned out our friendship wasn't real.

"Both of you were too chickenshit to come and speak to me face-to-face. Because you know what you're doing is so messed up. I can't *believe* you, Dan. Who the hell does that—stealing your best friend's fiancée? Telling them the day of the wedding? That's the lowest of the low. You always said family first. *Nothing* comes between family. I thought we were like that. You called me your second brother."

I shifted a quick glance to Miles, who met my eyes for only a brief moment before lowering them. Did he know what Dan had planned, or was he caught by surprise too? Maybe he was told to act unaware. Knowing how close the two brothers were, I couldn't believe Dan hadn't said anything to Miles. My anger grew as Dan fell over his words in his attempt to explain.

"Yeah…well…if I thought you really cared about her, maybe I wouldn't have, but you know it wasn't a love match. You said it yourself—it was like the merger of two companies. Lindsey deserves someone who loves her, and I'm going to give her everything she needs that you couldn't."

"Hopefully not an STD, considering the trash I've seen you with. Better get tested, Lindsey." I wanted to hurt them like they'd hurt me. Childish, maybe, but I was too worn out to care if I got down and dirty in the mud.

"Shut the fuck up," Dan snapped. "Once I was with Lindsey, I never looked at another woman."

"How very fucking noble of you," I snarled.

"Just deal with it, Lyon," Lindsey cut in with her brisk I'm-ready-for-this-to-be-over tone. "Tell people whatever you want. I don't care. But remember, we're still going to have to deal with each other, business-wise."

"You're kidding me if you think I'm going to stock your tequila in my clubs."

"We have a contract. Period. If you think of backing out, I'll sue you. And I'm bringing Dan into the business, so you'd better be prepared to see both of us."

"You're in for a rude awakening. Dan only managed to make it as far as he has because his grandfather started the company." In the early 1900s, Grandpa Herb had laid the foundation for what eventually became Halloran's, one of the world's largest luxury department store chains. The family sold half of it to a private equity firm, receiving an obscene amount of money. Dan pretended to go into the office, but from the number of hours he spent playing golf and drinking at my club, he didn't break a sweat over his cushy job as chief operating officer of brand development, whatever the fuck that was.

"He had enough brains to recognize you weren't appreciating me. Now you're alone, and we got married. So who's the fool now?"

The desire to terminate this conversation and put myself out of my misery far outweighed my need to further spar with Dan and Lindsey. "I hope you have the marriage you both deserve. And fuck you." With that sweet parting message, I hung up.

Instantly, Scott began to fire off questions to me. "What the fuck, man? Dan and Lindsey? That lying bastard. What the hell happened?"

"Three months they've been sneaking around, and yet they both act like it's my fault." I shrugged, pretending it didn't matter. But it did. God, I wanted to scream, but I refused to let anyone, even my own brother, know how deep the knife cut into my flesh. "They played me. I'm positive they're laughing about it, but I'll make sure I have the last laugh. Somehow."

My attention shifted to Miles, who sat in the corner, head down, focused on his phone, rapidly texting. I was sure Dan had reached out to give him the rundown, as every once in a while those big baby blues shifted from the screen to me, then immediately again to the phone in his lap. I jumped from my seat and stalked over to him.

"Did you know?"

His fingers stilled. "Wha-what?"

I didn't miss how he instinctively shrank away, pressing himself into the chair, trying to put as much space between the two of us as he could. Perversely, I leaned in closer, until my lips were a mere inch from his soft ones. I could feel the puff of his breath against my cheek.

"I asked if you knew that your brother, Dan, was fucking my fiancée. And that they were going to elope and leave me to clean up the mess they created. Did you know?" I poked his chest. "Did you, Miles?"

Long golden lashes fluttered. "I swear, Lyon. I didn't." A pulse jumped in his neck.

"You'd better not be lying to me." I captured his gaze, and his chest rose and fell. "Are you, Miles?" I licked my lips, and Miles's breathing accelerated. "You love Dan. Are you covering up for him and lying to me?"

# Chapter TWO

It had been a very long time since I'd been this close to Lyon Elliot. The last time was years earlier at a New Year's Eve party at Dan's apartment. Everyone but me was drunk off their asses on shots of tequila and bottles of champagne, while I'd pretended to keep pace, drinking club soda. On my fourth trip to the bathroom, I'd opened the door and found Lyon in front of me: eyes closed, his tongue down a woman's throat, his pants at his hips, her hands groping his exposed cock. I'd frozen in place. It was so filthy and primal, but I'd been unable to tear my eyes away from the sight of his big, beautiful dick in her small hands.

When his fingers crept up her naked thigh and hiked up her skirt, I'd grown afraid they were going to have sex right in front of me, and I'd fled. But the memory of Lyon half-naked and moaning fortified me for the cold winter months, when I would lie in bed and think of Lyon giving me his cock. Or me deep-throating him. Foolish, I knew, because Lyon wasn't into men. He always boasted about how much he loved tits.

But a guy could dream.

Now he and those delicious lips of his were right in my face. Unfortunately, it wasn't like my fantasy, where he kissed me and told me how he'd always wanted me. Instead they were twisted in an almost feral snarl.

"What? No. Of course I didn't know. I'm as shocked as you are."

Maybe it was a trick of light, but I flinched at the devastation behind Lyon's beautiful eyes. They'd always fascinated me—they could glow a rich indigo-blue or turn dark and menacing, like the angry gray of encroaching storm clouds. But today they were flat. Cold. Empty.

His mouth curled in a sneer of rage. "I don't know if I should believe you. After all, you'd say anything to protect him. He's your brother. You two stick up for each other."

While true, I knew Dan's faults, and there was no way in hell I could defend his actions today.

"Not this time. He's been sleeping with your fiancée, and they've eloped. That's pretty indefensible."

"He's fucking dead to me." Lyon walked away, his brother at his heels. The door to one of the bedrooms slammed, and I was alone. My stomach sank at the depth of Lyon's anger. This was a blow to their friendship that I doubted could be repaired. And while I was close with my brother and loved him no matter what, Lyon's hurt and embarrassment were palpable, and I felt sorry for him.

Dan's texts hadn't stopped, and I scrolled through the pictures of him and Lindsey at the Little White Chapel, getting married by an Elvis impersonator and drinking champagne. A video of them kissing was the last thing to pop up on my screen, and frankly, I wasn't in the mood. I clicked out of the message and slipped my phone into my suit jacket.

Scott and I were the only people in the suite, and with him taking care of Lyon, it was left to me to go appear before the assembled guests and make the announcement that there would be no wedding.

God, I hated this shit.

There was a reason I owned a bookstore—the customers kept mostly to themselves and only talked to me when they needed help. I didn't do well with large groups of people. Ever since college, I'd lost all trust in people. Except Dan. He'd always been there for me, the person I could turn to when I needed help.

Now with this stunt he'd pulled, I was adrift and confused. I loved Dan and looked up to him, but what he'd done to Lyon…

Heaving a sigh, I left the suite, wincing at the sound of breaking glass coming from behind the closed door. I hustled to the elevator, eager to put as much space as possible between me and all that furious rage.

When I opened the door to the room being used for the ceremony, fifty sets of eyes pinned me, and my heart pounded. A loud murmur rose, and I swallowed. I despised speaking in public. Sweat ran down my back.

"Uh…hi, everyone. I…uh…I'm Miles, Dan's brother. And…well…I'm sorry to say…uh…there isn't going to be a wedding today. So…yeah. Everyone is okay, no one's sick or anything. Sorry for the inconvenience. And thank you."

I tried to make it out of the room unscathed, but Uncle Harry, somehow as stealthy as a ninja despite his seventy-plus years caught up with me outside the double doors.

"Miles. You don't think you're going to make an announcement like that and walk away without talking to me, do you?" He peered up at me from behind his large, black-framed glasses. "What happened? He get cold feet, or did he come to his senses and realize she wasn't the one?"

Uncle Harry was an enigma. He was Lyon's great-uncle, but he'd always been more of a parent to Lyon and Scott than either their mother or father. While their parents went through partners like potato chips, Harry had never married and lived alone with his cats. It was Harry's house that Scott and Lyon would go to for Christmas and Thanksgiving, because Charles and Marianne Elliot were never home, too busy traveling the world, getting married and divorced. Last I'd heard, Papa Elliot was up to wife number six, and Mama Elliot had recently divorced husband number four and was working on number five.

Harry had become everyone's adopted uncle, and over the years, I'd come to think of him almost as much my family as Lyon's. He came often to my bookstore to browse, and I'd made him a special place, separate from the rest of the customers, where he could sit and read with a cup of tea.

I couldn't help but confide in him. "It's worse than that, Uncle Harry. Dan and Lindsey eloped to Vegas. They got married last night."

His jaw dropped. "That son of a B. And she…I told Lyon she was a snake in the grass, but he insisted she was his friend." He shook his head. "Poor Lyon. Where is he? Maybe I should go see him."

Thinking of how I'd left Lyon upstairs, I wasn't certain anything could help, but then I remembered Lyon's tenth birthday and how excited he'd been because his parents had seemingly put aside their differences and agreed to come home to celebrate his entrance to double digits. The party had started at six, and he'd waited hours for them to show. By nine, it had become blatantly apparent they were both no-shows and hadn't even bothered to send word, and Lyon was fighting back tears. Uncle Harry took him by the hand to a corner, and they sat, simply talking. I had no idea what was said, but Lyon finished off the evening with a smile.

Why that memory stuck with me I had no idea, but if anyone could help Lyon at this terrible time, it was going to be Uncle Harry.

"I think that's a great idea. I'll take you up to the suite." I took his arm, and we walked toward the elevator banks, away from the people streaming out of the room. I tried to close my ears to the murmurings I couldn't help but hear.

*"I'm sure he got cold feet. Lyon isn't the marrying kind."*

*"She must've found out he cheated."*

*"I bet she caught him in the act. I never liked him for her."*

I huffed out a sigh, as upset hearing the falsehoods as if they were speaking about me. Why, I couldn't say. Lyon and I weren't close. I could barely consider us acquaintances. But he'd always been a constant in my life as Dan's best friend.

And yeah, my secret fantasy lover.

Upstairs, I grew nervous as we approached the suite but also hopeful that maybe Scott had calmed Lyon down. When we walked inside, it was silent. Lyon sat on the couch, head in his hands, tuxedo jacket off and tie undone. He glanced up, and the rush of relief on his face assured me I'd done the right thing by bringing Uncle Harry.

"He stabbed me in the back, Uncle Harry. After all these years…" His lips trembled.

I'd never seen Lyon, a man who rarely expressed any emotion, as vulnerable as he was at this moment.

Harry left my side to sit by Lyon. "Miles said they got married. Is that really true?"

"Yeah. It is."

"That *bastard*." Hearing Uncle Harry swear shocked me. He'd always been unbothered and mild-mannered, so for him to use that language was a surprise. "I'm sorry, Miles, but I'm not going to sugarcoat it because he's your brother."

"I don't expect you to. I can't stand up for him on this."

Lyon's stone-cold eyes met mine, and I shivered as the chill rippled through me. There was no light or life behind them.

"I don't ever want to hear his name again. As far as I'm concerned, he's dead to me."

A painful jolt hit my chest. "You can't mean that. Emotions are running high now, but maybe one day you'll be able to talk to him."

"Don't you dare tell me what I will be able to do." With his lips curled and his eyes narrowed, if he could've hissed at me, he would've. "Get the fuck out of my face, Miles."

Uncle Harry threw me a comforting nod and tipped his head to the door. No one had to ask me twice. I ran my ass out of there and didn't stop until I got to my bookstore in Brooklyn, The Book Nook—not the most original name, but it served its purpose.

I received a few odd stares when I took my place behind the curved and pitted wooden counter, and I remembered I still wore my tux. Brittany, one of the college students I'd hired to help Gordon and me, smiled and waved before returning to shelving the books customers left scattered around the store.

Brow furrowed, Gordon scratched his bristly chin. "Why're you here? What happened? I didn't think you'd be in today. Did you leave the wedding early because you were concerned about the store? You don't have to worry. Brittany's been a big help, and Kelvin said he could come in if necessary."

"No, it had nothing to do with that." With a sigh, I sank into the leather chair I'd rescued from an antique store. "There was no wedding."

Gordon took off his purple-rimmed glasses to gawk at

me. "What? No wedding? Dan's friend chickened out? Guess you called it. You said he wasn't going to go through with it."

"Actually, no. Lyon showed up. It was Lindsey. She didn't."

Gordon's face was a picture of disbelief. "Get the hell outta here. She jilted him at the altar? *Damn.* I'm sure he didn't like that. The little I've heard of Lyon Elliot is he's a man you don't fuck with."

"Yeah. Let's just say he was not pleased."

"I'll bet. What happened? She realized what a prick he was? Maybe he sucks in bed."

Doubtful, I thought to myself, the heat of that one lusty eyeful I'd gotten seared on my brain. "I bet he sucks really well." When Gordon's brows flew up, I realized what I said, and my face burned. "I—uh, I mean…"

Blithely unaware of my inner turmoil, Gordon propped his chin in his hand and sighed. "I know what you mean. I wouldn't mind trying out the merchandise. I remember when he was in some Hamptons magazine I was flipping through in my doctor's office. They had him featured at a pool party in a tiny bathing suit, and *damn.*" Gordon fanned himself. "He's got it going on down there."

Saved by several customers who approached with armfuls of books, I pointed to the register. "You ring and I'll bag."

Gordon, as good-natured as he was clueless about my secret crush, chatted with the customers, keeping up a steady stream of conversation about the messy royal family, Hollywood gossip, and style trends. And while I was happy to see my business booming, I couldn't help wondering how Lyon was doing. Dan was frolicking in Sin City, and Lyon was left shattered and alone. It wasn't fair, but I sure as hell knew life didn't always play on the straight and narrow.

It was Well past seven by the time Gordon, Brittany, and I finished closing the store, and my feet ached. I wanted nothing more than to eat some spicy salmon and yellowtail sushi, lie on my couch, and watch something mindless on television. Accomplishing the first task was easy, and I juggled the bag with my dinner as I unlocked the front door of my town house.

It might seem odd for a single man to live all by himself in a hundred-year-old, three-story house, but I loved my home with all its creaky floors, sporadic heat, and constant need for repairs. While Dan lived in a super-modern high-rise with all the amenities, I preferred the old charm of tin ceilings, crown molding, and marble fireplaces in almost every room. It was the first thing I'd bought when I came into my trust fund. I wanted something of my own that I could make into a refuge from the outside world.

The shining wood floor of the long hallway led to the living room, which I'd established as my hang-out spot. I set the sushi on the coffee table, and lifting my hands overhead, took a deep stretch. Nothing felt as good as kicking off your shoes after a day of standing on your feet, and I'd untucked my shirt from my pants, intending to go upstairs, take off the rest of my clothes, and get comfortable, when the doorbell rang.

"Who the fuck is bothering me on a Sunday night?" Ignoring it in the hopes they'd go away, I unbuttoned my shirt and headed up to my bedroom.

But the bell continued ringing, and now someone was pounding on the door. Fearful they'd break the delicate original glass, I reversed course and hurried down to see who the hell it was. The neighborhood was one of the safest in the city, and I was on the annoyed side of being overtired from the emotional upheaval of the day, which was why I flung open the door without stopping to peek through the curtains.

"Lyon?" My astonishment couldn't have been greater if I'd seen William Shakespeare himself standing there. "What're you doing here?"

He leaned that long, muscular body against the doorframe and smiled at me with more warmth than he'd ever directed my way.

"Can I come in? I-I really don't want to be alone tonight, and I was hoping maybe I could hang out with you."

His hair lay in messy waves over his forehead, and his eyes were a bit unfocused, leading me to believe he might've had a few too many drinks before coming, but it was the slight tremble of those full lips that tugged at my heart.

"Of course." I held the door open, and he walked inside, but instead of passing by me, he stopped and put a hand on my shoulder.

"Thank you."

My stomach flip-flopped and went into a free fall.

*Oh, God. What the hell did I just do?*

Miles looked good enough to eat with his undone shirt exposing his pecs and ridged abs. I'd never had a nipple fetish with Lindsey, but those tight red buds of his surrounded by soft hair called to me, and I wanted to put my mouth on them and suck until they turned hard.

I smiled at him. "Thank you for letting me in."

His lashes lowered, and once again that blush stained his cheeks. "It's okay. I'm surprised to see you, but I'm happy to help any way I can."

*Oh, you will, baby. And I can't wait.*

My belly tightened, but I merely nodded. "Thank you. You're being kind."

"Come into the living room." Miles waved to me. "I have sushi, and you're welcome to share if you're hungry."

The house was charming and in keeping with the old-world sophistication of the historic neighborhood. I'd never been inside, but its understated elegance suited Miles. Dan's apartment had black lacquer and mirrors everywhere, even on the ceiling in the bedroom, and I'd always said he should make it a nightclub, it was so glitzy. Lindsey hated it, used to say she could never live in a place with so many reflections of herself in the morning. Now it would likely be her home. A stab hit my heart.

*Focus.*

Miles pointed to a large sectional couch. "Have a seat. I'll just run into the kitchen and get some plates for us."

I sat but didn't touch the food. "Don't bother. I'll probably only have one or two pieces." I lowered my gaze. "I don't have much of an appetite tonight."

Miles made a sympathetic sound and sank next to me. "Have you eaten anything?"

I shook my head. "I-I couldn't." A little white lie. Uncle Harry had made me a sandwich and I ate it to please him, but it'd tasted like straw.

"You're the last person I expected to see tonight. Why did you come here?" Immediately his cheeks turned fiery red. "That was mean. Of course I'm glad to see you're handling it so well, but I figured you'd be with your friends. Or maybe go home with Uncle Harry."

"He tried." I gave Miles my best smile. "But as persuasive as he can be, I didn't want to be with him tonight. And I sent Scott and Beth home. They have Lilah to worry about, and there was nothing they could do for me."

"So you showed up here? I'm just trying to make sense of it."

I shrugged. "I don't know. It's just that we've spent our whole lives together, but we've never really gotten a chance to know each other."

A puzzled frown rested on his lips. "You've always made it clear what you thought about me. We're not friends." His hands twisted in his lap, and he ducked his head. "I've heard what you call me—Miles the Mouse."

Hearing it come from his mouth made me wince. "I'm sorry. That was cruel of me."

Steady blue eyes met mine. "Yeah, it was. I had enough trouble being the younger, unpopular brother. It was hard as hell living in Dan's shadow with everyone looking down on me, calling me geek, nerd…" He gulped. "Or worse."

I knew. I'd heard the slurs and had laughed along. "Maybe I'm realizing the error of my ways."

He raised a brow but said nothing.

"Have you heard from him?" Why I wanted to know I couldn't say.

"I went to the bookstore after I left you, and I haven't checked my phone." His tuxedo jacket lay draped over the end of the couch, and Miles pulled out the phone and nodded. "Yeah. He's been texting me. They left Vegas, and they're going to Costa Rica for the honeymoon."

"Fucking bastard," I spit out. "That's where Lindsey and I were supposed to go. He jumped right into my place." A sour taste rose in the back of my throat. "I can't believe I was so clueless, that I had zero idea it was happening."

"They fooled everyone. I'm really disappointed in Dan. I thought he was better than that." Miles's face creased with sympathy. "I know he cares about you."

"The only thing he cares about is getting as much ass as possible. Sooner or later he'll get tired of Lindsey and cheat on her. They deserve each other."

"You still haven't answered my question. Why did you come here tonight? I'm not your friend. I'm Dan's younger brother. I should be the last person you'd want to see."

"Funny, right? I don't know why." I met his gaze, and in those blue depths, I recognized wariness coupled with a touch of desire. "You know how close he and I were." Unexpected tears formed at the corners of my eyes, and I brushed them away, fearful Miles would see and pity me.

*What the hell are those about?*

Miles inched closer and reached out his hand, letting it rest on my shoulder. My breath caught at his gentle touch. I didn't expect to feel this wellspring of desire flow through me.

"Why did he do this to me?"

"I don't know. I'm so sorry, Lyon. I wish I could help."

"I'm so confused. One minute he was my best friend, and the next he became my enemy. I feel so lost." My fingers skimmed his jaw, the muscles tense and quivering under my touch. "You are helping. Just being here with me. For me. Letting me unburden myself. You're so easy to talk to." I continued to map the elegant lines of his face while he sat frozen, yet I could see the rapid rise and fall of his chest and knew his heart would be furiously pounding. I leaned in close, taking a chance, and touched my lips to his. A violent shudder rolled through him, and I pressed harder. "Miles," I whispered and slid my fingers into the thick hair curling at his nape and took his mouth.

He whimpered under me, and that sound turned me on like nothing ever had before. My tongue pushed past those soft lips, and when he sucked it, so hungry and greedy, I nearly shot in my pants. It took all my strength not to rip off his clothes and fuck him into the couch cushions. I set my hands on his shoulders, and with one final, lingering kiss to those swollen lips, I pulled away.

And nearly lost it again at his flushed face, eyes so dazed with lust, I could've drowned in their blue depths.

*Get a grip, Lyon.*

"I didn't mean to come and take advantage of you."

*Liar.*

The sound of my hoarse voice, rough with want, shocked me, but it woke Miles out of his stupor, and he blinked and jumped away as if I had the plague.

"I...I didn't mean to...I don't understand..." Stammering and embarrassed, he buttoned up his shirt. "Wh-why did you kiss me?"

I ran my shaky hands through my hair. "Would I sound like an idiot if I said I don't know? I know that sounds terrible, but it's the truth."

His brow furrowed, Miles chewed on his lower lip for a moment. "I didn't know you were into men. I thought you were straight."

I allowed a thin smile. "I don't advertise my bisexuality, but I've been with men and women my whole life. Another thing only Dan knew."

"Are you ashamed of it? Is that why?" He'd retreated to the opposite side of the room from where I remained seated.

"No. I've never denied it. I like men and enjoy having sex with them." I grinned. "It's very different from having sex with a woman. I love getting my cock sucked, and I enjoy a fat dick in my mouth too." I licked my lips and watched his face pale with shock, then blaze red.

"Uhhh." A strangled sound burst from Miles, and he turned away from me but not before I could see the thick bulge in his pants. I rose from the couch.

"I'd better go. I'm sorry, Miles. I guess I'll see you around."

Not giving him a chance to respond, I left him and found my way outside, where I briskly walked away and turned the corner. I stopped there and called for a car, which took less than two minutes to arrive. Once I was settled, I replayed everything that had happened from when I entered Miles's house to the moment I left.

It had all worked out perfectly to plan.

All except how Miles tasted when I'd kissed him, making my dick spring instantly to life. Who knew Miles the Mouse could kiss like that?

I slowly ran my tongue over my lips, wishing they'd retained some remnant of the soft fullness of his mouth. As the car crossed over the bridge and into the city, I was busy imagining what he'd be like under me in bed.

If all went as I hoped, I wouldn't have to imagine for long.

It might've been my wedding day, but I'd spent the night planning my revenge.

Dan wasn't going to get away with humiliating me. He'd regret stabbing me in the back, lying to my face, and making me look like a fool.

If it was the last thing I did, I would destroy him.

He might be fucking my ex-fiancée, but I would have his brother in my bed and fuck him until he was so in love with me, he wouldn't know what hit him. Then I'd walk away.

Because nothing would hurt Dan more than Miles being hurt.

I'd stripped off my suit and lay naked in bed, my cock stiff, and I wrapped my hand around it. And while it should've been Lindsey here, sucking me off or riding me to oblivion, I barely remembered her kisses. It wasn't her I was thinking of. Instead, it was Miles's face in front of me. Those little whimpering sounds of pleasure he'd made while sucking my tongue lit me up, and I lost my breath, my heart hammering and my nuts drawing up tight.

"Oh fuck, oh fuck," I cried out, my orgasm so powerful,

I came over my hand and stomach before I knew it had hit. I twitched and shivered, laying limp and boneless.

This would be easier than I thought. I wouldn't have to fake desire when I kissed Miles, not with a mouth and tongue that talented. Plus, he was pretty sweet and kind of adorable with those big, round eyes. There'd be no problem getting it up for him, and my mind already raced, thinking ahead to my next encounter. Imagine, me finding Miles the Mouse sexy. That thought brought a smile to my face. The fact that Miles might be surprisingly satisfying in bed was just the cherry on top of a revenge sundae that would taste so damn sweet when I licked the spoon.

Dan would regret what he did to me, and I wasn't going to rest until I made Miles mine.

A week passed, during which I had to deal with curious, nosy people who kept trying to get me to unburden my problems to them on the pretense that it would help me. I knew better—they only wanted something juicy they could take back to their friends to have a laugh at my expense. Anyone who didn't think men gossiped was delusional. We did, and it was almost comical to see some of them fumble and attempt to show concern when they'd never given a damn about me. No one thought that maybe I was actually hurt by Dan and Lindsey's actions.

I sat in The Lyon's Den with Scott, enjoying a drink. He normally stopped by at least once a week after work so we could catch up, but since the fiasco, he'd come by every day. He was my rock, and though I had always been the one to help Scott, now I needed him.

The usual weekend crowd had begun to fill the space, and I scanned my surroundings with a satisfied nod.

"Busy, huh?" Scott accepted a drink from a proffered tray. "I guess it's good to keep your mind off everything."

"Yeah. It's doing very well. I knew the city was going to be happy with a place like this."

The Lyon's Den was advertised as a gentlemen's club, although, of course, we couldn't keep out women if they wanted to join. In the beginning many did, more out of curiosity, but now, after five years, it had settled down to one or two applications every six months or so. Admission was strictly by referral, and there was a lengthy, in-depth vetting process. Membership ran twenty thousand a year, and there was a wait list. I'd spent years studying the old-fashioned clubs of the rich and powerful nobility in London, like White's, Brooks's, and Boodle's, and wanted something along similar lines—a place where alliances could be made and deals struck, without the press catching wind.

The club was in an Upper East Side townhome and decorated in wood paneling, with polished wooden floors and wool rugs woven in subdued patterns. Tables for two and four were spread about the large open area. A bar sat tucked in the corner, but it wasn't the type where you could sit and order drinks. Upon acceptance, you filled out your preferences for food and drink and were served what you liked without being asked. If you changed your mind or wanted something different, you were accommodated and the new drink added to your profile. Meals were included, and you could choose from a variety of offerings.

For those who wanted to conduct a private business venture, rooms were available in the back of the club, but a request to reserve the space by the hour was required. It was all done anonymously with passwords and a personal code to enter the locked rooms. Many an explosive business deal had been conducted in those rooms. I'd toyed with the idea of having a "betting book" such as the one White's gentlemen's club once had, where the men would make bets on whatever they chose to, but I decided it could be too risky if someone took offense or if stock-market inside information was leaked. It wasn't worth legal action, considering how many lawyers and judges were members and knowing how quickly people sued each other these days.

There was also a cigar room, a separate room to play cards and chess, and a wine cellar where I stored rare vintages from a sommelier I'd hired to travel the world and find the best. I was intent on building up a private Scotch collection and had an expert attend auctions to bid on my behalf. My chef and pastry artist were Paris-trained and Michelin-starred.

There were other private clubs in the city to choose from, so I was always thinking of ways to make The Lyon's Den stand out. Personal, intimate service was what my club was known for. I met with everyone who applied to see if they were a good fit for the Den. I'd always trusted my instincts, although now, I couldn't be sure anymore…

None of this was done to make money—I had more than I'd ever need ten times over, thanks to a family that had made its money in banking and railroads in the nineteenth and twentieth centuries and invested it wisely.

Scott nudged my foot. "Any word from either of them?"

I grimaced and swallowed a hefty slug of my drink. "No, and why would I hear from them? They're probably fucking their brains out and on my dime." Of course Lindsey had used the trip we'd planned for the honeymoon. All she'd done was replace one groom with another. Easy-peasy.

"I still don't get it." Scott frowned. "Why not break up with you and be done with it? Why the sneaking around behind your back?"

My stomach soured, and I gazed into my half-empty glass. "Because she wanted her company tied into mine. That tequila contract? I checked it out, and the date we finalized the contract was the week after she and Dan began sleeping together. Maybe they had a thing for each other all along and planned it. Though I doubt Dan had an active part in that. Most likely he let himself get led by his dick and just did whatever Lindsey told him to do." I swirled the ice cubes in my drink. "Fool," I said bitterly, but I wasn't certain if I meant him or myself.

"I hope you're not sitting at home every night moping or being angry. It's not worth it. Not to mention it's unhealthy for you. Neither deserves you as a friend."

I squeezed his shoulder. "Thanks. And no, I haven't been doing those things. I've been trying to run a business."

*And planning my revenge.*

I finished my drink. "I'd better make the rounds."

Scott rose with me but held my arm for a moment. "Don't let this sour you on people. I don't like what I'm seeing."

I burst out laughing. "First of all, this didn't change my opinion of people or relationships. It only reinforced my belief that this whole love-and-marriage thing is pure bullshit. For me, at least. Second of all, I appreciate you and Beth trying to help, and you know I think she's a great woman, but I can't sit a whole night right now with someone who wants to tell me that I'll find the right one and fall in love."

Scott's eyes danced. "So I guess I shouldn't mention that Beth wants to set you up with a friend once you're ready?"

I patted his cheek. "Not if you want to keep that pretty face she loves so much." My smile turned grim. "Seriously. I do love you, and I hope you know that. And I know you'll always be there for me, just like I'll be for you. You and Uncle Harry are all I have in my corner. Please stop mentioning Dan and Lindsey. I don't want to talk about those two again. He's banned from the club as a guest. If Lindsey wants to bring him in as a business partner, good luck to her. I think we know how that's going to work out."

"Yeah. That's for sure. He's not like Miles, whose bookstore, I hear, is pretty successful. People are going back to the independent stores because they like the more personal service."

"I'll bet they do. Personal service is where it's at."

And I planned on getting a whole lot more personal with Miles.

# Chapter FOUR

The last customer finally left, and I locked the door with a sigh. We were supposed to close at seven, but I always let the stragglers stay a little past, so it was closer to seven forty-five by the time I shut down the computer and put the cash in my lockbox. I'd go to the bank in the morning to make my deposit.

I made a cup of chamomile tea and sat in one of the comfy leather armchairs, cradling the warm cup, but my mind still raced instead of calming. Five days had passed since Lyon's surprise visit and shocking kiss. Five sleepless nights where I'd tossed and turned, unable to forget the searing heat of his tongue in my mouth, his taste, the scent of his skin, the sound of him whispering my name.…I'd allowed myself to be swept into his sensual aura, and though it was only a brief moment, it was everything. Everything I'd dreamed about my entire life.

"Don't be an idiot," I muttered. "It was the confusion, and he was hurt, and more likely than not a little drunk. I'm sure he had plenty of whiskey before he came over."

My tea finished, I roamed the store, straightening the chairs moved out of place and reshelving the books customers left on the tables. I surveyed the space, planning ahead for the readings scheduled: a romance novel, a women's-fiction novel, and a self-help book written by a man who'd survived years of abuse from his parents, then his lovers, but who'd eventually broken free. I was most interested in listening to him.

A *knock-knock* drew my attention, and my eyes narrowed.

"Miles, open up."

Astonished at the voice I thought I recognized, I walked over to the front door and opened it.

"Lyon? What're you doing here?"

He squinted at me. "Can I come in?"

"I'm closed. I mean, the store is closed."

He put a hand on the wall by the door as if to hold himself up. "I tried to get here earlier, but I got stuck in traffic. I'd like to talk." He ducked his head and rubbed his eyes. *Dammit.* He was either really good at making himself appear pathetic, or he was honestly hurting. Either way, my heart softened. The past week couldn't have been easy for him, especially with Dan and Lindsey plastering pictures of their honeymoon all over social media, complete with videos of them kissing and looking blissfully in love. "Please, Miles?"

The beautifully dressed and put-together Lyon was always a feast for the eyes, but this Lyon? His tie hung loose, and his shirt collar was unbuttoned. The late-night stubble only added to his rakish, deliciously wicked appearance. The charming, slightly disheveled, sad man reached inside my chest and squeezed my heart. I wasn't sure I liked it, but I couldn't slam the door in his face.

"I'm going home. You can walk with me if you'd like."

I locked the door and set off down the street. I lived right around the corner from the store, and Lyon didn't speak while by my side. At the foot of the stairs to my house, I stopped and pulled out my keys. "Look, I don't know what's going on, but I think maybe you should see someone. Professionally."

"But I like talking to you."

The word "no" died on my lips. My stomach churned with a mixture of excitement and fear. "I-I think you're in a highly emotional state, and a therapist would help you more."

"They don't know me like you do."

I choked out a laugh. "I don't know you at all. We're acquaintances at best."

"Can't we be more? This experience has taught me I don't have any real friends. Maybe I've been wrong the way I've lived my life, and I want to change. You're such a good person. I need more friends who are willing to tell me the truth and be a friend like that."

"You're very persuasive."

"Am I? Is it working, then?" His smile was sweet and appealing, and I couldn't help but respond to it.

"All right. Come on. I'm tired of standing outside and giving my neighbors a show." I trudged up the steps, and he followed. "Can I get you something to eat?" I asked him once we were inside.

"What have you got?"

My response to his infectious grin was to roll my eyes. "I have leftover *moo shu* chicken and lasagna from a few days ago." When he wrinkled his nose, I pretended annoyance by shaking my finger in his face. "Listen. Beggars can't be choosers. Pick one."

His eyes lit up. “Let’s share. It’ll be a party.”

He trailed at my heels as we walked into the kitchen. In my wildest dreams, I’d never expected Lyon Elliot to be in my kitchen, joking with me about leftovers. “All right, I’ll heat them both up and—”

“No, don’t bother. Cold Chinese food is the best.” Without asking me, he opened the refrigerator, stuck his face in, and pulled out a container, then left me standing with my jaw hanging. “Bring some forks,” he called out before turning the corner.

“Who the hell is this person?” I muttered to myself but took out the lasagna and grabbed two forks and a knife.

I found him sitting on the living-room floor, his shoes kicked off and his suit jacket tossed over the arm of the sofa. “Come on, Miles, sit next to me.”

I sat, but not where he wanted, and I didn’t miss his frown. I wasn’t a total fool. I needed my space. Lyon Elliot was such an overbearing presence, I could probably be in Madison Square Garden and still sense him.

He forked some food into his mouth and chewed, closing his eyes and humming his pleasure. I cut the lasagna in half and ate from my piece. “I’ve never eaten cold pasta.”

Lyon’s eyes popped open. “What? You’re kidding. That’s like a rite of passage for every college student. Get drunk at parties and eat cold ravioli from a can in the morning.” He winked at me and scooped up more food, chewing noisily. “Ask me how I know.”

“Well, I wouldn’t. I was never invited to any parties and didn’t get picked for any fraternities, so…” I lifted a shoulder, surprised how old hurts could still feel so new. They lived right underneath my skin, like a living, breathing beast.

Stricken, Lyon set his fork on the table and scooted over to me. “I’m sorry. I didn’t mean to bring up bad memories.”

“Well, just so you know, none of my college experiences

are worth a first thought, never mind a second." I busied myself with reaching across the table for the *moo shu* but froze when Lyon grabbed my arm.

"Why? What happened? Was it a boyfriend? I never heard mention of anyone…"

And no way in hell would I tell him. I'd kept my hurt wrapped tight like a new book whose spine had never been cracked open.

"I've moved well beyond that point in my life where college has any meaning to me."

"I'm glad to hear that." Lyon's thumb tickled my wrist, then pressed the pulsing vein. "I think it's a time of new beginnings for all of us."

"New beginnings?" I gulped some air, desperately wishing I had the strength to pull away from him. This had been my fantasy since I realized I was gay, and my brother's best friend, Lyon Elliot, had always played the starring role. I'd put every other man up against him and found them wanting.

"Yeah. For me too." Somehow the space between us had vanished, and Lyon's mouth hovered over mine. "Because I don't know how I never saw it before, but I find you incredibly attractive."

"Do you? You never noticed me at all until now. I was Miles the Mouse, remember?" I licked my lips, and he tightened his grip on my wrist.

"No past hurts tonight. Everything is brand-new."

"Maybe for you. But some things are impossible to forget."

"I'm sorry my cruel nickname hurt you, but I'm getting the impression there's something more."

I shrugged, but his stare was laser-focused.

"Tell me."

"Why?"

He blinked as if surprised I was questioning him. I had the feeling people didn't do that to a man like Lyon Elliot.

"Because you know my biggest humiliation and hurt."

"And because of that you want it to be even? You should know mine? Sorry. I'm not into playing games like that. I don't play games at all."

Proud of myself for not capitulating to his overwhelming physical presence, I held his gaze and was rewarded with a faint smile.

"You're very different from how I imagined you."

"I didn't think you imagined anything about me."

"Maybe neither of us knows the other like we thought." He nuzzled into my shoulder, and like the first time he'd touched me, I struggled to hold on to my self-control because falling into him would be so damn easy.

I shivered as his warm, wet tongue licked a path on my neck. "Why now? I don't get it. I thought you'd hate me and you'd want nothing to do with anyone in Dan's family."

"Did anyone ever tell you that you ask too many questions?" Lyon breathed into my ear, and I shivered, goose bumps rising. My cock swelled, pushing against the zipper of my jeans. "How about if it feels good, just do it?"

He pushed me to the floor, lying on top of me, letting me feel the thrust of his heavy cock, while taking my mouth in a bruising kiss. His touch was like a drug, hurtling me into space, and I clung to his broad shoulders.

"What the hell, Lyon?" I moaned, unable to keep from arching up into that thick, pulsing shaft. His fingers teased my shirt out from my waistband and hiked it up. The bulge of his erection pressed into my thigh, and he rode me hard while I lost myself in this haze of sensuality between us. Then I felt his hand on the waistband of my jeans, and he popped the button and down went my zipper. He cupped my throbbing dick through the dampness of my briefs, and I whimpered, knowing if he touched my bare skin, all would be lost and he'd be inside me within minutes.

That couldn't happen.

"*Mmm.* Please, Miles. I haven't been able to stop thinking about you all week. So damn sexy. Let me? Can I?"

"No." But with my willpower fading fast, I knew how easily Lyon would be able to turn my no into a yes. Surprising me, he accepted my refusal and rolled off me with a loud groan of frustration and after sitting up, pressed a hand to his crotch.

"Fuck, Miles."

Anxiety pulsed through my blood, and I sat up. "Sorry, but you can't show up, put on a pitiful face, and think I'm going to sleep with you."

A dazzling smile, one I'd seen him use all my life to bend people to his will, curved his lips. "But you aren't kicking me out."

It was impossible to remain angry with him, and my lips twitched. "Should I?"

He laughed, eyes crinkling shut, and I wished I were the type of guy who could be sexually free and easygoing. I wanted so much for whatever this was happening between us to be real, but I waited for him to tell me it was all a mistake, and he should never have kissed me and tried to fuck me.

"Listen, Miles…"

*And here it comes.* I lifted my chin, staring directly into his eyes. "You don't have to say it. I know you're only here because I'm an easy target, but I'm not blaming you. You don't have to feel guilty."

His brow puckered. "Easy target? Why would I feel guilty?"

I sputtered. "Because you don't give a damn about me. You don't want me as a person. You needed to let your frustration out with anyone handy, and I was more than willing to be that person."

His lips thinned. "And you think that's why I came here? To have sex with you and walk away? Get my rocks off?"

"I don't have to think it. I know." I held his gaze. "Now if you don't mind, I'd like to take a shower and go to bed. I have to be at the store early tomorrow."

His jaw hardened. "You don't know anything."

I snorted. "I have a lifetime's worth of knowledge." Sending up a quick prayer that my shaky legs would hold me, I rose and zipped up. "So thanks for coming, and I'll see you around. But please don't think this is going to happen again."

In all the years I'd known him, I'd never seen Lyon Elliot left speechless by anyone, and I had to admit it felt good that I'd done it. He scowled and pouted, and I had to bite my lip to keep a smile from breaking through. He was so damn cute, and I wished I could trust him, but I'd been wrong too many times before.

"Why don't you believe me when I say this wasn't my intention? I came to talk."

"Is that so? And yet this is the second time you've 'come to talk,' " I aired-quoted. "And both times we've ended up… you know…"

"Mauling each other like wild animals?" he offered with that cheeky grin I knew had gotten him everything he'd ever wanted.

Except me. I was older and wiser, and as much as I wished it was so, I knew better than to trust myself.

It was my turn to scowl. "Not funny. I'm not falling for it. Now I want to take a shower and go to bed."

His eyes twinkled. “I could join you. I’m a great back-scrubber.”

“Good night, Lyon.” I set my jaw and marched out of the room.

Laughing, he walked past me and out the door.

At ten the next morning, I walked into the store with my coffee and a lemon poppy-seed muffin. Gordon was behind the desk, reading *What Men Want*, and looked up. “Well, hello and good morning, Miles.”

*Uh-oh.*

Instinctively, my antennae went on high alert, and I narrowed my eyes. “What’s going on? Why are you this cheerful so early in the morning?” My skin prickled, and I sighed and set my food on the counter. I knew without him having to say anything. “Okay. Where is he?”

Gordon’s brows rose. “Wow, you’re good. He’s sitting by the window.” He rolled his chair over so we couldn’t be overheard. “He’s gorgeous. Are you two dating?”

I scanned the store until I found him. An errant sunbeam spilled over his shoulders and touched his dark hair, reflecting its sheen. He lifted his attention from the book in his lap, and our eyes met. A slow smile tugged at the corner of that wickedly sensuous mouth.

“No. We’re not dating. I don’t even know if I like the man. Or trust him.”

Lyon rose and crossed the room, and Gordon murmured, “I’m betting you’re going to find out sooner rather than later.”

“Hello, Miles,” Lyon drawled. “Your coworker was

correct. He said you always show up exactly at ten, and here you are."

"I like to be punctual. What do you want?" I frowned and circled around to stand behind the wooden counter, using it as a barrier between us.

"It's a bookstore, and I found myself with nothing to read at home."

I could hardly snap at him for that, but I stubbornly refused to engage further. "I hope you find what you need. If you have any questions, Gordon can help. I have deliveries to open in the stockroom."

Leaving them both, I pushed the door marked *Employees Only* and found the boxes of books to be entered into the inventory system for shelving. I slit the top of the first one open.

"You forgot these."

Box cutter in hand, I whirled to see Lyon, coffee cup in one hand, muffin in the other.

"Can you please stop following me?"

"I'm trying to prove you wrong, but first, please put that weapon out of reach?" He set the bag and coffee on the shelving and crossed his arms.

Furious at how weak in the knees his proximity made me, I set the box cutter on the table.

"What am I wrong about?"

"That I only want to be with you for sex." He raised a brow and smirked. "Unless you want to lock the door and have a quickie. Kidding." Lyon put his hands up. "Look. I'm serious. I'm here in your bookstore because I was hoping to spend some time together and get to know you better without our tongues down each other's throats."

My face burned, and my head spun. Was he telling the

truth? Or was he hoping to get lucky? Either way, I wasn't sure I wanted to say no.

I waited, anxiously holding off from pushing Miles, surprised by how much I wanted him to say yes. His wide yet suspicious eyes searched my face, and I forced myself to remain neutral. Not an easy task for me. But for my plan to work, I had to have his complete trust. Miles needed to be totally enamored of me, and that meant reining in my capture-and-devour instinct and becoming a turtle. *Slow and steady wins the race.*

And the prize was hurting Dan as much as he'd hurt me. The benefit? Getting to fuck Miles. An unexpected pleasure for sure because damn, I couldn't remember the last time I'd been so hot for someone. Maybe it was because he didn't make it easy. Miles was a firecracker, and I wanted to be the one to light his wick and make him explode.

Nervous as a stray cat, he sidestepped me, putting the

box of books between us. I grinned, enjoying the game. It revved me up and got my juices flowing, which would only make the ultimate conquest even more enjoyable. I almost felt sorry for Miles.

Almost.

"Come on, Miles," I urged, using my most persuasive voice. "How about I take you to lunch—your choice. Then maybe you can come to the club later? We can have a drink."

Miles's brows shot up. "I'm not a member. And I don't really drink."

I winked. "I think I can get you in. And you can have one glass of wine. To celebrate our newfound friendship."

To give him credit, he was still suspicious. And he was smart to feel that way. But I wasn't going to stop until I had him. By the time Dan returned from his month-long honeymoon, Miles would be so in love with me, he wouldn't be able to decide what to have for dinner without my input. My belly tightened at the thought of Miles bending to my will.

"I don't know…" He picked up the box cutter and set it right down again. I didn't miss those long fingers trembling. I wanted them wrapped around my aching dick. I wanted to kiss that soft mouth and find him willing.

*Damn.* I just wanted him, any way I could get him, and so bad, I scared myself because it had nothing to do with the game I was playing. It was dangerous, but desire had taken control.

"Please, Miles? I'm so lonely, and I don't want to sit in the Den alone, having to answer all those questions from people who only want gossip. They don't care about me. All they want is some juicy tidbit about my sad life. Having you there with me would really help. Maybe if they see you're on my side, they'll leave me alone. You have no idea what it's been like."

A week had passed, yet I'd spent every evening fending off probing, personal questions, and I fluctuated between wanting to go home and curl up in a ball in my bed and lashing out and telling the nosy fuckers to shut up. My lower lip trembled, and I watched his resolve weaken.

"I guess I could." Miles gnawed his lip. "One drink won't hurt. But I can't do lunch. It wouldn't be fair to Gordon to leave him during the busiest time, and the college kids I hired don't come in until later."

*Dammit.* But I'd take what I could get.

"Not a problem. If you text me what you want for dinner, I'll have them prepare something for you. Unless you'd like me to surprise you."

"It doesn't matter. Anything is fine."

"I'll see you around eight at the club?"

"I just..." He sighed and lifted a shoulder. "Okay. Eight o'clock."

Much as I wanted to kiss that frowning mouth, I restrained myself.

Hopefully that would happen later tonight.

At 8:10, Miles still hadn't shown, and knowing how punctual he was, I had to assume he wasn't coming. I was shocked that I was more disappointed than angry. I'd casually chatted up Gordon before I left to get a sense of Miles's favorite foods, and I'd had the kitchen set to prepare a nice romantic dinner for the two of us.

Now he'd stood me up. That never happened.

"What's got your nuts in knots?" Victor, my bartender, handed me my second Scotch of the evening.

"What're you talking about?" I snapped, checking my phone for the tenth time.

"Listen, Lyon, I've been here since you opened the place, and I've never seen you this on edge. You still upset about Lindsey breaking off the engagement?"

"That bitch can go to hell and take her husband with her. As far as I'm concerned, I dodged a bullet."

"Whoa. Okay, then. So, again. What're you so jumpy about? You haven't stopped checking your phone. If I didn't know you better, I'd swear you had a hot date."

Victor was as loyal as they came and knew to keep his mouth shut. He was the closest thing I had to a friend at the moment.

"This is no ordinary date. Dan is going to regret what he did to me."

Then Miles appeared, and my belly tightened. He'd changed from his earlier outfit of jeans and a long-sleeved T-shirt into a sleek navy suit and bright-blue tie that matched his pretty eyes. His nervous smile when he saw me did funny things to my chest.

"Isn't that Dan's brother? I've seen his pictures on Dan's phone."

"Yeah," I murmured. "Make sure you have ready that red wine I sent in this afternoon."

"Are you…and him? *Daaaaaamn*," Victor whistled low. "I had no idea you swung both ways."

"No fucking reason for you to, either."

My glass empty, I set it on the table and strode over to Miles. "I thought you stood me up. I know you're always on time."

He touched his tie. “I forgot there was a dress code and had to go back and change.”

*How…sweet. Dammit.* I shouldn’t let his words affect me. I took him by the elbow and steered him over to the corner table, where Victor had poured his wine and given me another Scotch.

“It wouldn’t have mattered. You could’ve come as you were.”

His lips tightened. “I didn’t want to stand out and be different from everyone else.”

*You’d stand out anywhere you are.*

What the hell was that about? If I said that to him, he’d laugh in my face. But Miles *was* different. He had a fresh, almost innocent look about him, but there was nothing pure about those kisses we shared. My mouth watered in anticipation of possessing him.

*Slow down.*

“I have a nice red wine I think you’ll like.” I handed him the glass, and Miles took a sip.

“It’s very good. I don’t drink much, but I do enjoy a nice Cabernet.”

“I’m glad you like it. Are you hungry?”

Not answering, he gazed around him. “This is a nice place. Dan used to talk about it all the time, but I never paid much attention…” He put a hand to his mouth. “Shit. I’m sorry. That was wrong of me. I didn’t mean to mention Dan.”

Hearing his name was like a knife to my flesh, but I forced a pleasant response. “It’s all right. He’s your brother and you love him.”

Miles sipped his wine. “You can love someone and still be angry with them. There’s no way I can condone his behavior. In case you didn’t already know, I’m a hundred percent on your side in this.”

I put a hand on his shoulder. "Thanks, Miles. That means a lot to me."

"Miles? Is that you? What are you doing here?" Uncle Harry called out to us, and my stomach sank. Much as I loved him, his appearance was going to put a huge damper on my intended seduction.

Miles, unsuspecting of my devious ways, broke out in a huge smile of welcome, and set his wineglass on the table to hug my uncle. "Uncle Harry. It's great to see you. Uh…Lyon invited me for dinner."

Uncle Harry's bushy gray brows drew together, and his sharp eyes raked over me. "He did? I didn't know you and Miles were friends, Lyon. Or that he was even a member. Don't ever recall seeing him here in all the years the club has been open."

*Shit.* Now I'd have to waste my time and energy on convincing Uncle Harry that I was trying to forge an actual friendship with Miles, instead of wooing the man to get him into my bed.

"He has my personal open invitation. And Miles has been helping me through this week. It's been hard, as you can imagine." Putting on my best sad-sack face, I hoped it would be good enough to fool Uncle Harry. Unfortunately, he knew me too well and had no trouble calling me out.

"Aside from the embarrassment, I didn't think it would be so rough. I knew all along this was no love match with you and that girl. It had business arrangement stamped all over it, but you young people do what you want for whatever nonsensical reasons. Now, Dan is a different story. I'd like to get my hands on him for a few minutes to find out what was going on in that head of his."

This wasn't proceeding to plan. I really wished Uncle Harry would go away and leave me the hell alone, but just then, my extremely efficient server appeared with Uncle

Harry's favorite bourbon and water, and he took a lip-smacking sip. I searched the room for his friend Maxwell Grant, who seemed to always be around, and as expected, it didn't take me long to find him.

"Oh, hey isn't that Maxwell walking in? Are you meeting him?"

"Eh?" Uncle Harry gave a cursory glance over his shoulder. "Yes, but he'll wait. I'm talking to you and trying to make sense of what I'm seeing."

Holding on to the thread of my patience was growing tiresome. "I don't know what you're talking about. I'm here with Miles, and we're going to have dinner. What do you think is going to happen?"

Miles huffed out a sound of displeasure. "There's no need to talk to Uncle Harry in that tone. He's voicing the same feelings I had when you asked me here. And frankly, I'm still not getting it."

Two deep breaths calmed the anger waiting on my lips to be released. If I said what I truly wanted, I'd irrevocably damage my relationship with Uncle Harry, which would ruin any chance with Miles. Plus, I didn't want that to happen. For all his busybody, pushy ways, I truly did love my uncle. He honestly cared about me.

"I'm sorry, Uncle Harry. I guess you're right, but I'm still processing it all. That's why I invited Miles. Dan was like my brother, and I thought maybe Miles could give me some insight into why this happened. I thought I knew everything about Dan, but obviously I was wrong." My smile was one of patience and friendship that I'd spent the day practicing in anticipation for the evening ahead, and I turned its full force on Miles. "I didn't realize what a nice person Miles was until he helped me after Lindsey and Dan ran off."

"That's because you were never interested in knowing him as anything other than Dan's little brother. You were so hurt as a child, you kept all personal relationships at arm's length, compartmentalizing all your emotions, and I worry that it's made you cold and incapable of finding a true, loving relationship," Uncle Harry pointed out. "Like your namesake, you try to be king of the jungle and have everyone bow to you."

Stunned and hurt by his brutally honest assessment, my eyes burned from the humiliation. Pale-faced, Miles tried to catch my eye, but I refused to crumble. I was a little buzzed from the three quick drinks, and my nerves were on the brink of snapping. I should've shut my mouth and walked away, but instead found myself saying, "Guess that's why my parents could never be bothered with me, right? You're the epitome of a gentleman, so what the hell are you doing here talking to me?" And though it might send my plans down the toilet, I couldn't stop the self-hatred. "You too, Miles. I know you think I'm a selfish piece of shit. Go on. You don't really want to be here, I can tell. Leave. Both of you. I don't need anyone."

I got up and strode off, heading to my private office at the far corner of the club. I pulled out my key and twice attempted to open the lock, but my shaking hands failed me. I pounded the doorframe with my fist.

"Goddammit."

"Lyon."

That soft voice penetrated all the chaos in my head, but I was too embarrassed from my outburst to face him.

"I thought I told you to go away," I grumbled.

"I'm hungry." Miles chuckled.

I snorted but turned around to see him leaning that long body next to me, amusement brightening his eyes.

"You invited me to dinner, and I didn't eat lunch in anticipation of a delicious meal."

"You heard Uncle Harry. He's right, you know. You should be long gone by now."

"I did hear him. I know he loves you and knows you better than almost anyone. And it's nothing I didn't already know and say to myself as I was contemplating canceling meeting you tonight." He folded his arms. "But I also heard *you* this week. I know you loved Dan and how badly he hurt you. And maybe you didn't have that swoony type of love for Lindsey, but you knew her a long time. I'm sure you cared for her, and you were friends. It's like losing a piece of yourself when you're blindsided by someone you've known and cared about for so long." He blinked rapidly, his eyes shiny and the brightest blue I'd ever seen.

Was he crying? For me? That rocked me to the core. No one had ever shed a tear over my feelings. Scott, much as he cared, while angry over Dan's cowardice, was pragmatic and matter-of-fact about the broken engagement. Even Uncle Harry, who I knew loved me, was easily able to put that aside and count my faults out one by one like jelly beans. Only Miles seemed to understand how broken and lost Dan's behavior had left me. He took it to his own heart and felt my pain.

And somehow, despite my outburst, my plan hadn't gone awry. It wouldn't take much to get Miles in my bed, and I grew hard, imagining what I could do to him. How I would wreck him for anyone else. I brushed at my lashes, surprised to find them wet. Damn, I was a better actor than I thought.

"It's so hard. Thank you for understanding. I don't like how angry this has left me."

"I believe you. And I didn't want to leave you, knowing how alone you must feel right now." He hung his head. "I-I know what it's like to be used."

His words cut through my dirty fantasy of having him

naked in my bed. Curious, I tipped up his chin. "What happened?"

He pushed away from my touch. "It doesn't matter. It was in college. A long time ago."

My lips thinned. "My parents fucked Scott and me over left and right while we were kids. *If it's Tuesday, it must be home with Mother. If it's Saturday, it's time to be with Father. Oh, wait. He didn't show. Back to Mother's, but she'd already gone away with her new husband, so off to Uncle Harry's we go.* It was long ago, and yet I still think about coming home to find it empty, no one there, not even the housekeeper."

It struck me then that all my life, the people who should've stayed had left me. Over and over again.

And Dan's leaving me was the hardest to take of all.

"That must've been hard on you and Scott."

Sympathetic big blue eyes met mine, and I wanted to kiss him. Not because of any plan of revenge or to make him fall for me. I wanted to kiss him because he was sweet and caring and understanding.

He was Miles, and I wanted to kiss him, but I shocked myself by not following through because it didn't feel like it would be right for him. I wanted him to want me.

Steadier now, I managed to insert the key and open the door. "About that dinner. They can send it here. If you still want to eat with me."

His smile transformed the sadness in his face into shy happiness. I guessed it was a rare occurrence because in all the years I'd known Miles, I'd never seen it. It beamed from him like a torch lighting the darkness. And I liked it.

"Yes. I do."

"Good. Come on in."

He gazed around my spacious office that had a large sectional couch, a big flat-screen television, and a dining table in the far corner. It was set up like a studio apartment, and there were many late nights before the wedding when I'd fallen asleep on the couch.

"So is this what people mean when they say they're entering the lion's den?" Miles joked. "Should I be afraid?"

I grinned. "I guess we'll have to wait and see."

# Chapter SIX

"I have to admit I was wrong." I set my steak knife on my plate. "And by the way, that's the best filet I've had in years. It barely needed a knife, it was so tender. And the crispy onions on top were delicious. Everything was."

We were at the dining table in Lyon's office, finishing up the main course of filet mignon, whipped garlic potatoes, and creamed spinach. We'd started off with shrimp cocktail, and I spied both tiramisu and key lime pie on a dessert tray. I'd been reckless and had drunk my glass of rich red wine quickly, surprisingly, Lyon kept to ice water.

"Wrong about what?" Lyon patted his lips with the linen napkin. "You thought my food would be terrible? I think it rivals Michelin-star restaurants." He huffed, but I recognized the teasing and smirked at him, enjoying the easy conversation and banter.

"This." I waved a hand between us. "The conversation wasn't hard and strained, and I had fun."

"So you thought I'd be boring and dull, is what you're saying." His lips tugged up in a half smile.

"Hardly." I rolled my eyes, then grew serious and stared at my plate. "It's me. I'm usually the boring, dull one."

"Hey," he spoke sharply, rapping the table with his knuckles. "No put-downs at my table. It's not allowed. Unless it's about Dan." His eyes twinkled. "In fact…let's play a game. We can call it Dirty Dan, and each of us will tell something really embarrassing he did. I'll go first."

I knew this was a way for Lyon to exorcise his demons, and I also hoped that maybe it would alleviate some of his hatred of Dan and bring him a little peace.

"The first time Dan had sex, he came before he even got to put it inside the woman because he was so nervous. Made a big mess all over the poor thing."

My jaw dropped. "Get the hell out. He always boasted how he went the whole night and left her begging for more."

A belly laugh escaped Lyon. "Yeah. She was begging all right. Begging for someone to get her off." He smirked. "I had no problem helping her in her hour of need."

"Both of you were with the same woman?" Why did that not surprise me?

"Yeah. She used to come and watch her son's baseball practice. She was a single mom and hot and wanted both of us." He lifted a shoulder. "Her name was Leslie, I think. One afternoon, after practice, she asked us over. Said she wanted us to help her son with his swing, and afterward, he went next door to a friend's for dinner. We went straight to dessert." His lips twitched.

"Good God," I said faintly.

"Your turn," Lyon prodded. "Tell me something good."

I shook my head. “I don’t have anything like that.” I searched my memory. “Although…”

Lyon pounced. “What?”

Maybe I was being a traitor, but Dan *had* done Lyon wrong, and for the first time in my life, I was enjoying myself with him.

“It was summer, our parents were away for the day, and I was swimming laps in the pool. Dan sneaked some woman in, and they were fooling around on the lounge chair. I had no desire to see it and went into the house. They started having sex and were getting really into it.”

“Yeah. Dan can get loud when he’s doing the deed,” Lyon muttered.

“She did too. She was screaming, ‘*Oh my God, oh my God. Help me. Help*.’ I guess the neighbors grew concerned, and the next thing I knew the cops were in the backyard. They caught him mid-thrust.”

Whooping with laughter, Lyon fell over. “That’s a riot. He never told me that story.” He wiped his eyes and sighed, growing sad. “I wonder what else he never told me.”

Not wanting him to fall into the doldrums again, I raced to think of something to distract him. “When did you know you also liked guys?”

“Pretty early on.” Lyon raised his gaze to meet mine. “I used to like coming to your house and watching you swim.”

My throat went dry. “I-I didn’t think you ever noticed me.”

“I noticed. You in that tight swimsuit that left nothing to the imagination. Except what you’d be like in my mouth.” He licked his lips, and my dick stiffened. “I remember once you were practicing for some swim meet. You were only fifteen and so shy. I thought you were the cutest thing, and I was so horny every time I’d come over, hoping I’d see you.”

"I can't believe this. You never gave any indication you were interested in me."

"Well, you were Dan's little brother. Off-limits, you know?"

"What do you mean?"

Lyon broke off eye contact. "You'd come out as gay, and when I told Dan I was bi, he warned me to keep away from you."

"What the fuck?" I seethed. "Keep away from me? Who the hell was he to dictate my sex life?" I knew Dan was overprotective, but this was taking it too far.

"I mean, in all fairness, I was kind of a dog back in the day and hitting it with anyone who caught my eye." He peeked up at me from beneath those dark, thick lashes. "I probably would've fucked you and dumped you, so he was right. You would've ended up hating me, and we wouldn't be here, getting to know each other."

"I guess we can thank Dan for that, at least."

Lyon poured me another glass of wine, my second, and raised his glass of ice water. "To Dan, for bringing us together. However unintentional it might be."

He clinked his glass with mine, and uncharacteristically reckless, I drained it. "To Dan. I'm all grown up and don't need his protection anymore."

Lyon's smile was slow and set my heart racing.

"I'm glad to hear that."

He set both desserts between us, scooped up a little of the tiramisu, and held it out to me. "Taste."

I let him slide the sweet concoction between my lips and couldn't help the hum of pleasure at its deliciousness. "*Mmm*, so good."

"Yeah, it sure as hell is." His husky voice was everything

I'd fantasized about, and left me achy and on edge. "Can I ask you a question now?"

"I guess." Instantly on guard, I waited.

"What did you mean when you said you'd been used and dumped before?"

"I didn't," I forced out, and pressed my lips together as a wave of dizziness rolled through me. "I—please, Lyon. Don't make me talk about it."

Consternation spread across his face, and he reached across to tangle his fingers with mine. "I'm sorry. I didn't mean to dredge up something so painful. Are you all right? You look sick."

I might be. Nausea bubbled in my stomach, and a sour taste hit the back of my throat. "I…I…"

"Hold on, I'm coming." Lyon left his seat and slipped his arm around my waist. "Lean on me. Let's get you to the couch."

"I'm okay."

He hugged me closer, and I rested my head on his shoulder.

"Sure you are. That's why you looked like you were going to puke all over my nice table." I caught the edge of his smile and let him pull me to the couch, but I didn't anticipate him sitting with me, his muscular thigh pressed to mine, his arm heavy and comforting over my shoulders.

"I feel silly. I thought I was past it. I should be." I hung my head, ashamed at how with only a few words, I was that scared, miserable kid I'd hoped was gone for good.

"I think we all believe we should recover quicker than we're capable of from things that hurt us," Lyon mused. Was he talking about Dan and Lindsey or his parents? Maybe both? He'd always put on such a good facade, I'd never thought Lyon cared about anything but having a good time.

My phone buzzed with a call, and I ignored it. I wanted to hear more from Lyon, but as soon as it stopped, it started up again.

"Someone really wants to talk to you," Lyon said. "Go ahead and take it."

When I saw the name on the screen, my stomach dropped, and I tried to shove it back into my pocket, but in my haste, my fumbling fingers hit the wrong button, and Dan and Lindsey's faces appeared in the window.

"Hey, Miles. How are you?" Dan gave me his big, good-natured grin, which I hoped I responded to with equal enthusiasm. Lyon had stepped away from me the moment he'd seen it was Dan.

"I'm fine. What about you two? Why're you calling on your honeymoon?" I sensed something was going on. "What's so important you couldn't wait to call?"

Dan held on to Lindsey's hand. "We're pregnant. Two months. Can you believe it, dude? I'm gonna be a father, and you're gonna be the best uncle."

I should have been thrilled for my brother, but instead, I felt the depth of Lyon's pain. It couldn't be helped. I darted a quick glance at him, but he'd wrenched open the door and disappeared. *Shit*. Knowing how devastating this news must be for him to hear, I wanted to comfort him as he'd helped me only moments earlier, but I first had to talk to Dan.

"That's great, and I'm happy for you both, but I'm still upset over what you did to your best friend."

"Don't worry about him." Dan's smiling face creased with puzzlement. "Where are you? It looks familiar."

"I'm out."

"On a date?" His brows arched high. "With whom? I didn't know you were seeing anyone. You never told me."

I grew increasingly irritated. "You've been busy. And

since when do I have to check in with you about everything? Obviously, you didn't feel the need to tell me everything about your personal life and that you were with Lindsey."

"Dude, calm down. I thought you'd be happy. I know you love kids. How much fun will it be to play with a little niece or nephew? You can teach them to swim."

"And we're going to get all our children's books from you," Lindsey added, her face alight with happiness. "I want to learn everything I can about being a good parent."

It was hard to be annoyed when your brother was celebrating such good news, and I was growing more confused and nervous with each passing minute. Should I stop being so angry and upset with Dan, my brother and the person who'd always been there for me? Or should I side with Lyon, who'd absolutely been wronged and had been left behind to handle all the fallout, but—and here was a huge but—hadn't ever been a friend to me?

Goddammit, the choice should be an easy one, but it wasn't.

"Miles. What the fuck," Dan shouted. "Now I know where you are. I thought those walls looked familiar. What the hell are you doing in Lyon's office? You're not a member of the Den. Why are you there?"

"You were his best friend. He considered you a second brother. He loved you."

A brief flash of pain darkened Dan's face before he set his jaw in a hard line. "Listen, Miles. It takes a shit to know one. I was like him until I met Lindsey. But once I fell in love, I saw how empty that life was. That's why I don't want you to get caught up in his lies."

"Maybe you don't know him as well as you think. He sure as hell didn't know you."

"What does that mean?" Dan stuck out his jaw.

"You're kidding, right? A month ago you were busy

helping him plan his wedding while you were sleeping with his fiancée. Now you're on the honeymoon he should've been taking, and his fiancée is your wife, and you're having a baby." My head spun. "Jesus, it's like a damn soap opera."

Lindsey took the phone from Dan. "But Lyon and I didn't love each other. I mean, yeah, we were friends, but he's not nursing a broken heart."

"How would you know?"

Taken aback, she stammered, "Well, uh, I…he and I had an understanding. We both wanted to expand our businesses, and I mean, I'm in my midthirties and hadn't met anyone I'd considered marrying. It worked out for both of us."

*Wow.* Lyon wasn't kidding when he'd said she was cold.

"But you were friends. And he takes his friendships very seriously. Unlike others." I glared at Dan, who pointed his finger at me.

"I'm gonna fucking kill him if he comes near you."

Lindsey's brow furrowed. "What're you talking about? Lyon's not into guys."

"He's bi," Dan tossed out, and I watched Lindsey's mouth form an *O* of surprise, and I grew furious with Dan for outing Lyon so easily and without a care. "I never thought he was really that into guys. Yeah, he had some flings when we were in college and in our twenties, but he was always more into women. Besides, once he met you, babe, I know he was ruined for anyone else. You're special."

"Aww, baby." She sighed, and they kissed. I didn't know whether to laugh or gag.

"Well, I'd better let you both go." It was getting uncomfortable to watch them, and I wanted to find Lyon and see if he was all right.

Dan stopped sucking Lindsey's face long enough to

point a finger at me and say in a stern voice, "Keep away from Lyon."

I lifted my chin. "You're the last one to give relationship advice, since you screwed over your best friend. And I'm over thirty now, not a college kid who doesn't know better. I think I'm a damn good judge of character, and frankly, I find both of you wanting in that category. Congratulations on the baby."

I ended the call and headed out of the office, hoping Lyon hadn't run away. Once in the main area, I spotted Uncle Harry sitting with his friend Maxwell. He beckoned me over.

"Hello, Mr. Grant."

"Miles." Maxwell, who was a man of few words, smiled and drank his tea.

"Miles, what happened?" Uncle Harry asked. "I watched Lyon run out of here like the devil was chasing him."

Dancing on my toes, I vacillated between wanting to tell Uncle Harry and needing to go after Lyon to make sure he was okay. His strong reaction to Dan and Lindsey's news left no doubt in my mind he was still devastated by their elopement.

"I can't really say, but do you know where he went?"

"Probably home. He doesn't do anything but work and sleep, especially now." He peered at me over his glasses. "Maybe you should check on him. I would, but I'm tired and I'm going to go home."

"Do you feel all right?"

"Oh yes, don't worry," he reassured me with a wave. "Now go, shoo. Make sure Lyon is okay. That boy likes to think he's tougher than he is, but he's not who he pretends to be. You know where he lives, right?"

"Yeah. I've been to a few parties at the apartment." Courtesy of Dan. I knew I was a pity invite, the afterthought.

"Let me know how he's doing. Someone has to worry

about those boys. Their father has a head like a coconut—filled with water, not brains."

I laughed and kissed his cheek. "I'll text you. Good night, Uncle Harry. Mr. Grant." I sped out of the Den, possibly into the fire.

I lay on my sofa, head throbbing, stomach in knots. None of the physical pain compared to the mental anguish of hearing Dan and Lindsey joyfully sharing their news.

A baby.

Two months along.

She was too busy with wedding plans to be in my bed, and whenever I tried to get her to stay the night, she'd pull away from me.

*"You have no idea what I have to do, all the plans that go into a wedding, while still running the business. I'm so stressed out, sex is the last thing on my mind."*

Liar.

She wasn't too overwhelmed to lie down with him and get pregnant.

And my best buddy, Dan? Well, he'd been busy fucking her behind my back. I'd bet she wasn't staying with her parents because she was so stressed out like she'd claimed. She was probably with him, both of them laughing at my stupidity. I could hear him now.

*"Fuck it, babe. Let's do it without a condom. It'll feel so good..."*

My stomach cramped. And Miles...God, the pity on his face when he'd looked at me for my reaction made me cringe. Until Dan's call, the evening had gone better than I'd hoped. My plans were coming to fruition—a few persuasive kisses in my office, and then we'd come here and have sex all night long. By the time morning came, I'd have him wrapped around my finger.

And yet...Miles had shared some intimacies that made me hesitate. He'd hinted at past hurts and deception. Had his heart been broken? Had he been in love? Had he sat in the dark wondering if anyone had ever cared about him?

A line in the sand had shifted, blurring the edges between the game of revenge and the puzzle of my attraction to Miles, a man I hadn't thought twice about but now couldn't get out of my mind.

I wanted to know more. I wanted to know him.

The doorman buzzed, but I ignored it. I wasn't expecting anyone. Uncle Harry was at the club, and it was getting late. Scott and Beth had gone away for the weekend, and there was no one else. It had always been Dan and me.

Not anymore.

The bell rang, and my eyes narrowed. "What the hell is going on?" Ready to lay into the poor soul who'd gotten the apartment number wrong, I flung open the door, snarling, "What the fuck do you..."

Miles stood before me, casting a shy smile somewhere

between my knees and the floor. "Hi. I-I hope you don't mind me showing up here uninvited, but I was worried about you."

"Me? You were worried about me?"

He nodded, solemn as ever. "I can't imagine how you felt hearing Dan and Lindsey's news, and when I went to find you, Uncle Harry said you were upset and you'd run out of the Den."

"Uncle Harry should mind his own business," I grumbled.

"He cares about you." Miles twisted his fingers. "Uh… and I care too. I don't want you to feel like you're all alone. Can I come in?"

This wasn't how I'd planned our evening. But when had anything gone right in my life lately? Curious to see what other surprises awaited, I swept my hand out. "Be my guest," I said and closed the door behind him. "Come on in and have a seat. Can I get you a drink? Oh, no, I forgot. You had your two whole glasses of wine. Miles Halloran doesn't drink to excess." I followed him to the living room and watched him slip out of his suit jacket and carefully drape it over a chair. His ass looked as fine in a well-tailored pair of trousers as it had in a tight bathing suit, and I couldn't help wondering why he was alone.

"Maybe I will tonight. Maybe you don't know me as well as you thought you did." Miles sat on the couch, his hands clasped in his lap. "Since the two of us started talking, I've been doing a lot of things I've never imagined before." His nod was firm. "Pour me a glass. Red, if you have it, but I'll take white if you don't."

Lips twitching, I nodded and reached for a bottle of wine I'd kept from Lindsey's stash. I kind of liked this slightly bossy attitude. "I have what you like."

A smile tugged at the corner of his mouth. "You just might," Miles murmured.

My brows rose.

*Well, well.*

Was Miles drunk, or did he feel the same chemistry between us?

My phone buzzed, vibrating on the coffee table, but I ignored it. It continued, and I could see the screen lighting up with text after text. Closer to it than I was, Miles shot a quick glance at it, and his lips tightened.

"It's Dan."

"Screw him." But Dan was a relentless bastard, and I knew if I didn't answer his texts, he'd keep annoying the shit out of me all night. I huffed out a sigh and grabbed my phone to read the screen.

*I know you're with Miles.*

*He's too good for you.*

*You better not fuck around with him.*

*If you touch him, I'll make sure you never walk straight again.*

*You fucking bastard, I'm gonna kill you when I get home.*

*You know Miles is off-limits. You promised me.*

And in all caps:

*YOU BASTARD. STAY AWAY FROM HIM.*

I smiled as I scrolled through my emojis until I found the appropriate one. The hand with the middle finger sticking up. I clicked on it and hit Send, then turned off the phone completely.

"Now where were we when we were so rudely interrupted in my office?"

Shifting his position on the couch, Miles gripped his wineglass. "I don't remember."

I slid into the space next to him. "I do. You were upset by my questions, and I'm sorry if I came on like I was badgering you. But I'd really love to get to know you more. Like why you don't have a boyfriend."

"I've never had one. Satisfied?"

My curiosity outweighed my need to seduce him. There was plenty of time for that.

"Not in the least."

He shifted away from me. "Look. I came to talk about you. You're very unhappy."

"And I want to hear about your life. That would make me happy right now. Please?"

He stared into his wineglass. "It wasn't anything big. I thought I connected with someone and was wrong. No big deal. It wouldn't be the first time something like that happened."

"True, but is it preventing you from being with other people?"

A sheen of sweat glistened on Miles's brow, and he wiped it off with his sleeve. "Why're you so interested in me and my college life? We were going to talk about you. I want to help you. I think what Dan and Lindsey did affected you more than you're letting on, and it goes way beyond their betrayal. Much as that hurts, I think it's a sign of something deeper."

"What're you a fucking therapist now?" I snapped. "I'm fine."

"Really?" Miles raised a brow, which only infuriated me more. "If you were, you wouldn't be so touchy."

"I'm not touchy. I'm sick to death of talking about it. Dan and Lindsey fucked me over. It's nothing new. I should've expected it. That's what people do."

"That's a sad way to look at life. It makes you sound so jaded."

"So what? Maybe I am. How would you feel if this happened to you?"

"It wouldn't." Miles set his glass on the table, and the mildness of his tone irritated me beyond belief. Who the hell did he think he was?

"Why, because you're such a good person?"

"No. Because I wouldn't ever marry someone I wasn't madly in love with. It's not just the fact that it's Lindsey who left you, because you weren't ever truly in love with her. You're more hurt because Dan left you. And I think it's a manifestation of what happened with your parents, leaving you and your brother alone so much."

I barely knew Miles, and yet here he was, slipping under my skin, burrowing deep to get at my rotten core. And hitting the mark. Dead center.

I forced myself to smile. "Dr. Miles. Go on. Tell me more."

His brows drew together. "Don't make light of it. I'm serious. Are you seeing anyone? Therapy can help."

"Did it help you?"

He flinched but nodded. "Yeah. I went. And it did."

"If I say I'll go, will you stop talking about Lindsey and Dan?"

"That's not a reason to go to therapy. Come on, Lyon. I'm trying to help you."

I wanted to kiss that earnest mouth and decided it was time to stop talking. "I know you are," I murmured. "And I appreciate it." I leaned in and heard his breath hitch. "Let me thank you."

"You don't have t—*mmm.*"

My mouth settled over his, and I took the opportunity to slide my tongue in past those open lips. Like before, I discovered that when I was kissing Miles, the rest of the world disappeared until it was only us. His taste intoxicated me, and my hunger intensified. He held on to my shoulders, and

I pushed him down until he lay flat and my thighs straddled his. I wanted him. I had to have him. My blood beat hot and hard, and I forced my fingers to stop trembling enough to undo his tie and unbutton his shirt.

"God, you're gorgeous. Perfect."

Miles reddened. "Hardly."

"Be quiet. I said you're perfect, and I mean it." I licked his pointy nipples, then bit them, loving his squeaks and whimpers. "Look at you. What else do you want sucked?" My hands made quick work of his belt and the zipper on his trousers. "Can I, baby?" I lowered my face to the thick cock pushing out from his briefs and inhaled, growing dizzy with the heavy scent of his desire. It poured off him like honey, and I wanted to eat his sweetness. I nuzzled him, and he groaned and swelled more under my lips, the fabric growing damp.

"Lyon, what the hell?"

"No, baby. Not hell. I'm taking you to heaven if you let me." I hooked his briefs in my hands and pulled at them, taking his pants with them, until he was naked from the waist to his knees. "Goddammit, how did you keep this under wraps? It should be in a magazine."

My mouth and lips paid homage to the wide glistening head of Miles's cock, licking and sucking. Not wanting him to get off too fast, I squeezed the base and took his length deep to the back of my throat.

"Fuck, Lyon, oh my God." Miles pounded the couch with his fists while thrusting, and I welcomed it all. I hadn't been this turned-on in years, and I couldn't get enough of him. Who needed to breathe when I had the most beautiful dick in the world in my mouth? I clutched his hairy thighs, steadying him while I rose and fell on his shaft, feeling the big vein pulse under my tongue.

A low keening sounded, and Miles started trembling. I knew he was about to blow, and I increased my speed, hungry to take it all. He shook and shivered, then fucked my mouth hard and fast and came, his hot cream spilling down my throat. I swallowed every delicious drop and made sure to lick him clean. When it was over, I sat on my heels, my dick throbbing for release.

Miles's eyes were closed, but a catlike smile of satisfaction rested on his lips. He reached out a hand. "I know you're staring at me. And you must be hurting. Get out of those pants, and I'll take care of you too."

Didn't need to ask me twice, and soon his long, elegant fingers were doing a dance on my dick. I lay with my eyes closed and my legs spread, anticipating a nice hand job, when a very warm, very wet mouth enveloped my cock, and I jerked up to a half-seated position.

"Jesus," I breathed and couldn't tear my eyes away from a sight I hadn't ever expected to see: Miles's golden head between my legs, those luscious lips gliding over my aching cock. It triggered something inside me and without warning, my climax ripped through me like I was hit by a lightning strike, and I fell onto the couch, twitching and moaning while Miles sucked me like one of those old-fashioned ice pops.

When he was finished, I had no strength other than to lift my arm and give a weak wave for him to join me. "Come over here."

But he didn't. He rose to his feet and pulled up his briefs and slacks. "I—uh, that shouldn't have happened."

My eyes flew open. "What the hell are you talking about? You gave me the most amazing blowjob and you regret it? Why?"

Miserable and red-faced, Miles zipped himself up, looking adorable with his cheeks scraped by my late-evening beard and his neck littered with red spots. I liked seeing my marks on him, and a wave of possessiveness rolled over me.

"I already said it. Every time we see each other now,

it leads to sex. I don't think it's right. You're vulnerable and at a low point in your life. The last thing you need is a complication when you're trying to recover."

*Hold up. Stop and rewind this script.*

Miles thought he was taking advantage of me? The irony of it should have me laughing, but I couldn't because Miles was genuinely upset, and I didn't like seeing that.

I got to my feet and slipped on my briefs. "Hey, don't do that." Wary eyes met mine, but I ignored him and put my arm around his shoulder.

"Do what?" He stood stiff as a board.

"Beat yourself up over what happened just now." I tipped his chin, forcing him to look at me, and I smiled into his eyes. "If you're worried that you're taking advantage of the situation, you're not. I've come to terms with what's happened, and I'm trying to move on. You being here with me really helps." I brushed my lips to his.

But instead of kissing me back, Miles stepped away. "You say that, but I'm not so sure, when all you're doing is masking your pain. Some people use alcohol, but you're using sex, and it's not right for me to encourage you. So I'm sorry, but I'm going to say good night."

Giving me no time to respond, he grabbed his jacket and ran out, leaving me standing in the middle of my apartment, wondering what the hell happened. I paced the living room, my thoughts tumbling over each other.

*What did I do wrong?*

*Why doesn't he want me?*

Did Dan say something to him that changed his mind?

I turned on my phone and saw that Dan hadn't stopped his texting tirade.

*Motherfucker, you better not lay a hand on Miles. He's been hurt enough.*

Knowing how much it would hurt Dan, I answered him, getting an almost vicious satisfaction.

*I've laid more than my hand on him. He's sweet, and you can kiss my ass if you think I'm going to listen to you.*

Dan's response was immediate.

*When I come home I'm gonna break your neck.*

I laughed as I typed out my response.

*Why do you want to hurt your brother like that? By the time you come home, he's going to be in love with me. So fuck you.*

I hesitated less than a second before blocking Dan's number and then deleting him from my phone. After that, I went through all my social media and deleted and blocked Dan and Lindsey. I didn't need to see their smiling faces pop up on my screen, sharing their oh-so-happy times.

It wasn't that I wanted a wife and baby. I'd never had the paternal instinct to start a family—and who could blame me? I'd grown up with absent parents who couldn't be bothered to show up for birthdays, graduations, or any important events.

But it wasn't any of those reasons that had me staring out the window into the black of night, trying to make sense of my burning eyes and aching heart. It was the terrifying moment of clarity that maybe I'd never have someone love me because I wasn't the kind of person worthy of being loved.

Deciding that pushing Miles wasn't the best tactic, I let several days pass before going to see him. In the interim, I'd come up with a plan I believed would help me stay close to Miles while benefiting both of us, and I had to admit it was rather brilliant, if I did say so myself.

At four o'clock on Thursday, I pushed open the door to The Book Nook and spied Miles off to the side on a ladder, shelving books. I waved to Gordon, who gave me a conspiratorial grin, then crossed the store to Miles.

"Hi, there."

He jumped, flailed, and fell, knocking me to the floor. I grabbed him, using my body as a cushion for him to land.

"Jesus, you scared the shit out of me," he squawked, clutching me, and I chuckled, holding him tight.

"Nice to see you too."

His long lashes brushed my cheek, and I had to refrain from kissing him, knowing he wouldn't like such a public display. Why I cared now that it was Miles, when I never had with anyone else, wasn't something I dwelled on, preferring to move forward with my plan of action. He pushed at my shoulders, and reluctantly, I released him and got to my feet while he scrambled to his and put some space between us. He picked up the toppled ladder and stood beside it.

"Why are you here?" He scowled, that full mouth screwed up in a thin line.

*Because you're adorable and I wanted to see you.*

*Uh, whoa.* Where had that come from? But damn, it did put me in a happy place to see his face. The past few days had been one drama after the other with screwed-up deliveries, a short in the electrical system, and a mysterious complaint to the board of health that led to a surprise food inspection. I kept my cool throughout.

"I have a proposition for you." At the skeptical twist of his brows, I snickered. "No. It's not what you think. It has nothing to do with sex. Although if you've changed your mind…"

"No. I haven't." He responded way too fast, and I didn't miss the faint blush on his cheeks, but I pretended not to notice. If I moved too quickly now, I'd never get what I wanted.

Miles. In my bed.

The thought of that prize made the waiting all the sweeter.

"Just checking. I was walking through the Den today, thinking about how I could improve the services I offer members, and then it hit me and I came right over."

Miles hefted a box. "Do you mind if I keep working while you talk? These books are part of a promo, and I need to put them out on the shelf." He didn't wait for me to answer and took a handful of books out.

"Yeah, sure. Anyway, I want to start a lending library at The Lyon's Den, where my members can come and get the latest books. It will keep them occupied, and it's something I can offer them in addition to the various newspapers and magazines I have right now."

Miles placed several books on the endcap and adjusted them. "That's a nice idea. What do I have to do with it?"

"I want your help. I'd like you to run it for me. You can get me the books and order the stock. Stuff like that."

"Stuff like that? Do you think I just snap my fingers and the books magically appear? I have specific inventory, and my books are ordered well in advance. Who's going to pay for them? What kinds of books do you want—best sellers, mysteries, nonfiction?"

*Dammit.* This wasn't going according to plan. He was supposed to be all enthusiastic and want to help me.

"Please, Miles. I really want to make this idea a go, and you're the person to help. You know everything about books. Won't you help me?" I bit my lip. "I'm hoping this project will take my mind off…you know…everything else."

I peeked up at him and gave him my most winning smile.

He had to say yes.

# Chapter EIGHT

Was he kidding? With Lyon I couldn't be sure. And though I did think it would be a good addition to his club, I was suspicious.

"Why now, all of a sudden? The Lyon's Den has been open for five years, and you just now happen to think of having a library?" I folded my arms, hoping my body language would work as a shield to keep him at a distance, even if I wanted nothing more than to have him hold me again.

He grinned. "You're very inspirational." He took a step forward and lowered his voice to a rough sexy growl that shot through me like a flaming arrow. "Especially when you're coming and your face gets all flushed."

"Shut up," I hissed. "Someone might hear you."

"There's no one near. Come on, Miles. Say yes. Help me. I really do think it's a good idea."

"It…is," I admitted, begrudgingly. "Thing is, you don't need me. You can order books on your own."

"But I want you. It would be nice to have you at the Den, and you could help the members pick out the books. You're knowledgeable about what people want to read and what's popular. I'm not. Plus, I'd need someone to be there specifically to handle the library, since I'm always wandering around, keeping an eye on everything."

"I don't know…" Lyon's smile drooped, and while I hated disappointing him, I didn't want to give him expectations. "I have a full-time job here, and by the time I'm done, I'm tired. All I want is to go home, have dinner, and relax."

Lyon's eyes brightened. "Then it's perfect. You can work there and have dinner at the club. And it's not going to be like a store where people will be buying books or you'll have sales or promos. It's more like a lending library on the honor system. You can set it up any way you want. I'll give you free rein. Come on," he urged and knocked his shoulder to mine. "It'll be fun."

Fun? Working with Lyon Elliot would be many things, but I wasn't sure *fun* was a word I'd choose. And yet…the tiny glimpse I'd had of The Lyon's Den left me yearning for more despite my misgivings. I'd never been into exclusive memberships, but it would be nice to have a place to sit with others and talk about the news of the day while having a nice meal. Maybe Lyon was on to something, and starting a library would encourage more people to buy books. But I wasn't ready to say yes. Not yet.

"I'm not sure. First, as you well know, I'm not a member of your club. And second, I really don't like exclusivity. It makes people feel left out."

"Worried about the underdog, aren't you?"

There was that tone I'd always hated. How he'd managed to hide it for so long was beyond me. The sarcasm and arrogance, along with the expectation that everyone would jump to do his bidding. Well, not this guy. I glared at him.

"Someone has to think of others. I know what it's like being there. Sorry, Lyon, but I'm not interested." I turned away. "Now please excuse me, I'm busy."

His mouth fell open, and I knew it was wrong of me, but I couldn't help the smug feeling of satisfaction that I was probably the only person to ever tell him no.

Aside from Lindsey.

And while I felt sorry for Lyon and sincerely wanted to help him get over what Dan and Lindsey had done to him, I wouldn't allow myself to be used in the process. The bells over the door jingled, and I breathed a sigh of relief. I'd half expected Lyon to argue further with me, but I peeked out of the corner of my eye to see his tall figure stride away.

Gordon, of course, had something to say about it.

"I can't believe you let him go. That man wants you."

"What he wants is to use me."

"For what?"

When I explained the proposition, Gordon seemed perplexed. "It's a good idea. How is he trying to use you?"

Here came the tricky part. I wasn't ready or willing to reveal to Gordon that I'd fooled around with Lyon. Mainly because I was a little embarrassed that I'd allowed my common sense to be sabotaged by a teenage crush.

"Oh…I don't know.…It's just that I don't like being part of something that excludes people. I believe in being as inclusive as possible. As someone who was always on the outside looking in, I can't condone helping a business that only accepts you if you have enough money to belong."

Gordon pursed his lips. "Well…why don't you do something about it?"

"Such as? It's not my business. It's Lyon's. He decides how to run it."

Gordon rolled his eyes. "Damn, you're dense. The guy is obviously interested in you, so make some demands. You've got more money than you can ever spend. Use it for what you want."

A sudden rush of customers needing assistance gave me no chance to respond, and for the rest of the day, I had no time to dwell on Lyon or his business proposal.

Around six that evening, Uncle Harry strolled in, his face wreathed in smiles. A newspaper was tucked under his arm.

"How are you, my boy?" He stopped by the front desk as usual.

"Busy as anything. Would you like this week's copy of *The New Yorker*?"

"No, no. I'm going to sit and read the paper for a while."

"Sounds good. I'll bring you your tea."

"Splendid. Thank you."

He settled into his usual seat, and I switched on the electric kettle. When the water was hot, I brewed his favorite English tea and brought him over a cup, along with a few shortbreads I knew he enjoyed. He'd gone to prep school and college in London and picked up an affinity for British-isms. His eyes lit up as I approached.

"You're a prince. Now sit with me for a few minutes. It's slow, and Gordon can handle any problems that might arise."

That was the thing about Uncle Harry. He knew how to get you to do what he wanted because he was always one step ahead, preventing you from making excuses. I chuckled and took the comfy club chair next to his.

"What would you like to know?" I stretched out my legs

and wiggled my toes inside my sneakers. "It's wonderful to see you as always, but I have a feeling you didn't come by just to sit in my store and read the paper when you have a beautiful home and your own personal space at The Lyon's Den."

"All true, but the boys are shedding like mad and I'm tired of being covered in cat hair. Besides, I want to know how it went with you and Lyon when you went to his apartment the other night." He folded up his paper. "I can't help worrying about him."

Hoping my face didn't turn the furious shade of red it always did whenever I thought about Lyon, I managed to keep my voice as steady as possible. "It was fine. I didn't stay long. A man like Lyon Elliot can take care of himself."

Uncle Harry's hand shot out to hold my wrist in a surprisingly strong grip. "Don't kid yourself. Lyon has been holding it together for many years—since he was a child, in fact, but everyone has a breaking point."

I opened my mouth to correct him, then remembered that young ten-year-old boy waiting for his parents to show up to his birthday party and decided to tell him. "Dan and Lindsey called while I was there. She's pregnant. Two months along."

"I can*not*…" Harry pressed his lips together. "I know he's your brother, but I am so incredibly disappointed in Dan."

"I am as well. Don't think I'm not. Even more so because he's so cavalier about it. There's absolutely no remorse for what he and Lindsey did."

We sat for a few moments, and then I decided to broach the subject of the lending library Lyon had suggested. I was curious to get his opinion.

"Lyon came here earlier."

Harry cocked his head. "Did he? I haven't seen him in a few days. I haven't been to the club."

"He wants me to work with him to set up a lending library at The Lyon's Den."

"Lyon always was a smart boy," Harry murmured and fixed me with a gleam in his eye. "I think it's a brilliant idea."

"I'm not so sure. The thing is, I'm not even a member of his exclusive club—"

"Which is very easily rectified," Harry brushed off my objection. "I'm sure he'll make you a member if you ask."

"Which I'm concerned about as well. Why would I want to be in a club that keeps people out? I don't like gatekeeping, it goes against my principles."

"I see." Harry steepled his fingers under his chin. "Well, then…why not make a condition of your helping him to change that? Or, you have the ability yourself to sponsor people. Suggest to Lyon that you'll work with him, but you want him to allow you to sponsor several people—pick a number—and have them become members of the club. Or maybe instead of that, make it a condition that The Lyon's Den contribute *x* number of dollars to a scholarship fund or your favorite charity. I know you're on the boards of several."

"Uncle Harry, I love that. And you came up with all these suggestions so quickly." My mind raced with possibilities.

"I'm full of good ideas, my boy." His eyes twinkled.

By the time I got home and ordered my dinner, I was too tired to get dressed again to go to the Den and make a proposal to Lyon. Besides, I knew when I spoke to him, I'd have to have everything in order because while Lyon Elliot might be a hedonist, he was definitely a businessman and wouldn't accept what I wanted simply to get into my pants.

At least I didn't think so.

I popped a piece of sushi into my mouth and was about to turn on the television when my phone rang with a FaceTime call from Dan. I sighed, brushed my hands off, and hit the screen to accept.

"Hi. Don't tell me you're calling to say you're having twins now."

But Dan, tense and unsmiling, didn't laugh at my attempt at a joke. "You're alone, right?"

"Yeah. Thanks for reminding me of that fact."

"Look, Miles, you need to cut off all ties with Lyon."

"What?" I stretched out on the couch and picked up my beer. "What does that mean?"

"Exactly what I said. He's bad news, and I want you to stay away from him."

Annoyed as fuck didn't begin to describe my emotions. "Who the hell do you think you are?"

"I'm your older brother, and I know Lyon. Just do what I say."

"I don't even know what you mean—'stay away from him.' "

Well, I did, but it wasn't like I was going to let Dan know what went down between Lyon and me. Especially me going down on Lyon.

"Don't fucking lie to me, Miles. I know you've always had a massive crush on him, but he's a user."

"Jesus. Let me ask you something. Why were you his best friend all these years if you have such a low opinion of him?"

Dan's lip curled. "It was fun, but now I'm married and I'm gonna be a father. I see who he really is."

The irony of it all wasn't lost on me. "You break your best friend's trust by sleeping with his fiancée and getting her pregnant, and you want to warn me about Lyon? What's wrong with this picture?" I picked up my beer and took a gulp. "You've got to be kidding me."

"Lindsey said you're too smart and would see right through what he's doing, but I'm not so sure. Lyon is a cold, manipulative bastard."

Hurt beyond belief, I smiled tightly. "Yeah, I am smart. So you're saying a guy like Lyon could never be interested in someone like me."

And Dan, wrapped up in himself as usual, nodded. "Exactly. It's all to get back at me. He'd never be with you if it wasn't to get revenge on me for marrying Lindsey." Relief spread across his face. "I knew you were too smart to fall for his bullshit."

"And you warned him off me years ago anyway. To protect me from him, of course. Even if he might've been interested in me."

Dan shrugged. "Well, yeah. I knew better. He didn't want you. It's all about the chase for him. He'd never be into someone like you."

My palms grew sweaty. "Thanks, Dan. I'm glad we had this talk."

"I was so afraid he'd already gotten to you and I was too late."

"No, you're right on time. I was thinking about making a decision that I now see wasn't in my best interest. Talking to you made it all clear."

He gave a thumbs-up. "Awesome. Well, I'm gonna go wake Lindsey up now. She took a nap, and we're gonna go to the beach for the sunset. It's so fucking awesome here."

He could have his cake and eat it, but I should sit home alone every night. "You have fun. When are you coming home again?"

"We're here for two more weeks. This is the life, dude. You need to find a boyfriend and come to Costa Rica. *Pura vida*, you know?"

I grinned. "Sounds like a plan. See ya."

I finished off my sushi and took a shower. When I'd finished dressing up in my suit and tie, I still hadn't dealt with all the anger and hurt from my conversation with Dan.

I wasn't Lyon's type? He couldn't possibly want someone like me?

I picked up a bottle of rarely used aftershave I'd gotten from Uncle Harry as a birthday gift and slapped a little on my face.

"Let's see what happens tonight. I have my own plans."

The Den was crowded, which should have made me happy, but instead I slouched at my table, sipping a double Scotch. I'd been invited to join several ongoing conversations concerning potential real estate developments or stock investments, where my participation would bring me a tremendous return, but my head wasn't into business at the moment.

Why didn't Miles want to work with me? After what had gone down between us at my apartment, I'd thought it would be an easy thing to get him to fall for me, but this plan of mine was proving harder to jump-start than I'd thought. Miles was stubborn and unpredictable, but…I liked talking to him. And kissing him. He was sexy and adorable and…fun. That wasn't part of the game. I frowned.

"Why are you in such a bad mood?" Victor asked. He

braced his arms against the chair opposite mine, dark eyes questioning. "The Den is hopping and has been every night. You're doing great—business-wise."

"I'm not in a bad mood. I'm fucking fantastic." I raised my glass to him. "See?"

"I've seen mug shots with happier faces. Are you still upset about Lindsey and Dan eloping?"

Was I?

"Not really. I'm resigned to the fact that they're together and having a baby."

Victor's eyes popped open. "A baby? Damn, that was fast work."

"She's two months along," I said dryly.

"Man, Lyon. I'm sorry. I hope you told Dan off."

My smile was thin. "As well as you can imagine. Plus, his membership has been revoked and refunded."

"So lemme ask you something." Victor took a seat. "What do you want with his brother? I saw the way you looked at him when he came to see you, and man…you were ready to eat him alive."

And here I'd thought I hid it so well. "Miles is a nice guy."

"That he is. Which is why I was wondering what you saw in him. This is all so sudden. I didn't know you were into guys, and even so, I didn't picture someone like him."

A faint smile touched my lips. "Why do you need to know anything, and who said it's all of a sudden?" Miles's soft mouth clinging to mine and his breathless moans of pleasure had carried me through the week, and my thoughts turned to that night in my apartment. Had he always been this sexy, this sensual, and I'd been too busy on the scene to notice? Well, I was damn sure noticing him now. "Maybe I've always had a thing for him."

"Hmm." Victor remained unconvinced. "I dunno. You're free to hook up with anyone and everyone like you used to before Lindsey, and yet you pick the brother of your former best friend who fucked you over? What's really going on?"

"Why do I have to have an ulterior motive? Maybe I just like spending time with Miles."

Victor frowned, but a waiter came to the bar, so he had to go fulfill the order. I left my seat, intending to make a sweep of the Den, when I spotted Miles at the entrance, speaking to Anton, the front-door host. My heart kicked up, and a thrill ran through me. When Anton shook his head, I hustled across the floor to stop Miles from walking away.

"Stop. Wait, Miles." Both he and Anton turned to face me.

"Lyon, he's not a member." Anton's brows drew together in puzzlement. "I know he came in the other time as your guest, but you don't have him on the sheet to allow entry."

I couldn't fault Anton for doing his job, but I sure as hell wasn't letting an opportunity like this slip away. "I know, but he's okay. Put his name on the list. Miles Halloran. He's to be allowed entry at any time." I gave him a quick nod and turned my attention to Miles, who'd remained standing by the door. "Sorry. I didn't know you were coming."

I ran my gaze over him, appreciating that once again, he'd gotten dressed up. This time he wore a gray suit with a blue-and-white-striped shirt and a dark-blue tie. His golden hair glistened in the overhead lights, and his cheeks were dusted with a darker-blond scruff. Damn, he was sweet and fucking hot, and I wanted another taste. This had nothing to do with Dan and everything to do with how amazing he'd felt in my mouth and arms the other night.

"I-I should've let you know, but it was a spur-of-the-moment decision."

*Will you walk into my parlor? said the spider to the fly.*

The old poem I'd learned years ago popped into my head as I put my hand on his shoulder and smiled into his crystal-blue eyes. "My favorite kind. Follow me."

I steered him toward my corner table, giving Victor a head tilt. With a shake of his head, he poured out a glass of red—the same vintage Miles had enjoyed the night he'd come for dinner—and brought it over. I refused to make eye contact with Victor, uninterested in his psychoanalysis of what I was doing.

We sat across from each other. Miles, his usual quiet self, studied me. I raised my glass of Scotch. "To a new beginning? Is that why you're here?"

He rubbed the stem of his glass. "When were you first interested in me?"

Not the question I expected, but I was willing to go with it. Maybe he needed more reassurance I was attracted to him, and that wouldn't be a hardship. "I guess I became interested in you around the time you were fifteen and I was getting ready to graduate from high school. I thought you were cute, especially in your bathing suit."

"And you mentioned it to Dan, right?"

"Yeah. He was not having it." I shook my head, remembering Dan's fury when I told him I thought his brother was hot.

"He told you to keep away from me."

Ah, now I understood. He was pissed at Dan. That I could get behind, but I could see there was something more behind his eyes—genuine sadness and anger. An unfamiliar emotion twisted inside me. Whether this was a game or not, I didn't like to see Miles hurting.

"Yeah. I did it to keep our friendship, but I was stupid, wasn't I?" On impulse, I reached over and took his hand, rubbing our fingers together. "I should've gone with my heart." His hand in mine relaxed the tension coiled like a snake in my belly. It was nice sitting here with him, not drinking away the evening or gossiping about other people or even talking business. Dan was into partying, and Lindsey was all about scoring another contract to sell her tequila. Maybe we never scratched below the surface to find out who we really were.

Miles was different. He saw me—even saw right through me.

Funny how I didn't mind.

I could get used to this. With him.

Miles licked his lips. "I-I wanted to talk about your idea. For the lending library."

"Sure. Tell me what you're thinking."

There was such sincerity in those blue eyes, I actually stopped thinking of seducing him and concentrated on his words.

"I'm trying to figure out how to make it work, without compromising my principles. I don't believe in exclusivity based on wealth."

"So what's your suggestion?" My fingers tangled with his.

"How many charitable events do you have here?"

My stomach sank. "Uh, none." My cheeks burned in embarrassment. "I never thought of it."

Disappointment clouded Miles's face. "Really? Wow. I'm surprised. A business like this, with so many wealthy patrons, could do incredible things for the people of this city."

Ashamed over the rebuke, no matter that it was gentle, I hung my head. Miles was right. For all the issues I had with my parents, they were relatively minor when compared to others' problems. My life had so far been an easy glide. I'd never had to worry about food or shelter…anything. If I wanted something, I got it. Simple as that.

"Yeah. You're right. I'm a selfish fuck."

A fleeting, sweet smile touched Miles's lips. "Well, I wouldn't go that far. You're not a deliberately hurtful person. I think you have the potential to do positive things for people."

I nodded, eager for him to see that there was good in me. I could be the type of person Miles would respect. Maybe it was sudden, but I wanted to convince him that I wasn't the cold, heartless bastard Dan had made me out to be. "Tell me what you're thinking. I'm open to suggestions." I winked. "Putty in your hands."

"Hardly," he scoffed, and he was so damn cute when he screwed up his face and chewed on that delicious lower lip while thinking. "Maybe you could donate a portion of the membership fees to a charity—we can pick one and decide. Or you could have an actual event where members would have to pay a certain amount to attend."

"I like the first idea better. What about…" I tapped my fingers on my chin. "What about if I had a check-off box on the application and the yearly membership renewal form that listed several charities? The Lyon's Den would then direct a portion of their yearly dues to a separate account. It would be mandatory in the sense that if they don't pick one, I'll do it for them."

Miles's entire face shone. "That's amazing. I love it. And I knew if given the chance, you'd come up with something. I think it's wonderful."

*I think you're wonderful.*

The words almost tumbled out of my mouth. What the hell? I had a plan I couldn't deviate from. This was all working so well, I almost forgot the ultimate goal of hurting Dan. Maybe using Miles wasn't as appealing as I first intended, but Dan couldn't get away with screwing me so bad. I attempted to flirt and squeezed his arm.

"Thanks. But it's all because of you. You're such an amazing influence. You make me want to be a better person."

Christ, did people really fall for this shit? It seemed the answer was yes, as the smile Miles gave me rivaled the brightness of the sun. It warmed a part of me I didn't know existed until that moment.

"It wasn't me. I was just a catalyst. It was always in you, waiting." He cast me a nervous glance. "I'm sorry. I shouldn't have doubted you."

*Oh yes, you should have.*

"It's okay. I didn't give you much reason to trust me."

*And you still shouldn't.*

"I do now."

"Good. Maybe then you'll go on a real date with me?"

He flushed pink. "A date? Why?"

Apparently, he hadn't yet fallen under my spell, and that had to change quickly.

"Silly. So we can get to know each other better without all these distractions." Still holding his hand, I teased his palm with my fingers. A shiver ran through him, but I held on. "Let's go to dinner, and I'll get tickets for a show."

He sat and pondered while I grew increasingly nervous. Finally, he said, "Can I ask you something?"

"Anything."

"Are you doing all this to get back at Dan?" He lifted his chin. "Don't lie to me, Lyon. Not when we're just starting to become friends."

*Fuck.*

I had no idea how to respond to that.

He sighed. "Silence is golden. I think I have my answer."

"No." I held on to him tighter. "You don't. Not really. Can I explain?"

"Sure." He withdrew his hand. "But I don't think you need to. I know what it is."

"Oh?" I arched a brow. "Tell me, then."

"You want to get back at Dan for fucking you over with Lindsey. So you're hitting him where you know it's going to hurt the most. Me."

"It's not—"

"I said don't lie." He slapped the table, causing the glasses to rattle and drawing stares from other patrons. I'd yet to see Miles truly angry, and after years of him melting into the woodwork, it was a turn-on to see the fire in his blood. And then, amazingly, the anger faded. His eyes danced, and that sweet mouth tugged up in a knowing smile. "And you know what? I'm pissed at him too."

"I know you are. And I appreciate your support, because he's your brother and you could stick by him and tell me to go to hell."

"I could," he admitted. "But I won't." He leaned in close. "And I want to mess with his head too. He deserves it. Not only for the terrible way he treated you, but because he thought he had the right to interfere in my life and dictate who I should and shouldn't be with."

In my thirty-five years on this earth, I'd never been more shocked. Not when Dan and Lindsey eloped. Not when they told Miles they were having a baby.

No. Here was nice boy Miles Halloran, the person who'd never had a bad word to say about anyone, the man who wouldn't even step on a bug because it had feelings, sitting across from me, with sparks flying from his eyes and a deliciously evil grin, offering to be my partner in crime to fuck his brother up and pretend we were a thing.

"Wait a second." Before I said something I might possibly regret, I had to make certain I read the room correctly. "Are you saying you want to pretend to be a couple to Dan?"

"Yeah. When he told me he warned you away from me, I can't tell you how angry I was. How many other men has he kept away from me, all in the name of protecting me? Who the hell does he think he is?"

Eager to egg Miles further on the hate-Dan train, I encouraged him. "That bastard has no right to dictate who you can and can't be with. If you want to have one-night stands, it's your life. And if you want to be with me, he has no right to say no."

"But you were going ahead with your plan to use me in your war with Dan, weren't you? That's what all this is about, right? The lending library, the cozy dinner for two, the invite to join The Lyon's Den…it's all right if it is. I just want the truth. I think we both deserve it, don't you?"

*Dammit.* I couldn't lie to him. That would make me a huge shit. It would be like lying to Uncle Harry. A big fat no. But here was where I'd have to make my own stranger-than-fiction confession.

"I'll admit it started that way, but the more we've spoken and gotten to know each other, the more I found I really do like you. It actually made me angrier at Dan because maybe you and I could've been friends too. Or more. Instead, he warned me to never come near you." I slid my hand across the table to tangle with his fingers. "The other night wasn't a hardship to be with you, if that's what you're thinking. So I guess it's my turn to ask—do you still want to go through with this?"

I waited, holding my breath, unsure what his answer would be.

# Chapter TEN

It shouldn't have surprised me. Lyon wasn't the type to let someone get the better of him, and his anger at Dan and Lindsey was way greater than a simple annoyance over a wrong meal delivered or even an expected business deal gone bad. This was a blow to his heart, and Dan might think Lyon was cold and calculating and didn't give a damn, but it showed me that maybe it was Dan who was the cold one and didn't care whom he hurt.

Plus, I was pissed as hell at my brother for pulling the strings behind the curtains of my life. If I'd wanted to have a fling with Lyon, I was an adult and should've had the opportunity to make my own decision. Considering Dan often thought with his dick and not his brain, he had no right meddling in my sex life.

Could I believe Lyon when he said he really liked me? I guessed time would tell, but I had no hesitation in answering.

"I'm all in. Dan had zero right to stick his nose in my business. If I want to bang every guy in the city, that's my choice."

Lyon's jaw hardened, and those indigo-blue eyes turned an angry gray. "You can't say shit like that, Miles."

I laughed in his face. "Coming from the man who used to brag he slept with half of the sorority girls in college? Come on. Double standard much?"

Apparently, Lyon wasn't used to being challenged, and this part might be just as much fun as my actual revenge against Dan.

"Me, yes, but not you, Miles. You're a nice person. You'd never use someone or have sex with them just because they made it easy."

"So what you're saying is I'm predictable." God, I hated being placed in a box.

At Lyon's dismissive shrug, I rose from my chair abruptly and stood over him. He arched his brow, which only infuriated me further.

"How about this?" I took him by the shoulder and planted a kiss on his open mouth. If I was hoping to shock Lyon, maybe I did, but I was even more stunned by the absolute hunger that slammed into me at the touch of his tongue to mine. Thoroughly rattled, I barely heard the loud murmurs in the background. I was too aware of Lyon's hands at my waist, his lips hot and demanding on mine.

When we finally broke apart, a flush had settled over Lyon's high cheekbones, and his breath came unsteady. "Wh-what was that for?" he croaked.

I refused to let him see how that one kiss spun my world out of control, and I waited until I could speak without my voice cracking. "You called me predictable. I wanted to show you I'm not the person you think I am."

"You're not kidding," he muttered as he ran a hand through his hair, then huffed out a sigh. "So this means it's a go? You want to fuck with Dan's head?" His eyes blazed. "Be forewarned: I don't half-ass things. This isn't going to be a situation where we only act cutesy in front of him."

"I figured you were a whole-ass type of person," I responded, hoping he'd pick up on my sarcasm. "What're you thinking?"

"We begin well before they come home—like tonight. We show everyone we're into each other, that we can't keep our hands off each other."

"Like how I just kissed you?"

His intent gaze caught me off guard, and when he stood and put his arms around me, I couldn't stop the shivers running through me.

"Lyon?" I breathed.

"No. Like this." He took my chin in between his thumb and forefinger and plundered my mouth, stealing the very air from my lungs. I strained toward him, my lips clinging to his, while I sucked his tongue. A deep rumble vibrated into my chest, and Lyon murmured against my cheek, "You see the difference? Not that I'm complaining about how you kissed me. I like that too."

"Hmm?" I sighed, dreamy-eyed and ready to swoon. "Oh. Yeah. I do. Me too. I think we can manage it."

Chuckling softly, Lyon nuzzled me for a moment. "Great. Looks like we started here tonight. We have quite an audience." Facing the dining room filled with smirking faces, I could see a few men didn't look thrilled about our very public display. I didn't care. I didn't care about anything other than Lyon's warm, hard body pressed to mine.

"S-so, what about my suggestions for the lending library?"

"You can do anything you want," he whispered in my ear. "With the library and with me."

Holding on to my sanity was proving harder than I'd imagined. I drew in a deep breath and extricated myself from Lyon's grip. My brain now unscrambled, I could finally think about something other than kissing and touching Lyon, and I began to make plans.

"I think the library is a hell of a lot easier." My smile was guarded but gentle. It would be so easy to start an affair with Lyon, but I already knew how that story ended—with me falling in love with Lyon while he kept me around to have his fun, but nothing more. "I like the idea of you donating a portion of the membership fees to charity, and I think you should also put on an event to bring awareness, so how about focusing on literacy?"

"Okay. I'll leave it up to you. You have full rein, and I'll give you access to the club. Whatever you need." Lyon's eyes twinkled. "You can have access to me as well."

"Do tell." I shook my head at his flirtation.

"If we want to make this work and fuck with Dan's head, we have to make it look as though we're together." Lyon cupped my jaw, threading his free hand through my hair to hold me steady, and ran his nose along my cheek. "It's not too hard a stretch. You know I want you."

"I know. But I want to take it slow." As I was rapidly learning, my brain switched off whenever Lyon touched me. I closed my eyes and fell into his kiss, becoming a needy mess of emotions. I sighed into his mouth and allowed him liberties I would never have with anyone else.

"This is as slow as I go, baby," he murmured, and a thrill ran through me, hearing him use that term of endearment. It might all be for show, but I could feel the swell of his dick against my belly. He wanted me.

"I can't imagine you at full speed."

His steady gaze pierced me to the core. "You won't have to imagine for long. I don't intend to wait forever to get you in my bed. The little taste I've had of you isn't enough. I want you. And I get what I want. Always." He gave me another lingering kiss that left my toes curled. "Do you want to see the space I was planning for the library?"

"Huh?" Still dizzy from his mouth on mine, I blinked rapidly to bring myself down to earth. "Oh, uh, yeah. Sure."

*Get it the fuck together, Miles. Look at Lyon. He's fucking cool as an iceberg and isn't letting your kisses get to him.*

I pushed aside all my dirty fantasies of me and Lyon so I could concentrate. "Show me." Holding my head high and ignoring the leers and grins of the men we passed, I followed Lyon around the corner of the main salon to a set of intricately carved wooden doors. Lyon unlocked them and we stepped inside. A large empty room boasted built in, floor-to-ceiling empty bookshelves and narrow soaring windows.

"It's like it was waiting for you." Lyon strolled around the room. "All you need is a computer system and a desk to check people out."

"And inventory. Don't forget that. It's a major expense."

He waved me off. "I'm not worried. I'll give you a credit card from the business, and you can order whatever you need."

"Okay." I walked the space. "When do you plan on having this open? If I start right away, I'd need at least a week to get stock, plus I have to see about my own store's schedule. But also, I can't work here until closing time. That's not until midnight, right?"

"Yeah." Lyon crossed his arms. "You could give your

assistant more responsibility. I'm sure he'd love that, and then you can be here."

"Nice try, I hate to break it to you, but I like working in my store. I could make the library on the honor system and leave a ledger for people to sign books in and out."

"I worry about honor with this crew." He scoffed. "You know these people."

"Okay, well…maybe Gordon could come work here?" My smile was mischievous, and his face fell, as if he were a little child and I'd told him there was no more candy.

"That's not what I want."

I patted his cheek. "I know. But sometimes you can't get what you want. Even you. I have to go. I'll talk to you soon."

I left him standing with his mouth open.

The following afternoon I was in my store, looking up best sellers and nonfiction books I believed would be of interest to the Den's members. Books about finance, investing, along with biographies of warriors, ex-military, captains of industry and the like, were all on my list. As promised, Lyon had messengered over a club credit card, and I'd begun to make purchases. When my phone rang, I was in the middle of debating whether to also include hobbies such as gardening, wine-tasting, painting, fishing, and boating. These men had to do something besides thinking of making money all day, didn't they?

"Hello?"

"Are you fucking crazy?"

Dan's heavy breathing filled my ear, and I clicked out of the computer screen.

"Hello to you too, and last time I checked, no."

"Do you know how many texts and pictures I woke up to of you kissing Lyon last night in the Den?"

"Hmm." I cast a glance to the ceiling. "My guess is quite a few."

"It's not funny," he roared. "Please tell me you haven't had sex with him."

My stomach dropped, and I knew my face was red. "Are you kidding me? What right do you have to ask me that?"

"I'm your brother, dammit. Did you?"

"You know what? Fuck you." God, it felt good to say it. All the years I'd let him boss me around and tell me what to do…I'd been so stupid. Not anymore.

"See? He's already affecting our relationship."

"No. I've finally got my eyes open. I'm with Lyon, and there's nothing you can do to stop it."

"We'll see about that," Dan said grimly. "Wait until I come home."

"Don't hurry back." Heart pounding, I ended the call, ashamed I'd aired my personal life in public. A quick scan of the store left me feeling a little better, as there were only two customers browsing the shelves, well out of earshot of my conversation. Gordon stared at me with newfound respect.

"Damn, that was epic. I bet you feel good. And props to you for telling him where to shove it. He's always talked down to you, and it pissed me off."

My hands still shook, and I pushed them through my hair. "I've never spoken to him like that. I always looked up to him. Our parents both worked long hours, and so many nights it was just him and me and the nannies. He wasn't only my big brother; he was my best friend. I wanted to be just like him." There was a huge lump in my throat. "Now, I don't know…was I stupid?"

Gordon folded his arms. "It's not like he's such a great role model. It's time for you to do what you want instead of listening to him."

Remembering my conversation with Lyon from the night before, I hitched my chair closer to Gordon's. "Lemme ask you something. How would you feel about taking on more responsibility here at the store? It would mean staying late to close every night. Obviously there would be a pay increase."

His eyes lit up. "Really? I'd love it. And I don't mind staying late. I've been seeing this guy, and he works at a coffee shop, so he doesn't get off until after ten o'clock anyway." His smile was coy. "Does this have anything to do with the library idea Lyon proposed? Which you know I think is great."

Having grown up so close with Dan, I'd never needed a best friend—Dan was the one I'd turned to—but now with us polarized, I found myself gravitating to Gordon and opening up to him. He listened without judging. He was there for me and me alone. I felt he truly had my best interests at heart and no ulterior motives.

Except for wanting me to hook up with Lyon.

"Yeah. He wants me to be there at The Lyon's Den to run it, and since they're open until midnight…" I shrugged. "I'm still not sure…"

"About what?" Gordon's brows drew together, his face scrunched up in puzzlement. "He has the hots for you. Have you banged him yet?"

I winced. Damn, I felt old. I was so not into the twenty-speak of boning and banging. "Uh, no. I didn't want to seem too easy." Not like I hadn't been lusting after him for half my life. No big deal.

"Are you kidding me? Make that happen as soon as possible. I bet he's an animal in bed." Gordon winked. "Like his namesake."

"You're being ridiculous." Face flaming, I returned to the computer and started the order process, but Gordon was like a dog with a bone and wouldn't drop it.

"Man, you have one of the hottest guys in the city after you, and you're not doing the deed. And you say I'm ridiculous? Guys like that only wait so long."

I heard what Gordon said, but Lyon would wait because he wanted to shove it in Dan's face. It had nothing to do with me.

"Whatever will be will be. Now let's figure out a schedule for you. I'm not sure how long this library thing Lyon is suggesting will last, but I'm happy to give you the promotion and responsibility no matter what. You deserve it."

"You deserve good things too, Miles."

Did I? I wasn't so sure.

# Chapter ELEVEN

The shocked expression on Miles's face was so damn adorable, I leaned in for a kiss but was met with air. He hadn't even invited me inside, and I remained on his stoop. I gave him my most disarming smile, but when he stayed silent, forehead puckered, I wasn't sure my plan would work.

"What? You don't like apple-picking?"

"Don't pout. It's not a cute look for you. And yes, of course I do. But since when do you commune with nature? That's something I'd never picture Lyon Elliot enjoying."

I tried for fun and flirty. "Why not? I'm sure I'll be a master apple-picker. And I checked—they do the corn-maze thing and the hayride, although I'm not a fan of straw up my butt."

Did I sound too chatty? I was trying hard to convince

Miles I could be on a date with him and not expect sex. Not that I didn't want it, but he would trust me so much more if I did the unexpected. And apparently, being a master of autumnal pleasures was the thing, because he graced me with one of those full-blown Miles smiles, and that, plus a sparkle in those big baby blues, sent a ridiculous jolt of warmth surging through me.

"I just don't know what to do with you."

This time I managed to kiss those pursed lips. "Anything you want, baby. I have a million ideas." I winked. "Now let's go. I've rented a car, and the thruway traffic can be a bitch."

It took us two and a half hours to get to the town I'd researched as being one of the quaintest for this kind of stuff. Granville, New York was east of Hudson Falls and more rural than I'd anticipated. But I figured Miles would be into all the greenery and cute, kitschy, country stuff, and from his shining eyes and the way he would point every five minutes, oohing and aahing at cows and sheep, I knew I'd done well.

A hand-painted wooden sign directed us down a bumpy gravel road, and soon we were parked along with over fifty other cars at High Point Orchards. Not only were there apples, but also the ubiquitous country market where you could purchase all sorts of homemade and homegrown goodies.

Miles nudged my shoulder. "This is a perfect way to spend a gorgeous fall day. Thank you."

I opened my mouth to make a snarky comeback about how my idea of perfect was him under me, but it seemed out of place up here, where the air blew so fresh and clean and the birds chirped in trees blazing with autumn colors.

"You're welcome. Your eyes perfectly match the brilliant blue of the sky. In other words, gorgeous."

"That's sweet. Thank you." He squeezed my hand.

*Maybe this is what happiness is.*

I rubbed my hands together. "Let's go get some apples."

For the next two hours we wandered the orchard, where I discovered I had a preference for tart but sweet, and I might've crunched a few instead of putting them in our baskets.

"Really?" Miles raised a brow when I tossed the core of my third.

"I should become a taste tester. Granny Smiths are too tart, but Macs don't have the taste I'm looking for. I like the Pink Lady and the Honeycrisp best, followed by Winesap and Fuji."

"Maybe you'll bake me an apple pie after all this," Miles joked up on the ladder, but I didn't laugh. It puzzled me that I enjoyed being here, so far away from the hustle and crowds. I couldn't remember ever taking a day for myself to disconnect and disengage, and I liked it.

I was discovering there were a lot of things I'd never known I liked.

"You never know."

I stayed below and admired his ass in jeans so worn and faded, I knew without touching how velvety soft they'd feel. That didn't mean I wasn't aching to run my hands over their softness, but I refrained because Miles wouldn't like it. He wore a blue sweat shirt that rode up when he reached to pick fruit, and I made no attempt to avert my eyes from that dark-gold trail of hair disappearing beneath his jeans. I was shameless in my staring. He caught me several times and shook his head as he climbed down the ladder.

"You're terrible. You don't even try and hide it."

"Hide what? That you're hot and sexy and I want to jump your bones? I'm not dead. And if it's going to be right there in my face, I'm going to look at it." I grinned. "I like to look at pretty things. Like your ass."

"Oh, brother. Let's go pay for this, Romeo."

After we loaded the bags into the car, I took his hand.

"I'm hungry and I want a snack. It's apple-cider-doughnut time; then the hayride starts at five. They serve mulled wine."

Waiting on the long line for our food, Miles gave me a funny look. "You're really into this. Did you go apple-picking a lot as a kid?"

I'd have choked with laughter if it wasn't so fucking sad. "Are you joking? Who would Scott and I go with, our nanny? No, I've never been. I guess I didn't expect to enjoy it so much, but I'm having a good time. I remember your family went upstate every year."

It was one of the few times Dan and I didn't spend vacations with each other. The Halloran family took one family-only week upstate a year, just the four of them, and I recalled that week being a lonely one. I'd wander around feeling like I'd lost my best friend. Scott and I would play together and our nanny would attempt to keep us busy, but I missed Dan.

"Yeah, to the house in Woodstock. You and Dan used to go there in the summer when you were in college." Was that a flicker of pain in his eyes, or was it a shadow from the clouds overhead? "My parents sold the place a few years ago. They hadn't used it in years."

We took our paper bags and cups to one of the wooden swings set about the grounds and sat. The doughnuts were hot, greasy, sticky-sweet, and better than anything I'd had at the last Michelin-starred restaurant I'd eaten in, and I stuffed two in my face and licked my lips. Miles had gone quiet since our conversation, and I nudged his foot with mine.

"What's wrong?"

"When I was eight, we were up at the house, and I decided to get up early one morning and do laps in the pool. I'd made the swim team and was anxious to prove I could swim faster than anyone else in my group."

"You were like a fish. Rarely got out of the pool. When

you were in high school, your team was chasing the state championship, and Dan and I would go to cheer you on. I couldn't stop staring at your ass. You in that Speedo played a very big part in my bisexual realization. So thank you."

I expected a snarky comeback or at least a smile but got neither. A haunted expression took over. "Yeah. Well, that morning I pushed myself harder than ever and got a cramp when I was in the deep end."

I sat up quickly, setting the swing in motion. This wasn't fun or about sex. This was Miles sharing an important moment in his life. With me. "Shit. What happened?"

"I started to go under. I would've drowned for sure—it was early, and I was alone."

"Eight years old was pretty young to swim alone." I couldn't imagine how scared he must've been.

"I thought I'd be able to show off to my parents." His sorrow hit me like an arrow through the heart. "I wasn't popular in sports like Dan, and I wanted them to be proud of me for something."

*Dammit*. I wasn't supposed to like Miles as much as I did. But I wanted those sweet Miles smiles, not big sad eyes that tugged at a heart that wasn't supposed to care.

"Your parents are great. They loved you no matter what. You know that. What happened?"

"Dan was also outside. He was going to meet a football coach to practice his throwing and was getting his bike out when he said he heard me screaming. He jumped in and pulled me out." His doughnut and cider forgotten, Miles wrapped his arms around his waist. "I swore Dan to secrecy. I never wanted anyone else to know what an idiot I was."

"Why would you say that? It wasn't your fault. I mean, it was dangerous for you to swim alone at that age, but we all do things we shouldn't when we're young." It dawned on me then. "Is that what Dan said? That you were an idiot?"

"Yeah. He never lets me forget that if it wasn't for him, I might've drowned. He's right. I know I shouldn't have gone swimming without an adult. But he went over the top on the protective-older-brother part."

I found all this fascinating since it was a side of Dan I'd never known. "How so? Were there more instances?"

"Yeah…there was the time I stood up in the rowboat and fell in the pond. The rowboat trapped me underneath. Dan got me out." Red splotches covered his cheeks. "I was kind of a walking disaster, and when I got older that bled into my dating life."

I waited for him to explain further, but he stayed silent, and I wasn't going to push to hear about the men who'd broken his heart.

"We all make mistakes. No one is perfect."

"Yeah, well, some of us make more than others. That's why I decided I'm better off with books than people."

"And why Dan appointed himself your guardian." In a way, I understood Dan's thinking. You want to protect the people you love, and Dan, for all his shitty behavior and faults, did love his brother.

"Yeah. But now it's to the extreme. I determine my sex life, not my brother."

"And I'm damn glad to hear you say that."

Taking advantage of the moment, I scooched over to him and pressed a kiss to his frowning mouth until it softened and he met my tongue with his. When we finally broke apart, Miles wasn't the only one breathing heavily. It took a few seconds before I could find my voice to speak.

"I think it's time for the hayride."

We wiped our fingers on the napkins, tossed everything into the garbage cans, and then I took his hand in mine. He gave me one of those sideways smiles, and I laced our fingers together. There were eight other people already seated in the wagon, and I picked the corner so I could squeeze Miles in next to me. The promised mulled wine was handed around, the horses started up, and we were off.

Miles said, "If you would've asked me six months ago where I would be on a Sunday afternoon, going on a hayride with you wouldn't have even made it on the top one hundred list. The top one thousand, to be honest."

My arm rested on the back of the wagon, and I slid it over his shoulder so I could play with the ends of his golden hair. "Yeah? Where does it stand now?"

The sparkle had returned to his eyes, and he settled against my shoulder with a sigh. "I'll let you know when it's over."

"Challenge accepted," I murmured in his ear. Miles had been taking pictures, and I plucked the phone out of his fingers and took a selfie of us, with me kissing his cheek and his smiling mouth. The horses clip-clopped along the dirt road, and in the distance a cow mooed. I sipped my spicy wine. It was pastoral and out of my comfort zone, but so was me on a date in the country with Miles Halloran. "I always come out on top."

Night had fallen by the time we returned to the city. Miles's house was blessed with a small driveway, which meant I was lucky not to have to look for parking. I cut the engine, and we stared at each other. He cleared his throat.

"Thanks for the day. It was exactly what I needed."

"Aren't you going to ask me inside?" I undid my seat belt.

Instant wariness spread over his face. "Uh, well, it's getting late."

I grinned. "I have to pee. Must've been that coffee we stopped for on the thruway. I'll help you carry your stuff in." Without waiting for an answer, I popped the trunk and got out. I handed him several bags of apples and other stuff he'd picked up and followed him into the house.

"The powder room is the third door on the left."

I didn't really have to go, but I'd wanted an excuse to get inside. I washed my hands and returned to find Miles hadn't moved from where I'd left him. His guard was up, as it should be. I wasn't leaving until I had another taste of him.

"No cup of coffee for the road?"

"I'm out of coffee."

"How about tea? That's your drink of choice."

"But not yours. I know what you're doing."

"Good. Then you won't be surprised when I do this." I pulled him to me and kissed him, sucking his tongue, tasting the sweetness of the apples and doughnuts we'd eaten. His mouth was like a drug I was becoming addicted to. "You drove me crazy all day, do you know that?"

"N-no," Miles stuttered, his eyes wide and hazy.

"So fucking sexy. I could kiss you for hours." Holding him against the wall with my body pressed to his, I took my time trailing kisses down his neck. He whimpered and squirmed, which only ramped up my desire because I could feel him grow hard and thick. "You know how much I want you."

"Lyon, please, no."

At his words, I immediately withdrew and gazed at him with concern. "What's wrong?"

"Nothing." He rubbed his face. "But I'm not sleeping with you just because we had a nice day upstate."

Annoyed, I shoved my hands into the pockets of my jeans. "Nice? I thought it was a fucking fantastic day."

A half smile teased his lips. "All right. It was fucking fantastic. But this?" He waved a finger between the two of us. "Still not happening."

"Spoilsport," I muttered, and he cackled.

"You look like a three-year-old who was just told no dessert."

"I was." I moved in on him and squeezed his ass. "No cake for me."

"Will you knock it off?" Miles said breathlessly, and I kissed him again.

"Are you sure you want me to?"

He put his arms around my neck and turned the tables on me, pushing his tongue past my lips to sweep against mine. His lips grew hard and demanding, and I cupped his ass and rocked my pelvis with his. A deep shudder ran through him, and he let me go.

"Yeah, I do. I'll talk to you about the library during the week."

I scowled but said nothing. By now I knew him well enough to see his steely determination and know he wasn't going to change his mind.

"Fine. Night." I turned and walked away.

"Lyon?" I stopped and peered over my shoulder. "I had a great day. Definitely number one on my list."

Something funny twisted in my chest, and without thinking, I smiled at him. "Me too."

On my way to drop the car at the rental place, I found myself replaying moments of our day together. The moan of pleasure when he sank his teeth into the apple-cider doughnut. His bright face, alive with laughter as he lugged the basket filled with apples he'd picked.

The taste of our last kiss lingered on my tongue, and I physically ached for him. How was this happening? It was all supposed to be a joke, revenge on Dan for what he did to me.

Now it looked like the joke might be on me after all.

# Chapter TWELVE

To avoid thinking about Lyon, I buried myself in the bookstore, using the excuse that if I was going to run the library at the Den, I had to make sure everything was running smoothly with my own business. Gordon was doing a great job managing on his own, and the additional help was working out perfectly. The fact that I'd taken off a Sunday when I'd never done so before wasn't lost on Gordon.

"Why won't you tell me where you went?" He trailed after me. "Were you holed up in his apartment having wild, tantric sex?"

I stopped in my tracks and gaped at him. "What the hell are you talking about?"

"I've been doing a lot of reading in my downtime."

His brown eyes twinkled. "Don't knock it till you try it. My boyfriend is definitely reaping the rewards."

Astonished I was having this conversation at all, I shook my head. "Let's get ready for this author coming in today."

"Did you read his book? *The New Boyfriend*? It's all about the expectations we place on other people to make us happy, when we should really look to ourselves. We need to love ourselves first."

"I read it, and it all sounds good on paper, but in practice, it's not so easy."

I'd set up a table with the author's books, and his personal assistant had delivered a stand-up floor banner with a picture of him holding his book. Roscoe McAllister had certainly hit it big, and I was glad to have him at my small store. People were already milling about, waiting for him to arrive, and I had both Kelvin and Brittany handing out small bottles of water to the crowd, so Gordon could handle the sales.

The bells jingled, and McAllister strode in like a conquering prince. He was around sixty, with short gray hair, piercing black eyes, and a closely trimmed beard. I hurried to him.

"Mr. McAllister, I'm Miles Halloran, the owner of The Book Nook. A pleasure to have you at my store."

"Glad to be here. I'm grateful indie stores still exist, and I happily and wholeheartedly support them."

We shook hands. "I have your table set up, but before we start, can I get you anything? Water, tea, coffee?"

"Just water is fine. Nice little spot you have here. I grew up spending my weekends in bookstores like this."

Warmed by his praise, I grew chatty. "I wanted a place where people could feel comfortable. That's why I made it more like a living room in the front with all the couches and chairs."

"It certainly seems to be working. You have a nice crowd."

"That's for you. How about we get you situated?"

His PA arrived, and she took over, getting him seated and ready for the signing. I'd ordered over a hundred books, and three hours later, every one of them was gone. McAllister flexed his fingers, and I rushed over.

"Can I get you a hot towel for your hand? The authors I've had here before have told me that helps."

"No. I'll be fine." He smiled at me. "Come and sit with me. Tell me a little about yourself."

Caught unawares, I froze. "Uh, okay, sure."

"Was I being too forward?" He chuckled. "I tend to forget not everyone is like me."

"Few people are, Roscoe." His PA laughed and closed up his banner. "I'll go put this in the car."

"Penny's known me for years. Puts up with all my shenanigans."

More relaxed now, I pulled up a chair and sat with him. "I'm sorry. I'm just not used to authors wanting to mingle. Many of them consider me the help."

"Without bookstores, authors aren't able to exist."

"I hope we can say that in five years. It's a dwindling business."

"I agree, which is why I love doing these small tours. I get to meet people like you, who love books as much as I do."

"I always have. They can be an escape."

Roscoe frowned. "Only if you allow it to. If you need someplace to hide." This was becoming more intense than I liked, and I guessed it showed on my face, as Roscoe leaned in close. "Are you in a bad relationship?"

"What?" I laughed. "No. No relationship at all."

"But there's someone…I can tell."

Curious, I pressed him. "How? I only said a few words to you."

"It's your body language. As soon as I asked the question, you grew a little stiff. Like you weren't sure how to answer."

"That's amazing."

"Am I right? Is there someone? Are they foolish enough not to reciprocate?"

I laughed out loud. "Now I know you're giving me a line. Maybe I'm the one who's pushing him away."

"Are you?"

The laughter fizzled out of me. "It's a complicated situation."

"Is he married?"

"No. Absolutely not. He's not married. In fact, that's what started the whole thing between us."

McAllister's brows knotted. "Care to explain?"

Maybe an outsider's opinion would help. I laid out the events, leaving out the parts where I'd kissed Lyon. McAllister listened intently, and when I was finished, I grabbed a bottle of water off the table and gulped it down.

"That's quite a tale."

"I know it sounds silly, but my friend is so hurt, I wanted to help him."

"Even though it's against your brother's best interests."

I frowned. "My brother has sailed through life, never worrying about anyone but himself. This time, in my opinion, he's gone too far."

"So you and this man are playing a joke on him."

"Yes."

"But it isn't a joke for you, is it? You like the jilted groom?"

Well, that didn't take him long to figure out. I shrugged. "I feel sorry for him."

"Doesn't answer my question. But maybe it does." He ran a hand over his beard, thinking. "I think if it's the only way for you to explore your true feelings for this man, there's nothing wrong with it, but you need to learn to put yourself first at some point. On the other hand, you can't regret a chance you never take. I know I'm bastardizing the original quote, but you get the gist of what I'm trying to say. Don't spend your life worrying about what other people think of you. You can't think about opening your heart to someone else until you love yourself, but you can have both. Now I have to go because Penny is sending me smoke signals."

I turned to see his assistant standing by the door with a harried face.

"I didn't mean to keep you."

"Stop diminishing your wants and needs. I sense you're used to that. It's time to step out of the comfortable place you've settled into and break some of the barriers you placed around yourself. Would you like one last piece of advice before I leave?"

"Yes, please."

We both rose, and I walked with him toward the door.

"Do something new and breathtaking. Something that makes you nervous. Forge ahead and make it your own. And when you succeed, do it again. And again." He placed a hand on my shoulder. "It was very nice meeting you, Miles. I hope you get what, and whom, you want."

After he left, I thought about what he'd said. What would make me nervous? The question wasn't what, but who.

Lyon.

Being close to him made it impossible to think of anything else. Overpowering didn't begin to describe his presence. If we were going to play this game, I had to see myself as an equal and set the pace sometimes. I couldn't allow him to take control. The thought was a little terrifying but also thrilling.

At the end of the evening, I slipped my phone and keys into my jacket pocket. "I'll see you tomorrow, Gordon. I'm leaving you to close up. I figure if I'm going to give you the responsibility, I shouldn't be hovering."

Gordon's smile was bright. "Thanks, Miles. I won't let you down."

"I know you won't. As a matter of fact, I might take a half day tomorrow."

"Take a full one. Live dangerously."

On my way to The Lyon's Den, I knew I was about to do exactly that.

Lyon's front-desk person, Anton, gave me a welcoming nod. "Good evening, Mr. Halloran. Welcome to the Den."

"Thanks, Anton. But please call me Miles."

He blinked. "We've been told not to get too familiar with the members and never to call them by their first name."

I set my jaw. "Well, I'm okay with it, and I'll make sure to tell Lyon. Don't worry." I passed the large table he sat behind and stopped. "Is he here, by the way?"

"Lyon? Yes. Would you like me to locate him for you?" He picked up the cordless phone.

"No. I'm sure I'll find him. Thank you."

Inside the main salon, I immediately spotted his broad frame. He was sitting with a group of men I'd never met, and I had no desire to interrupt him, but I didn't need to.

Scott, Lyon's brother, waved to me from his table. Glad to see someone I knew, I joined him. Scott and I were about the same age, and we'd always been friendly, but he had a large circle of friends, and I was way too introverted to ever try and fit in.

"Hi, Scott. How are you? How are Beth and the baby?"

"Both well. Beth is out with her friends on a girls' night, and Lilah is with Beth's parents. I figured I'd come and see how Lyon's doing."

It made me happy to know Lyon had a strong support system in his brother and great-uncle. Recalling what McAllister had said to me, I decided to put it to the test. Because nothing made me more uncomfortable than talking about my personal life.

"He seems to be okay. We spent the day together yesterday. Apple-picking." I waited for his reaction and wasn't disappointed.

"You're shitting me."

I couldn't help smiling. "Would I do that?"

Scott cackled. "Pictures or it didn't happen." He waggled his fingers. "Show me something."

Laughing, I pulled out my phone and showed him one I'd taken of Lyon stuffing a doughnut in his face. Scott's eyes crinkled shut.

"This is priceless." Without asking, he scrolled, and I froze when he came to the one Lyon had taken of us kissing in the wagon during the hayride. Scott handed back the phone, a pucker of concern between his brows. "I didn't know you and Lyon were…close."

"Since what happened, we've started talking," I began and then figured to lay it all out there. "Actually, we've been seeing each other a lot."

"That looks like you've progressed beyond talking. Way beyond." Scott huffed out a sigh. "Look, Miles. I think you're a really nice guy, but I don't want my brother hurt again."

"You think *I'm* going to be the one to hurt *him*?" I laughed. "That's the funniest thing I've heard in a long time. You do know we're talking about your brother, right?"

Scott's eyes flashed. "Yeah. And if you knew anything

about him, you'd know my brother isn't the unapologetic slut he likes people to think he is. He uses sex to hide his pain, but his hurt runs deep. Our parents' behavior traumatized him." He pressed his lips together and shook his head. "I didn't mean to snap at you, but I love him, and I hate seeing him so angry and bitter. That's not him."

My gut twisted. "I-I'm sorry. I didn't mean to joke about it. I don't know Lyon well, but I'm learning there's much more to him than I thought."

"When we were young and our parents would disappear and leave us with the nanny, I'd cry a lot, and Lyon would sneak into my room at night and sleep with me. He'd never leave me to play alone and included me in everything until I was old enough to make my own friends. He helped me with my homework and taught me how to swim, hit a ball, and ride a bike." When Scott smiled, I could see how alike the two brothers looked. "He was with me the first time I got sick from drinking too much, and he told me all about sex and how to protect myself. When I met Beth, it was Lyon I brought her to meet first because I wanted him to love her as much as I did. He's my hero, and I'm not sure he knows how much I love him."

Stunned by Scott's heartfelt confession, I reached across the table and squeezed his hand. "I'm sure he does. He's told me you and Uncle Harry are the most important people in his life."

"Your brother used to be in that company." He played with his tumbler. "Can I ask you something? Do you really have no idea why he did what he did?"

"No. And I can't forgive Dan as easily as he wants me to." I lifted my chin. "My brother is completely in the wrong. The more I hear of the story, the worse it sounds for him. I'm not going to stand by someone who thought nothing of throwing away a lifetime of friendship."

Scott stared hard at me, then gave a quick nod. "If you mean it, I'm happy. There's nothing I want more for my brother than for him to have someone who truly cares, man or woman. It's not that I don't trust you, Miles, because I know you're not a player, but you have to admit that all this"—he spun his hand in the air—"happened pretty fast. Coming off a broken engagement, Lyon is the most vulnerable I've ever seen him."

Fascinated by this deep insight into Lyon, I wanted more. "I understand, but what draws me to him is how different Lyon is in private compared to the face he shows to the public."

Scott studied me. "If he's shown you that side, you're much closer than I imagined." My face flamed, but I said nothing, and he gave me the same cheeky grin Lyon used with me. "I get it. And I'm all for your newfound friendship. It might be exactly what Lyon needs."

Lyon left the men he'd been talking to, and my thoughts tumbled rapidly. I was so confused, maybe I should go home and take a few days before I spoke to him. There was still time for me to leave. He hadn't seen me. He didn't need to know I was here.

Scott tapped the table between us, jolting me out of my head. "Don't think I was warning you off. We've known each other all our lives, and I think you have feelings for him."

*Damn.* This was the second person today who saw right through me.

"I do like him."

Scott rose to his feet. "One more thing, and I'll be as direct as him: Lyon doesn't do anything he doesn't want. If he didn't want to spend time with you, he wouldn't. I hope it continues between the two of you." He gave me a conspiratorial wink, then left, and I wondered how I didn't incinerate in flames of embarrassment.

Did I want Lyon? Was I willing to take a step forward on the road of no return?

Exactly how far I'd go to get what I really wanted was something I wasn't sure of, but I was taking that first step… onto a runaway train named Lyon Elliot.

Uncle Harry had been trying to talk to me, on the phone and in person, but I'd been ducking him. I knew what he wanted, and I wasn't ready to lie to his face. But after an entire week of successful avoidance, he caught me with my pants down.

Literally.

I was in the restroom at The Lyon's Den, using the urinal, when he came in and locked the door behind him.

"Why are you hiding from me?"

I cast a rueful glance at my crotch, finished my business, and tucked myself away. "Considering you just saw me naked, I'd hardly say that was true." I washed my hands. "What can I do for you, Uncle Harry? Have you eaten dinner? Would you like to join me?"

"Don't waste that charming smile on me. I'm not one of your sycophants."

"Uncle Harry, you wound me." I touched my chest. "You know I love you."

"As I do you, otherwise I wouldn't care." He tipped his head. "I want to know what you're doing with Miles."

*No, you probably don't.*

Uncle Harry was no fool, so I had to tread carefully. "I needed a friend, and he's been a shoulder to lean on."

*And a mouth to kiss.*

"But he's Dan's brother, and those two have always been incredibly close. You can't imagine Dan will allow you to come between them."

A conversation like this did not belong in a bathroom. "Let's go somewhere more private?" I walked past him to unlock the door, and he followed me in silence until we reached my office. I poured him his favorite bourbon and me a Scotch. Knowing that the best defense was a good offense, I turned the question to him. "What do you think is going on between Miles and me?"

A half frown tugged at his lips, and clever eyes regarded me thoughtfully from behind those thick-rimmed glasses. "After your performance here last week, and hearing how you two were spotted having a cozy *tête-à-tête* and dinner, I think everyone assumes you're having an affair. Are you only doing this to hurt Dan?"

Was I?

"Performance? Do you mean when I kissed him? He actually kissed me, you know." I let the Scotch linger on my tongue. "I don't understand why you characterize it that way. We're exploring options."

He was not amused. "You're smiling. Do you think this is funny?"

My grin faded at his fierce tone.

Uncle Harry set his glass on the desk and leaned in close. "I love you to death, Lyon, but I'm well aware you've got something up your sleeve when it comes to this sudden interest in Miles. I understand how hurt you are by Dan's actions, but Miles is no match for you. He's an innocent in whatever game you're playing. I'm afraid all the growth I'm seeing in you will be overtaken by your desire for revenge."

Didn't anyone understand my side? I knew Uncle Harry loved me, but his words hurt and caused me to strike out.

"Go on. Tell me more about what a terrible person I am. But if that's the case, why do you bother with me?"

"If I thought you were beyond redemption, I would tell you and I wouldn't try so hard. But I know better. I know *you*. Deep down, where you don't let anyone inside, you're a wonderful person, and you deserve someone who truly loves you. I understand why you don't let anyone get close to you."

Doubtful. How could he, when I didn't understand why myself? And he was wrong. I wanted Miles close to me. But as much as I could love anyone, I loved Uncle Harry. He and my brother were the only people who'd never hurt me.

"Do you? Maybe you'd like to explain it and enlighten me?"

A troubled expression replaced his normally agreeable one, and he sighed. "While your brother has been able to put your parents' behavior aside, you always had a harder time of it. Perhaps because you were older and felt like you had to be the strong one, I don't know. But what I am sure of is that it couldn't have been easy seeing the revolving door of mothers and fathers over the years."

I bit the inside of my cheek, welcoming the pain. It kept me focused on not breaking apart. "I got used to it."

"Of course you did. But getting used to it and understanding it are two different things. I was an adult, and childless, and I still couldn't fathom their utter disregard for your welfare."

My throat was as dry as the desert, and my hand shook slightly as I lifted the tumbler of Scotch to take a sip. "What I've always found interesting is how the two most selfish people on the planet found each other. Why did they even get married? Did they ever love each other? Did they love us?"

It took Uncle Harry a while to answer. He drank a bit of his bourbon, took off his glasses, and rubbed his eyes with a sigh. All while I waited, irritated I'd even asked the question. Not like I cared, but still, I wanted to hear what he had to say.

"I don't know."

And that was why I loved Uncle Harry. Because as brutal as that was to hear, I knew it hurt him more to have to say it to my face, and yet he'd never been anything less than honest with me and Scott.

"The night your father brought your mother home to meet us all for the first time, I remember how surprised I was because she was younger than him. He was a senior at college, and she was a freshman. He told me in confidence she was the one girl he hadn't been able to 'get.' " His smile was wry. "I'll leave it up to you to figure out what that means, but I think you understand."

"I do. And you think I'm like him? That I only care about getting someone into bed?"

"Until recently, yes. Your father always loved pretty things and the chase. Once he got what he wanted, he grew bored." His gaze was pointed.

"I didn't get bored with Lindsey. She cheated and left me. Don't forget that."

Uncle Harry nodded. "I haven't. I'm not saying you're like Charles. He was a cheater from the start—when your mother got pregnant right away, he returned to his old ways."

I clutched my glass harder. "But she was just as bad. She was never there for us."

"Perhaps she grew disillusioned and gave up. She was young and had the money and freedom to do what she wanted."

"She had children," I spat. "If she didn't want us, she didn't have to have us. Did you know that our old nanny, Sonya, always sends us birthday and Christmas cards? After all these years, she still cares. But not our own parents. Well… not true. Once Scott and Beth had the baby, seems our mother remembered she had a family, and Scott tells me she's always sending Lilah presents. Not visiting her, though, because that would take effort and time on her part."

I didn't resent it. Scott was younger, and I'd shielded him from their neglect by always being there, hoping he'd lean on me with whatever he needed.

"When was the last time you heard from Charles or Marianne?"

There was nothing more I wanted than for this conversation to be over. I'd rather face Dan and Lindsey than be forced to acknowledge the ugly truth.

"I can't remember. She sent me a wedding announcement, two years ago I think? Or was it three?" I tapped my chin. "As for him, it was so long ago, it's faded from my memory." I shrugged. "It doesn't matter."

"I think it does."

My laughter rang out in the still room. "Well, Uncle Harry, you're wrong."

He remained infuriatingly calm. "I don't believe I am. To me, you're still hurting from them not being there for you at your most important moments—school functions, birthdays, graduations. I'm sure you rarely, if ever, had a family meal together. As you grew older, it made you incapable of forming lasting attachments with people. You've never fully healed from Charles and Marianne's abandonment."

"You don't always heal from pain. You just learn to live with it." At that point, it might've been Uncle Harry, but I'd had enough. "I tried, didn't I? I knew it was all a farce, but I tried. I didn't love Lindsey, but we liked each other well enough and had the business connection. I thought we could make it work. And look how that turned out. What's worse, the person I truly loved, someone I believed would always be there for me, stabbed me in the back and left me. Was that my fault too?"

"I never said it was your fault, Lyon. None of it was. You're a product of the environment you grew up in. Which brings me back to the initial question. What are you doing with Miles? Are you with him because you want to hurt Dan?"

I might hate lying to Uncle Harry, but it didn't mean I wasn't going to do it. It was a matter of self-preservation—his delving into my past had to stop. "Look, Uncle Harry. Miles is a big boy and perfectly capable of making his own decisions. If we're attracted to each other, so be it, and let nature take its course, I say."

Those wise eyes regarded me, and then he sighed and rose to his feet. "I hope you know what you're doing."

"Do any of us?" I opened the door for him, and we reentered the main salon area, where I found Miles sitting at a table.

Uncle Harry pursed his lips as if intending to speak but shook his head and walked away. He didn't understand. Miles and I, we were adults and knew what we were doing. Dan had always treated Miles like his little brother—emphasis on *little*—never treating him like an equal. I'd never paid attention, as Miles had a knack for blending into the background if you weren't looking for him.

Now I couldn't look away.

"Well, who do we have here?" I sat next to Miles. "Couldn't stay away from me, huh?"

A snort escaped him. "Hardly. I wanted to talk to you about the library."

I put a hand on his elbow and leaned in as I drew him close and dragged in a deep, tantalizing breath of his spicy aftershave. "You could've called. Have a drink."

"Okay." Those bright-blue eyes glowed, and he wet his lips. Goddamn, I wanted them on mine. I'd have them too before the night was over.

Behind the bar, I found Victor's gaze on mine, and I tipped my head to Miles. Victor understood, and within a minute, we had our drinks.

We sat across from each other at a small table for two, tucked in the corner, but that didn't stop the others in the room from nearly breaking their necks to see us.

Miles lifted his glass. "I see there's a severe case of giraffe-itis—all those long necks trying to insert themselves into our business."

"And what business would that be?" The tension from my conversation with Uncle Harry was dissipating, and I began to enjoy myself.

"Whatever you want it to be." Miles blinked and turned a fierce shade of red, which normally would be a turn-off. I had little interest in flirting or pretend-innocence. My partners and I knew exactly what we wanted from each other. Hot, greedy sex and lots of it.

Not so with Miles. I was certain he wasn't the type to have had many lovers—there was no pretense in his quiet, shy behavior because I'd seen how he'd lived his life. In Dan's shadow.

The little tastes I'd had of him only increased my desire

to discover more of who he was. This man I'd spent half my life with but barely knew.

I always did like a good mystery.

"Tell me about the library. The kinds of books you've ordered."

"Really?" Realizing he'd given himself away, his blush returned, and he gulped half his wine.

"Really," I almost purred, happy to see him a little off-balance.

"Uh, sure."

I knew I shocked him, and I grinned to myself. We might've agreed we were both out to teach Dan a lesson, but I enjoyed a little bit of cat and mouse. I didn't want to make it too obvious how bad I wanted to rip his clothes off and get him naked.

That could come later. It would. Tonight.

"I placed an order for a load of nonfiction, mysteries, biographies, food and wine, and travel books. I think you'll have them by the end of the week. Should be around a hundred fifty copies."

"Sounds perfect. And I was right. You knew exactly what I wanted." I ran my foot up his leg. "Thank you."

"You're welcome," he whispered.

"Did you eat dinner?"

He shook his head, and I raised my hand without breaking eye contact. The same server who brought our drinks appeared almost immediately.

"Yes, sir?"

"What would you like?"

Miles blinked, and a hint of that banter I enjoyed returned. "Surprise me."

"Bring us the Dover sole with vegetables. And for dessert, the tiramisu, but in a box to go."

"Right away, sir."

Miles bit his lip. "You're going to make me wait for tiramisu? That's not fair."

I raised my glass. "Whoever said I play fair? I play to win."

The meal was faultless, but I could barely eat. Each slide of the fork into Miles's mouth turned me on. Those full lips enticed, and I avidly watched him chew and swallow every bite.

He finished and set the cutlery on the plate. "Are you done eating me with your eyes?" He raised his brows, his eyes twinkling.

"I'm ready to get to the main course." I rose from my seat. "You. Are you coming home with me tonight?"

Clearly surprised by my abrupt candor, he didn't answer, and his smile faded. But he got to his feet and slipped on his suit jacket, which he'd removed when dinner was served. I picked up the box with our dessert and followed him out.

We didn't speak until I unlocked the door to my apartment. "Make yourself comfortable." I tossed my keys aside, took off my jacket and tie, and unbuttoned my shirt collar with a sigh of relief.

Miles walked into the living room and stopped by the pictures of Dan, Scott, and Uncle Harry I had on the credenza. He picked up one of Dan and myself taken on our twenty-fifth birthday. We were born a couple of weeks apart and had always celebrated together. That year the party was in Cancun.

"I remember that trip. Dan invited me to come." Miles snorted. "I think I'm still traumatized."

I had no memory of Miles being there, but I wasn't surprised. We were all about partying, getting as drunk as possible, and getting laid. I barely noticed him on a regular day, but on my birthday when he was Dan's brother and sat in the corner? Not at all.

"It was a crazy time." I took the picture from his hand and placed it, facedown, on the credenza top.

Miles cocked his head. "I bet you didn't even know I was there, right? Miles the Mouse," he said bitterly, turned, and walked away.

"Hey, hey, whoa, stop. Why are we taking twenty steps backward when we're about to jump a hundred forward?" I followed him, slipped my arms around his waist, and kissed his hair. "It's been years since, and we're both different people now."

He turned to face me. "Are we? I'm not so sure I've changed."

Those lips had tempted me long enough, and I touched my mouth to his. "You're here. With me. Isn't that a change?"

"Yeah, but we're both doing this as a fuck-you to Dan."

*Oh, hell no.*

"I don't see Dan in the room, do you?" My fingertips ghosted over his face, and now it was my turn to shiver, thinking of all those golden bristles rasping along my body. "What happens here tonight is for us. We're both good at pretending—we can fool Dan in public without me doing this." I buried my face in the sweet curve of his neck and nipped, wanting to mark him so when he left me, I'd still be there. "In private." His late-night scruff rasped against mine as I continued my exploration with my lips. "And this." I covered his mouth with mine and kissed him as if I needed his breath to live. When he pulled at my shirt, popping the buttons off, triumph surged through me.

"What're you doing to me?" Miles groaned, but that didn't stop him from kissing me back, sliding that warm, velvety tongue of his along mine. We held each other, kissing and rubbing up on each other.

"Anything you want, baby. Should I tell you?" At his nod, I gave him one long, lingering kiss before resting my hand on the waistband of his pants. "Or show you?"

"Both," he whispered, and I was lost in the absolute fiery brilliance of his eyes.

I popped the tab of his slacks and unzipped him, releasing his erection. "I plan to get you naked and do every delicious thing you've ever imagined me doing to your beautiful body. All you have to do is let me know what you like." I slid them past his hips, and he kicked off his loafers and let them fall to the floor.

"I like you."

With those words, Miles undid his tie, and I made quick work of his shirt. I pushed it off until he stood almost naked. The silence grew between us like a living thing, pulsing and all-enveloping.

"Now," I said, trailing wet kisses down his neck. "Do you really think things are the same between us?"

"Take off your clothes too. Please."

Surprised by the uneasiness in his voice, I stepped away and peered at him, shocked to see his white face and heaving chest. "What's wrong?"

He blinked, his eyes wary and uncertain. "Nothing."

But his fingers trembled as they reached out to undo my trousers. I covered them with mine. "Has it been a long time? Is that why you're hesitating?" His hand in mine, I pressed it to my groin. "It's been a while for me too. Almost four months."

"A lifetime, huh?" Miles teased, and I smiled, relieved his humor had returned.

"Feels like it. But I'm thinking being with you is going to be an unforgettable event." When Miles rolled his eyes, I took the opportunity to swoop in for another skin-tingling kiss, and with his help, I undressed to my briefs like him. "Better now? I know you just wanted to see me naked."

Not answering, Miles pressed his lips harder to mine, and I cupped his firm ass. The frantic thumping of his heart was all I needed to hear, and I gave him a juicy squeeze before whispering, "Let's go to the bedroom."

He nodded, and for whatever reason, I felt protective and took hold of his hand. Miles's face was tense, and I hoped he wasn't going to bolt on me. I stopped in the doorway, more certain than ever that Miles hadn't had many lovers. I wanted to erase all his bad experiences and be the one he'd never forget.

"You sure you're okay with this? I don't want you to do anything you're not comfortable with."

With shining eyes, he touched my face. "I've never been more certain of anything in my life."

Once inside, I pulled him down to the bed and wrapped my arms around him, letting him feel me.

"Lyon, God." His moan in my ear was everything I needed to hear. "I can't believe this is happening."

A nervous lover I could handle. And I was ready to handle every beautiful inch of Miles, from top to bottom. In one smooth move, I peeled his briefs off and braced myself over him.

"Believe it, baby. This is what I've been dreaming of for weeks now."

"What?"

Was he kidding? I brought my face close to his and kissed him. "You. Naked and under me."

With a sigh, Miles accepted my tongue in his mouth and sucked it. I could feel the rise of his hunger as his cock thickened and poked me in the belly. "More," he whispered. "Please. I want it. You. I want everything."

I left those soft, beautiful lips for the delicious red nipples tickling my chest. "I'm going to give you everything you want. And more."

I teased and nibbled those tight nubs, not leaving them until Miles cried out and writhed under me. The ultimate prize lay waiting for me, and I blew a cool stream of air over the gleaming tip of his cock.

Miles clutched my arm. "I need...please. Lyon, fuck me, come on." His hand gripped his cock, thumbing the tip. Sweating profusely, his eyes closed, Miles moaned, bucking his hips. This wild abandon surprised me. Even though we'd fooled around a little, I assumed he'd be more passive.

*Damn*. I liked it.

"Let me get you ready." I kissed the smooth crown of his dick, and he shuddered, releasing soft, pleading sounds when I licked the slit. "So gorgeous." I grabbed my lube and condoms and quickly slicked my fingers, eager to feel his heat. When I slid one finger inside him, he went quiet and began to breathe heavily. After I added two more fingers to stretch him, a high-pitched wail of pleasure burst from his lips and he stiffened and came, shooting ropes of come over his taut abs.

"Damn, you're sexy. I can't wait to be inside you."

He panted but said nothing, and I figured if he was like me, he'd be too blissed out to speak after hitting his climax. I rolled the condom on and teased the outside of that sweet little hole before pressing into him.

"Uh, oh God." He tensed, and those big blue eyes widened.

"Shh, baby, I know it's been a while. I can take my sweet time because you're so damn delicious. You tell me when." I waited until he met my eyes and gave me a brief nod. "Now just bear down on me and breathe." I pushed one leg up to give me more depth, and I closed my eyes briefly as the warm velvet of Miles's passage squeezed my throbbing dick. "Oh God, you're so fucking tight. You're killing me." The deeper I slipped into him, the harder I fell.

"Lyon, Lyon…" Head thrashing, Miles whimpered and flailed, hitting the bed, then gripping me. His blunt nails dug hard into my flesh, and the pain was exquisite, lending itself to the raging fire pouring through my blood. Outside, a storm blew in, pelting the windows with rain and booming cracks of thunder and lightning.

I couldn't hold back and thrust hard, needing to own him, possess him, make him mine. My heart pounded, my head spun, and I pumped fast and furious. "Oh Jesus, oh God." I dissolved in hot pleasure as I exploded, my orgasm tearing me apart.

Our sweaty bodies lay tangled as the storm raged outside, and I nuzzled close to Miles, kissing the damp hair plastered to his brow, his cheek and jaw. "How do you feel? Fantastic, I hope?"

Instead of speaking, he grasped my nape and met my lips with his. Our tongues played, and when we broke apart, he smiled up at me. "I'm sure I'm feeding the beast, but it was amazing. *You* were amazing."

"So were you," I whispered, a bit overcome by how much he'd affected me. I touched his chest, feeling the pump of his beautiful heart, wondering if there was room inside for me.

His eyelids fluttered, then shut. Careful not to hurt him as I knew he'd be sore after not being with anyone for a while,

I eased out of him, but he merely sighed and rolled over. Leaving him sleeping, I went to the bathroom to toss out the condom, wash my hands, and catch my breath for a minute. *Damn.* I felt great. How fucking stupid of me to think sex with Miles would be a chore. He might be the best lover I'd ever had, and I couldn't wait to get back into bed and see what else happened between us.

But when I came out, he was gone.

Thoroughly soaked, I made it up the stairs to my house. I couldn't stop shaking. Once I'd undressed, I showered slowly and carefully and put on pajama pants and a sweat shirt.

It might only be September, but I made a fire and sat staring at the flickering flames, a cup of tea warming my hands.

All these years of dreaming about Lyon Elliot…thinking about what kissing and touching him would feel like…

Finally making love to him had blown all my fantasies to the moon and beyond.

And yet, all I could see was my nineteen-year-old self, surrounded by my grinning roommate, Robert Clifton, and a sophomore from the football team, Dickson Monroe.

*"You like guys, huh?"*

*Shocked, I met Robert's eyes. We weren't best friends, but we hung out. He was way more popular than me, but he'd always acted cool. Now his gaze was filled with disdain and hate.*

*"Wh-what? What're you talking about?" I thought I'd been so careful. Jeff and I had met in an English Lit class, and after studying together a few times, we'd made out a little. He was the first guy I'd kissed.*

*"C'mon, Miles. Don't deny it. We knew something was weird about you, and we've been watching. Dickson saw you making out with a dude in the library." They sniggered and made kissing noises. Robert wiped his mouth and said, "When you said you were gonna bring someone to the room, I wanted to know if you were doing it here with him. I didn't wanna walk in and see you getting railed. That shit's not natural. So we set up a camera. We got you on video, making out with him. Gave the guys at the frat house a good laugh."*

*I'd invited Jeff to my room when I was certain we'd be alone. Neither of us had ever been with another guy, and we'd decided to take it slow. I liked all the kisses and touching. It was nice. He was nice. I wanted him to be my boyfriend.*

*My mind whirling, I fought not to cry or throw up. "Why would you do this to me?" My nausea grew. "You had no right to spy on me."*

*Robert sneered. "What're you gonna do about it?"*

*Unable to sit there any longer, I jumped up and pushed past them, then took off running. I ran and ran until I came to a thicket of trees behind the dorms. Once I determined I was safe, I sank to the ground and pulled out my phone and called my brother.*

*"Dan?" I burst out crying.*

*"What's wrong? Are you hurt?"*

*"No, but..." In between hiccups, I told him the whole story.*

*"Fuckers. I'll handle it. I was president of the fraternity, and I'll make sure to take care of that camera and deal with those shitheads."*

*"Thanks. I-I can't stay in my dorm. Do you think they'll let me change? I don't want Mom to know the real reason. She'll just get all upset and hover over me."*

*"You sure?"*

*"Yeah. Please? Just tell Dad, but not about the camera... it's too humiliating. Just say I want a single. I'm too upset to talk to him."*

*"Whatever you want. I'll make some shit up. You're my baby brother. You can always count on me."*

*"Thanks. I gotta go."*

The next day I was told to move dorm rooms, and I ended up in a single for the rest of my time in college. I'd see Jeff, but he would turn his back to me. Nothing ever happened to Clifton or Monroe. But the end result was a fear of being watched and spied upon. I tried not to let it get to me, made attempts to date other guys, but they'd all failed miserably. In the years after that incident, I'd rarely allowed anyone close enough.

It didn't help that I had Dan telling me that guys only wanted sex. That they didn't care about me.

*"You don't need those losers. Fuck them. You'll meet someone eventually. I can hook you up when you graduate."*

But that never happened.

I might've had a crush on Lyon, but I would never have acted on it. Turned out, he was right all along about me. I was Miles the Mouse.

The rain continued to pour from the sky, and thunder shook the house on its frame. I hoped the roof would hold. I sipped my tea, but as hot as it was, it didn't warm me. It would take more than a cup to unfreeze the coldness I'd lived with all these years.

The bell rang, but I ignored it. I had no delivery planned for the night. My belly was full, but my heart was sore and aching.

I heard pounding on the door and the knob rattling. Fearing a break-in, I approached the entrance, holding the heaviest thing I could find—*The Complete Works of William Shakespeare.*

Peering through the sheer curtains covering the glass front, my jaw dropped. "What the fuck?" I yanked the door open and was greeted by a blast of wind and rain, but it was nothing compared to the fury of Lyon Elliot.

"What're you doing here?"

Without bothering to answer, he barreled past me and stood dripping in my foyer.

"What am I doing here? That's what I'd fucking like to know. I left you sleeping in my bed after we had a fucking awesome night, and when I came out of the bathroom, you'd vanished. Poof." He waved his hands around. "What the hell, Miles?"

The fact that he'd come all the way in this storm wasn't lost on me. I set the book on the small antique marble table and faced him. "You didn't need to come out here. You could've called."

"I could've called?" That handsome face turned incredulous. "That's all you have to say?"

There was so much more I could tell him. But I never would. That trust thing again.

I spread my hands wide. "Sorry?"

Furious eyes spit fire. "Oh, no. No way." He folded his arms and placed himself in my path. "You need to explain what happened to make you run. Now."

Little did he know I'd become a master at avoidance, and I slipped past him. "I wanted to sleep in my own bed."

How stupid was I to think a man like Lyon would accept that lame excuse? Of course he followed me, his feet making wet, squelching noises inside his sneakers. I took pity on him.

"If you want to get out of those wet socks before you have to leave, I can put them in the dryer."

"You have got to be kidding me," he muttered. He took my arm in a firm grasp, but his voice was surprisingly gentle. "I didn't come here to get my laundry done. Miles. Please. What happened? Why did you run away?"

I twisted out from his hold. "Stop pushing me. It was too much…you…were too much. Everything. Just go, please." Humiliated, I left him and ran upstairs to my bedroom, where I started pacing. Footsteps pounded up the stairs, and my heart hammered.

There he was, at my door.

"I thought I told you to leave."

Cocky as ever, he sauntered in. "Yeah, but I know you didn't mean it." He stopped in front of me. "Besides, I don't leave people when they're upset. And if I'm the cause of it, I need to know what I did."

"It's not you. It's me." I forced my lips into a smile. "See? Now you can go."

"Miles, you're a terrible liar." He touched my face. "Now tell me. Why did you run away? Did I hurt you?"

"No."

"Good. I thought it was amazing between us. Was I wrong?" His lips brushed my cheek, and a shudder ran through me.

"N-no, you weren't."

He splayed a hand across the small of my back and

moved close to whisper in my ear. "What, then? My bed wasn't comfy? My pillows were too hard? Tell me."

"It was silly. I don't know why I did it, but I guess maybe because it was you? After all these years of looking down on me, now suddenly you were there, and we were…you know." My face burned. "I think I just got overwhelmed and needed some space."

"I'm sorry. I never meant for you to think that."

My eyes narrowed. "Come on. Miles the Mouse? That's not a name you call someone you like or admire."

A flush darkened his cheeks. "You're right. And I'm living with that regret every day. I regret a lot of things in my life now." He raised his hand from my waist to cup my jaw. "All I want is to make it right with you."

*Oh, hell no.* I wasn't going to fall for him. This was all part of his plan to get revenge on Dan.

"You did. I guess I didn't expect to have it turn physical so quickly."

"Sometimes what we plan changes course, and we don't see it happening until it's too late."

He studied my face, and I grew increasingly nervous that he could see right through me. I batted his hand away. "Do you want me to dry off those socks for you? It won't take long."

He nodded, that piercing gaze unrelenting.

"Great. Follow me to the laundry." Only too happy to leave my bedroom, I walked with him down the hall to where I had my machines. When I tossed them inside the dryer, he also pulled off his sweat shirt and sweat pants, leaving him wearing only his boxers and that damn cocky smile.

"These are damp too. You wouldn't want me to catch a cold, right?"

"No," I croaked. "I-I can give you something to put on while you wait."

"I'm fine as is." His eyes, that unusual shade of indigo now, danced with amusement.

*Bastard. He knows exactly what he's doing.*

"Okay, well, um. Do you want to go downstairs? I can make you coffee."

"Why are you lying to me? If we're going to be partners in getting back at Dan, we have to tell each other the truth."

"I don't see how the two things are related. You're mad at Dan for betraying you. I'm mad at him for thinking he could control my personal life. That's all we need to know."

I walked away, but I didn't miss hearing Lyon's muttered curse. That was fine. Let him get angry, annoyed, frustrated. Whatever. As long as he didn't find out he was my first lover, we'd be okay.

I made his coffee and some tea for me, and we sat before the fire.

"I'm not going to push you to let me stay if you don't want me to." Lyon surprised me with his insight.

"I didn't say that."

The words tumbled out of my mouth before my brain could stop me, and he smiled.

"No? So should I tell you what I like for breakfast?" He waggled his brows.

As much as I wanted to wake up next to Lyon, how could I tell him I was too sore and my body still ached from being with him earlier to sleep with him again? A man like Lyon Elliot expected sex and lots of it.

"I—uh…I'm not ready for a repeat performance."

His face grew grim. "Do you think I'm only here for sex?"

"Aren't you?" I tipped my chin up, meeting his startled

eyes with defiance. Where I'd gotten the courage to speak to Lyon like this, I had no idea. Maybe we were both wrong about each other—him for calling me Miles the Mouse and me for thinking he was arrogant and invincible.

"I can control myself. If you want to take it slowly, I'll respect your wishes. I'm able to keep my hands to myself." His dimples appeared. "But I can still hold you and sleep next to you, can't I?"

"You promise to be good?"

His grin grew wicked. "Baby, I'm always good."

"I walked right into that one, didn't I?" God, I was acting like a kid with a crush. "You're making it impossible for me to say no."

He set his coffee on the table. "That's the point. Let's go to bed."

It took me five more days to set up the lending library as I liked, and Lyon, true to his word, had hyped up the new charitable requirement to the members. There was no grumbling, mainly because these people were always searching for another tax deduction.

Gordon, who'd come to help me shelve the books, stood in the center of the room with his hands on his hips. "This is great. I can't believe you put it together so quickly."

Adjusting the computer on the desk to where I wanted it, I gave him a satisfied smile. "Well, it's a case of when Lyon wants something, he gets it."

"Not always."

That deep voice tinged with amusement sent tingles through me, and I saw Lyon leaning against the doorframe.

"Oh, hey. We're just about finished here. It looks great, right?"

"It does. I had no doubts." He strolled inside. "How are you, Gordon?"

As the two of them chatted, I sat at the desk and continued to enter all the books into the system. Once I'd discovered there was a software program I could adapt for a lending library, it was easy.

The door clicked shut, and at the sound I glanced up. Lyon smiled at me from across the room. Nervous, I wet my lips. "Where'd Gordon go?"

Three long strides brought Lyon in front of me, and he braced his hands on the desk to bring his face close to mine. "I sent him to get us lunch."

"I didn't say I was hungry."

Lyon came around the desk and stood behind me, encircling me with his firm, muscular arms. He'd left his suit jacket off, and the heat poured off his body, soaking into mine. With each passing second, I grew more faint with longing.

"I am." He kissed my neck and hummed, the sound reverberating through my veins. "I'm famished."

"Really?"

His breath puffed along my cheek, and his lips found mine in a hard, demanding kiss. "Mmhmm. Starving."

"Y-you should eat breakfast."

He sucked my tongue, and my head spun.

"Yeah. But I'd rather eat you."

We clung to each other, our lips and tongues battling for control. I'd thought that once we'd had sex, it would be enough for me—I'd achieved my fantasy, and I could stop thinking about Lyon. Instead, I remained up every night since, edgy and restless. Wanting his kisses. Craving him inside me. How was it possible to physically ache for someone? I'd always laughed at romance novels, believing them to be filled with impossible longing and pent-up desire.

I wasn't laughing now. The mere touch of this man unleashed a torrent of emotions I'd kept banked for all these years. Now the dam broke, sweeping me away. Right into his arms.

"Lyon," I moaned, and he held me tighter.

"Say my name again. I like hearing it."

"Lyon, please." I wasn't sure I liked what I was feeling, but my body was all for it, and he smiled against my cheek.

"That's it. Much better. I like having you here. Makes it easier for me."

"Easier?" My blood turned cold, and I pushed him off. "Easier for what? For you to come and get off whenever you want? God, I knew this was a stupid idea. I should've never agreed to it. I'm not your boy toy."

He frowned. "All I meant was that I wouldn't have to go to Brooklyn to see you." He pouted, and I hated how even sulky he was adorable.

"Oh." Feeling foolish, I ran my hands through my hair. "Sorry. I didn't mean to accuse you of anything."

"Yeah, you did." His brows drew together in consternation. "You still think the worst of me, don't you? No matter what I do or say, you're always going to default to believing I'm a selfish bastard. I can't win, so why am I even trying?" With a thrust of his hard jaw, he strode to the door and left, slamming it on its hinges.

A moment later Gordon hurried in, carrying a tray. "What happened? Why is Lyon so mad? I just passed him, and he grunted at me and didn't want the food he asked for."

"Who knows with him? He's temperamental."

But I'd lied. Lyon was wrong. The problem wasn't that I believed he was the same self-centered person I'd known. In truth, he was kind and considerate, and though I'd had little experience and he was my first, I knew he was a wonderful lover. He made me laugh, and I liked it when he called me baby.

Lyon was the exact opposite of who I thought he was, and that was terrifying.

I genuinely liked him.

Maybe even more.

What the hell was I going to do about it?

The bad thing about running your own business was that you couldn't take off whenever you wanted. I had responsibilities, one of which was going to prove a huge pain in my ass.

In preparation for the launch of Lindsey's tequila, the first shipment of bottles was due today, but the last thing on my mind was fulfilling my commitment to the contract. We were supposed to be on our honeymoon, and Dan had agreed to take care of accepting it for me. Instead, he was the one enjoying the sun, sand, and surf, while I was getting cock-blocked and insulted at every turn.

Frustrated, I sat at my table and watched the trickle of suits walk in for lunch. Normally I'd be hanging out with Dan, maybe nursing a hangover and listening to his bullshit stories, and then I'd wander around, schmooze with the members, pick up on the gossip, and discover stock tips or investments. Now I had to deal with sidelong glances and smirks and knowing I was the subject of their chatter.

Victor himself delivered my drink, and I eyed him when he took the chair opposite me and straddled it, resting his thick forearms on the top. “What’s wrong, Boss?”

“Nothing. I’m hungry.”

A dark brow arched high. “Didn’t anyone ever tell you frowning gives you wrinkles? Just saying.”

“Shut up.”

But of course, no one listened to me, Victor being no exception. “Girl trouble?” His eyes crinkled with laughter. “Or is a certain man not falling for the bullshit?”

“I should fire you,” I murmured idly, sipping my Scotch. Miles hadn’t left yet, so he couldn’t be too angry with me.

“You should do a lot of things. Like admit you’re crushing on Miles and make a move.”

“Crushing? Make a move? What is this, an afterschool movie?” I fluttered my lashes. “Gee, golly, Victor. I wonder if he’ll wear my jacket to the prom.” Snorting, I shook my head. “You’ve got to be fucking kidding me.”

“I never thought I’d see it.”

“See what?” Growing more annoyed by the minute, I wondered if I should just trash this whole revenge plan. Who cared what Dan thought? He could go to hell.

“You like this guy. And you have no idea what to do about it. It’s kind of fun watching you be all dopey and pathetic about it.”

“You’re an ass. Get to the kitchen and make me something, please. That kid Gordon was supposed to bring in my lunch, but I left.”

Victor, however, didn’t move. “It happens to the best of us, you know.”

"What? Gas?" Irritated, I tapped my fingers on the table, and a waiter appeared.

"Can I get you something, sir?"

"About time," I snapped. "I shouldn't have to ask. Get me the chicken sandwich. And another Scotch."

"Yes, sir," Pale and sweating, he threw a slightly panicked look at Victor, who nodded and tipped his head. The waiter scurried away.

"Why're you taking it out on the staff? Poor guy was ready to piss his pants."

Guilty because he was right, I hung my head. "I'll apologize when he comes back."

"Whoa, wait a sec. An appropriate response instead of an answering snarl, telling me to fuck off? Who are you, and what have you done with the real Lyon Elliot?"

"Was I really that bad?" I chewed my lip. "Not just to the waiter, but to everyone? Before, I mean."

"Yeah. I hate to say it, but you were more often than not pretty obnoxious. I knew you weren't always a bastard because whenever your uncle comes around, he brings out another side—who you are, I'm guessing. Or could become." Those big dark eyes glinted. "It's the same whenever you're with Miles."

I grunted. "Can you please stop bringing him up?"

The young waiter approached again with a full tumbler of Scotch and a chicken sandwich. A heaping order of fries accompanied it. He set it in front of me, and I made sure to smile.

"Thank you. And I'm sorry I bit your head off earlier. I shouldn't take my bad mood out on others. What's your name?"

Wide-eyed, the man stared at me. "Watson."

"Well, thank you, Watson. I appreciate the heavy pour as well." I lifted the glass to him.

"You're welcome." Shoulders straight and smiling, he left for another table.

"That wasn't so hard, right?"

"I can be nice. I *am* nice," I grumbled. "Except when people piss me off. Like you are."

"Because I'm telling you the truth? Suck it up, buttercup. You like me because I'm *not* afraid to tell you the truth."

"Don't you have drinks to make?" I took a bite of my sandwich.

"I think sitting here with you is more important. Because you're still upset, and it bothers me."

"Thanks." I met his frankness with my own, astonishingly candid answer. "It still hurts like fucking hell."

And in another shocking development, Victor stood and squeezed my shoulder. "Be who you just were. To everyone. I think you'll be surprised at what might happen. You have a potentially good thing going."

I finished my sandwich and was contemplating another drink when I spied Miles on the outskirts of the salon. He scanned the room and walked toward me with a purposeful stride. I admired the square cut of his jaw and the intensity of his blue eyes.

Fuck, he was hot.

"I want to talk."

I tipped my head. "An empty chair awaits."

"No, not here with all these eyes. I'm finished setting up the library, and I need to go to my store and get some things done there before I start spending so much time here with the library. So, uh…can you come to my place tonight after you close the Den?"

He was correct. Though the people around us tried to

be discreet, they failed miserably. I'd spotted those curious stares.

"If it's just to tell me you're not interested in going through with our plan, we can end it right here."

"Did I say that? You're being defensive for no reason."

Damn, he was being bossy. I kind of liked it.

"You call it defensive. I say reasonable."

"Jerk," he muttered. "Please, Lyon?"

"Now that's better. I like hearing you ask me nicely. You said that before. Remember? I like hearing you call out my name." I allowed a smile when I leaned in close so only he could hear me. "When I was kissing you? And inside you?"

A fierce blush covered his face, and those big eyes grew even larger. "What? Stop it. Shut up. I can't believe you… *ugh.* What am I saying? Of course I can."

Damn, he was cute. Who knew I had a thing for sweet guys who blushed at the slightest hint of naughtiness? I'd always known Miles was sexy, but Dan's threats and warnings had made him invisible. Why bother to look if I couldn't touch? Now the gloves were off. And I wanted to touch him.

"You really want to talk?"

Still pink-cheeked, he nodded, and I wasn't quite sure what this tingling feeling in my stomach and chest was. I hoped the kitchen wasn't serving spoiled food, but no one else in the room seemed to be having any issues.

"Okay. I have stuff to take care of this afternoon, but I promise I'll make it after closing. It might be late, though."

"I'll wait up."

As I watched him walk out of the Den, I heard my name called from the opposite side of the club. Victor waved me over, and when I saw who was with him, I winced.

"It could be worse," I muttered, and grabbing one more

bite of my half-eaten sandwich, I chewed and swallowed before joining him and the petite woman by his side. "Hello, Belinda."

Belinda Florence, Lindsey's COO, waited for me. "Nice to see you again, Lyon. We're all prepared for the upcoming launch." We'd always had a cordial but cool relationship when dealing with each other, and she'd never been anything but properly efficient. An organization whiz was how Lindsey defined her.

Which was why I was surprised when her hand lingered in mine at our greeting, those long, pointy, red fingernails scraping against my palm. I shot her a questioning look, to which she gave a slow smile and lowered her lashes.

"I have the final numbers for you, and I wanted to get a feel for the space and bring over the uniforms for the girls." She reached inside a box on the bar and pulled out a skimpy, sparkly outfit.

"Girls?"

She handed me the contract. "It's right here. Dorado girls will be handing out samples in branded shot glasses."

"Lindsey's thought of everything, hasn't she?"

"She always does." Her hand rested on my arm. "Can I be frank?"

I was busy reading the contract, searching for a loophole. "Sure."

"I was horrified to find out that Lindsey cheated on you. And with Dan, no less."

My hands tightened on the contract. "Thanks, but I'm fine. This is purely business now. There's nothing else between us."

"Glad to hear that," she purred and slid her hand up my arm. "If you ever want to get a drink and, you know, talk business, let me know."

Amused, I gazed down at her. Long, silky black hair was pinned to the top of her head, and she was stylishly dressed in a figure-hugging sheath of hot pink and sky-high stilettos. Smiling full lips gleamed, and her heavily-lined brown eyes glowed. Funny, I'd only ever remembered her in dark suits, wearing little to no makeup.

Belinda was giving me every signal that she was ready and willing to get much more personal. I'd always enjoyed a sexy, confident woman, and if I took her home, she'd probably be a tigress in bed.

And yet I felt no desire to discover if that was true. My mind was on a golden-haired, blue-eyed man whose sweet and fiery blushes captivated me.

"Thanks. I'll let you know." I flipped through the rest of the contract and handed it to her. "Looks good. You can coordinate with Victor." I gave her an absent smile. "I have to go to my office now. I'll talk to you soon."

Her eyes narrowed. "Okay, sure. Thanks, Lyon."

Once in my office, I powered through my monthly paperwork, then checked the library system Miles had installed. I was pleased to see there was already a list of book requests in the queue.

"Maybe he's really on to something."

The door opened and closed, and the lock clicked. Surprised, as no one ever entered my office without knocking, I peered over my desktop computer.

"Whoo—whoa, what the hell." I jumped up and backed away. Belinda let her trench coat slide to the floor and pulled the pins out of her hair. It hung like a curtain of ebony silk around her naked shoulders. She'd changed into one of the Dorado girl outfits she'd shown me—tiny, sparkly shorts and a sequined bikini top that barely contained her full breasts. Long, red-tipped fingers toyed with her belly ring, then slid down her tanned stomach below the top of the shorts. A pink tongue swept over her lips.

"I thought maybe you'd like to see what the costumes looked like on someone." Husky-voiced, she swung her hips provocatively while crossing the office. "And if you like it, I'll let you take it off me." She popped the top button of the shorts.

"Uh, Belinda, you really shouldn't be here." I continued to retreat until my back hit the wall. "I think you'd better leave."

"Come on, Lyon. I know you don't mean that." Her arms wound around my neck, and she pressed that lush, curvy body to mine. "Lindsey and I used to talk all the time—girls do that." Her fingernails scratched a path from my stomach to my groin. "I know what you like. Lindsey said—"

I pushed her away. "You don't know anything, and I don't care what Lindsey said. She knows nothing about me. Obviously. Now please leave. And in case you think of crying wolf and claiming I tried to take advantage of you, I have everything that happens in this office recorded."

Face flushed with anger, Belinda's full lips thinned and those magnificent breasts bounced as she marched across the office to pick up her coat from the floor.

"Lindsey was right about one thing. You're a big fat dud." With that scathing retort, she slammed out of the office.

"Jesus."

Looked like I'd dodged a bullet. If I hadn't had Miles on my mind, I might've taken her up on her offer and had sex right on my desk. I sank to my chair, wondering why the hell that didn't bother me. I'd thought after Lindsey, I'd be hitting up the club scene, plowing my way through hookups, eager to find solace in whomever was willing to give it for the night.

None of it—not the pounding music, not the inevitable next morning hangover, nor the indistinguishable sex—was worth losing the potential of what I might have with Miles. Because if I knew only one thing, it was that Miles wouldn't stay with me if he thought I was sleeping around.

Now if I could only figure out why the hell that mattered so much to me.

“No, Dan. I don’t want to talk about it.” I paced the stacks of The Book Nook, trying to keep my voice down, but my exasperation level was about to go through the roof. It was near to closing, and I had tons of things I still had to take care of before I spent the rest of the week at The Lyon’s Den. New stock needed to get put on the shelves, and I had to go over the daily schedule with Gordon, since it was the first time he’d be on his own. Plus, I still wasn’t sure what the hell was happening between Lyon and me, and at such a whirlwind pace, I hardly had any time to process it.

“I’m an adult, perfectly able to make my own decisions, and certainly capable to choose who I wish to spend my time with.”

“Don’t you get it? This is going to be college all over again.”

My knees shook, so I sat on a step of the wooden ladder out of fear of falling. "What the hell does that mean?"

"You were taken advantage of by people, remember? I'm trying to prevent a repeat."

"It's been over ten years, Dan. I'm not the same person."

"Yeah? Well, I remember some guy who stole your credit card information when you were on a date, and another who sold you on some pyramid scheme, and I was the one you called for help. But this time might be the worst one of all."

"And yet it's okay for you to do what you did and hurt someone."

"Who? Lyon? Pfft." He snorted. "Trust me, he doesn't care, and if he tells you otherwise, he's lying just to get in your pants."

A wave of humiliation swept through me. "That's disgusting. And you're wrong."

"Listen, Miles. You've had such a massive crush on him all these years, you'd probably roll right over for him."

"What the hell did you just say?" I couldn't see through the furious red haze his words unleashed.

"You heard me. You'll thank me in the long run."

"Yeah? Well, time for you to listen. *Butt the fuck out of my life.* I'll do whatever I want, with whomever I want. Repercussions be damned. Just like you did."

And with that, I hung up the phone, but I couldn't stop shaking. The blinders were off. All Dan wanted was to treat me like a kid. Everyone made mistakes, and hopefully I'd learned from them. Dan was the one stuck in the past—my past—and refused to move on.

I had no idea how long I sat, attempting to regroup, but it must've been enough time that Gordon peeked his head around the bookcase.

"Everything okay?"

My attempted smile must've failed miserably, as Gordon nodded. "There's no one left except us. It's five to seven, so I'm gonna close early."

He disappeared, and I huffed out a breath and ran a sleeve over my burning eyes. Hearing Dan put it so crudely, that I'd roll over for Lyon, humiliated me worse than anything anyone had ever said to me.

Gordon reappeared with a cup of hot tea for me and his usual coffee mug for himself. I took it from him.

"Thanks. You didn't have to do this. I'm fine. I'm sure you have better things to do than babysit me."

"Yeah, sure, but you're upset." His brows drew together. "Want to tell me what happened?"

Leaving out the incidents Dan had brought up, I gave Gordon the gist of the conversation. "So as you can see, he can do whatever he wants, but when it comes to me, he thinks it's okay to tell me what to do, and when I don't, he calls me names."

"Not cool, for sure, but can I ask you something?"

"Yeah." I sipped the strong black tea.

"What is the deal with you and Lyon? Do you like him? He's obviously into you."

The irony of Gordon's words wasn't lost on me.

*He sure was into me the other night. Deep into me. And I never felt so alive.*

I wasn't about to share with Gordon the little plan Lyon and I had agreed to—it sounded so childish when I thought about it. "I don't know. I'm not sure I can trust him, but I also think Dan's wrong. There's a lot more depth to Lyon than he lets people see."

"Why is that?"

I shrugged and finished my tea. "I don't know, but I plan to find out."

I'd barely had time to set down my keys when the bell rang. When I peeked through the curtain, I couldn't help but smile.

"Uncle Harry. What a nice surprise. Come on in."

He strolled past me to the front parlor, where he sat on the love seat he favored whenever he visited, a find from one of my antique store browsings. "Thank you. I apologize for popping in on you unannounced, but I wanted to make sure I caught you early enough, in case you had evening plans."

"It's not a problem."

I took his tweed cap and umbrella and set them on a small table in the corner, then took the club chair opposite him. "To what do I owe this delightful visit? Can I offer you anything?"

"No, no. I'm full up with tea, and I'm having dinner with Maxwell later tonight. I wanted to stop by and chat with you about Lyon."

"Good God, does anyone in New York City have anything else to talk about besides my friendship with Lyon?"

A twinkle lit Uncle Harry's eyes. "Not at the moment. And certainly not from people who've known both of you for years."

I huffed out a sigh. "Would you be upset if I said I didn't want to talk about it? I spent enough time this afternoon being berated by Dan."

Harry's good humor faded. "Did you, now? I'd say that's the epitome of the pot calling the kettle black. Was he saying negative things about Lyon?"

Watching Harry grow angry surprised me. It was a rare occurrence for the older man to lose his temper. I said cautiously, "I know you and Lyon are close. But even you have to admit he doesn't have the best reputation."

"But that doesn't answer my question. Was Dan talking negatively about Lyon? He's got one hell of a nerve," he insisted, his ire rising. "A man who doesn't have any moral character and would sleep with his best friend's fiancée? This is the man who dares to speak about my great-nephew?" His face was turning red.

"Uncle Harry, don't get yourself worked up. I know Dan is wrong."

"Wrong isn't the half of it. He's spreading lies about Lyon, and I won't stand for it. Trust me, Dan doesn't know him as well as he thinks. Lyon, for all his faults, loved your brother. He would never deliberately hurt Dan the way Dan destroyed him. Don't let Lyon's ruthless businessman facade fool you. When it comes to the people he loves, he would do anything and everything to help them."

Hoping to get a little more intel on Lyon, I leaned forward. "I always suspected there was more to Lyon than he let people see."

Uncle Harry steepled his fingers beneath his chin and fixed me with his thoughtful gaze. "He's a very complicated person and not the complete hedonist most are led to believe. Is he a saint? By no means, but I'm sure we've all done things in our past we regret." His smile was wry. "I know I certainly have."

"I have as well," I said softly. "And I agree with you."

"Good." Harry nodded with approval. "Because Lyon needs a person like you in his life—someone who cares about others, someone who knows the true meaning of friendship and trust."

But I still wanted to know more. "I always thought Lyon hid his true feelings. Do you know why?"

The twinkle returned to Harry's eyes. "That's something you'll have to find out, my boy. And I'm sure you can do it."

My heart swelled at Harry's praise, which I knew didn't come lightly. "We've gotten friendly. Closer than before, for sure. It's sad that it took Dan's bad behavior for it to happen."

"It's all about turning a negative into a positive. Now, I've taken enough of your time." With a grunt, he heaved himself up, and I rushed to his side to help him rise. "I'd best be on my way."

"I'm always happy to have you. Are you sure you can't stay?"

"No, no. Maxwell and I have tickets to the opera, and I don't want to be late." His smile was sweet, and my heart beat faster. Was Uncle Harry telling me something? His close lifelong friendship with the hotel mogul and philanthropist was no secret, but I'd admit to being curious if there was something more between the two men. Neither had ever married, and they'd been staunch friends forever, going on vacations and appearing at social functions together. Perhaps the times they grew up in made them wary about revealing too much of their own personal lives, but all I wanted was for Uncle Harry to be happy.

"Then I'll walk you out." I handed him his umbrella and cap, but he stopped at the door and put a hand on my arm.

"I think we're of the same mindset, which is enough to set my heart at ease. I'll leave you to a pleasant evening."

Impulsively, I kissed his cheek. "I'm happy you stopped by."

"I am too."

Once I made sure Uncle Harry was safely inside his car, I took the stairs two at a time to get ready for Lyon's visit.

This time there was no banging on my door. When Lyon rang the bell, I answered it. He'd come straight from The Lyon's Den, still in his suit and tie from the day.

"You could've changed. I said I'd wait up." I held out my hand. "Give me your jacket, and I'll hang it up." I took it from him and hung it on a peg, and then we walked into the living room.

"I didn't want to waste time." That disarming half smile tugged at his lips. "I'd rather be here."

"Well, now you can take off your tie and get comfortable. Do you want a drink or some coffee?"

"Coffee would be great. It'll perk me up." He pulled me into his chest. "I don't want to fall asleep on you." That delicious, naughty grin broadened. "Unless we're naked and I'm on top."

"Uhhh…" My stomach did a crazy swoop, and my breath caught. Lyon took advantage of my unsteadiness by settling his mouth over mine, but I didn't exactly push him away. When he released me, I swayed for a moment, and he chuckled.

"Go get me my coffee."

With my lips still tingling, I hurried to the kitchen to get his coffee and my wits together. I refused to let him take the driver's seat tonight.

When I carried in a cup for him and tea for me, I found him gazing at the mantel covered with family pictures.

"How are your parents? Are they in the States or at the apartment in London?"

"Last we heard, they were heading for the South of France. My father can't sit still in one place any longer than a month, so who knows where they'll be by the end of the year?" I handed him the mug.

"Mm, good. Nice and hot. Give them my regards the next time you speak."

"I will. Now can we sit?"

"Oh, yes, sir. Getting right to the nitty-gritty." He sat on the couch, spreading his legs to showcase those powerful thigh muscles so they pulled the trousers tight. For once he'd listened to me and taken off his tie and unbuttoned his collar, so a peek of dark chest hair swirled out.

It was still hard for me to believe I had Lyon in my house. That he'd been my lover. Did one time make someone your lover? Did I want to have sex with him again? All the questions swirled around in my mind, and I swallowed hard.

"With me starting full-time at the library, I thought we needed to talk and set some boundaries. Just to reiterate and make it clear, I'm not there to make it easier for you to have sex with me."

He tipped his head. "As we've discussed. But does that mean we can't have a little bit of fun? All work and no play makes me cranky."

"You're incorrigible."

"I've been called worse," he teased.

"No surprise there." I huffed and took a seat across from him. "Look, I know we agreed on this game of revenge against Dan. And if we're sure we're alone, I don't mind a kiss or two." His grin broadened, and I hurried to continue before the conversation derailed. "But I think…at least for me…it's changed from simply a game."

The good humor vanished, and his face grew taut. "Go on."

Maybe I was shooting myself in the foot, but I'd strayed

so far out of my comfort zone by that point, I might as well lay it all on the line.

"All this time we've spent together—the apple picking, and especially when we talked about the charities—I saw a different side to you. I like that person and would love to know him better, but he doesn't stick around long enough for me to get that chance. That Lyon is someone you keep hidden away, and I wonder why."

A shadow dimmed his eyes. "I don't know what you're talking about. I'm the same everywhere I go. Maybe I was too caught up in the party scene to have thought about the charitable work I could be doing, but now I'm on board. You've enlightened me."

I knew he'd be evasive, but I pressed him anyway. If he grew angry, so be it. I had to reach him somehow. "I know there's something more than the Lyon Elliot who only cares about pleasure…about getting laid."

He sipped his coffee. "Maybe. Maybe not." He shrugged.

He was making it very difficult to sit still and not smack him. "God, you're frustrating. Why are you being like this?"

Eyes flashing, he set the mug down abruptly. Coffee slopped over the side, but he didn't seem to care. Fingers dripping, Lyon pointed at me. "Like what? This is who I am. Take it or leave it. Me changing into your ideal man wasn't part of our deal."

"Neither was me sleeping with you," I shouted, and we stared at each other.

"So you regret it?"

I met his gaze unflinchingly. "No. But if I'm sleeping with someone, I'd like to know them better. I saw a different man than the one I thought I knew, and I liked him." I left my chair to sit next to him. "That man is charming and funny without being cutting and cruel. He's a tender, sweet lover. I want *all the time* the Lyon you give me when no one else is around."

Lyon sat very still.

"The nonsense with Dan aside, is sex all you want from me?" I held my breath.

The slight shake of his head made my heart leap.

"Then tell me why. Why do you think you have to keep up this fake persona when I know there's so much more to you? What are you afraid of people discovering about you?"

With a sneer, he faced me. "Nothing. There's nothing more to me. This is what you get. There's never been anything else. It's why even my parents don't give a damn, okay? The only people who care are Uncle Harry and Scott, and sometimes I wonder if I'll end up driving them away too."

Recalling what Uncle Harry had said about Charles and Marianne, I knew to tread carefully. Lyon's emotions were a minefield, ready to explode at a wrong step. "I care." Taking a chance he'd pull away from me, I took his hands in mine, and when he tensed, I gripped him tighter. "I care."

"Why? I know Dan's given you an earful of all my faults."

"He didn't need to," I teased lightly. "You forget I've known you my whole life."

But Lyon didn't join in on the joke. He stared over my shoulder, his grim face hard, as if carved from stone.

"No, you don't. You saw what I wanted you to. Remember when I came by the first time and said that you knew me? And you laughed in my face and told me I was wrong? Well, you weren't. You were right. I said it to get you to feel sorry for me. I wanted someone to care."

My heart pounded, and my stomach dropped.

*Oh God, don't make me fall in love with you.*

I gathered my wits. "These past weeks made me suspect

that the man I see when no one else is around is who you are. Although I do like the snarky Lyon." I gentled my tone to almost a whisper. "All I'm saying is, if you'd given that man more time to develop, you wouldn't have had to work that hard to seduce me." I paused. "Again, that is."

His eyes widened, and the anger in their depths died, replaced by a glow of desire. "But you said at the Den that you weren't there for me to get my rocks off. That you had a job to do."

"And I meant it. Business is business, and I'm there to work. But we're not working right now."

Lyon's eyes blazed with their beautifully unique indigo fire, and his lips twitched. "No. We're not. Although I'm working hard to get you to where you were the other night. Naked." He took advantage of me holding his hands to draw me close, although truthfully, it didn't take much effort.

"Is this all still part of the revenge to get back at Dan?" I whispered against his mouth.

Lyon dipped his head and kissed me, releasing my hands to cup my face and suck my tongue hungrily. When he let go, his eyes glittered.

"Dan who? I'm here because there isn't anyplace else I'd rather be. Or anyone else I'd rather be with."

We lunged at each other, and our clothes went flying as we ripped them off. All the inhibitions I'd surrounded myself with since college fell by the wayside. The other men who'd used me vanished into nothingness. There was no one but Lyon, and when we were naked, I pushed him to the couch and sank to my knees.

"You're beautiful." I took his thick cock in my mouth, slowly running my tongue over the heavy pulsing shaft, and sucked. Precome spilled down my throat, and I swallowed it like the finest wine.

"Shit, Miles, your face. Oh God, baby. You're amazing." He touched my hair, and everything else faded away.

I loved hearing him call me baby....I loved...him. My admission to what I'd always kept hidden spurred me on.

Moving faster, I played with his sac and teased his quivering thighs but never let up on licking and swallowing that gorgeous dick. He was huge and hot, stretching my jaw to the limit, but I'd never felt more alive.

I hummed, holding him at the base of his cock and returning to the wide, smooth head. I tickled the slit with the tip of my tongue, and Lyon squirmed and moaned, his fingers tangling in my hair, holding me in place.

"Yeah, baby. God, you're amazing. Wanted you for so long."

Those words sent me reeling. The powerful thighs under my fingertips tensed, and his balls drew up. I increased my pace and slid my lips along his erection, eager to feel him explode in my mouth.

"Oh God, I'm there...fuck, Miles."

He thrust into my mouth hard and came, bringing tears to my eyes, but I loved it and took every drop he gave me. When he finished, I let him slip from my mouth and gazed up at him. His head lolled to the side, and a blissful smile curved his lips. Lyon cracked one eye open.

"What're you doing down there? Come up here."

I snuggled next to him and gasped when he kissed me, his tongue playing with mine. "I like my taste on you," he murmured, and I sighed.

"Me too."

"And I'm not about to leave you hanging." He licked his palm and gripped my shaft, and with his tongue plunging in and out of my mouth, he pumped my dick until I saw stars and came all over his hand. Eyes sparkling, Lyon licked his fingers clean. “Delicious.”

I couldn’t help trembling. Where did we go from here? I was lost in the woods with no compass or stars to guide me, only a heart that urged me toward an uncertain path. One I’d never dreamed possible.

“I can see your mind working, and I’m not sure I like what you’re thinking.”

“Maybe we should get dressed and finish that talk.”

Lyon frowned. “Talk is overrated. As are clothes.” But he relented. “Okay, fine.”

We put on our clothes, and I was about to suggest we go to the kitchen, when the bell rang. Instantly alarmed because it was after midnight, I hurried to the front.

“Fuck.”

“Let me in, Miles.”

Lyon stood in the hallway. He hadn’t bothered to button his shirt, and his feet were bare. At the sound of Dan’s voice, Lyon frowned, but then his eyes brightened and his smile turned crafty. “Let him in. Are you ready for showtime?”

My heart sank. “This isn’t a game. Can you finish getting dressed, please?”

Lyon’s expression was troubled, but he disappeared into the living room, and I hoped he was doing what I’d asked.

The bell rang over and over. “I see you through the door, Miles. Open up,” Dan yelled and banged on the glass.

Reluctantly, I unlocked the door, and Dan burst inside.

“What the fuck, dude? Why were you standing there waiting instead of letting me in?”

“What’re you doing here? Where’s Lindsey?”

“Resting in the apartment. I cut our honeymoon short to come home and make sure you weren’t doing anything stupid.”

"Like what, Dan?" Lyon walked out, and I could've died a little. He'd put his socks on, but his shirt was still unbuttoned.

"You fucking son of a bitch. I'll kill you."

Dan ran past me, leaped at Lyon, and punched him.

*Ow. Fuck, that hurt.* I'd never been hit in the face.

Chest heaving, Dan stood over me. "Get up, motherfucker." His fist drew back, and I rose up on my elbows to scoot out of reach before jumping to my feet. I worked my jaw and winced.

"If you break it, you pay for it, remember that."

"Not if I kill you first, you bastard. I warned you to stay away from my brother."

"And I told you to go to hell, and yet here you are." I could feel some swelling in my lips when I attempted to smile. I hoped he hadn't loosened a tooth. I hated going to the dentist.

"Dan. Shut up and leave Lyon alone." Miles pushed at him, but Dan outweighed him and remained in place.

"Are you fucking crazy? Look at you. God, I don't even want to know what I interrupted."

"I can tell you if you want." I grinned, hoping to instigate another furious outburst.

An ugly flush turned Dan almost purple, and a growl burst from him. "Shut up." He took Miles by the shoulders. "Tell me I'm not too late."

"Too late for what?" Miles turned red, and I didn't like how I could see him shrink in front of my eyes. I'd never noticed how Dan overwhelmed Miles with the sheer force of his larger personality. "I don't know what you want me to say."

"I do," I interjected. "He wants to know if we've had sex yet."

Miles faced me, those big blue eyes wide, and I could see the longing in them as well as humiliation, confusion, and hurt. I could have my sweet revenge against Dan right now and tell him everything. That would set him off, and I might get my ass beat to a pulp, but it would be worth it to know I'd caused him pain.

But it would hurt Miles more.

Dan's mouth continued to run. "I told you he only wanted you for sex."

White and visibly shaken, Miles whispered, "It's not like that. It's not what you think." He wrenched away from Dan, and I wanted to go over and hug him, but it wasn't the time, so instead I turned my attention to filleting Dan alive.

"Listen, you selfish prick. Don't talk to Miles like he's a fool. Nothing's happened between us. Not that I haven't tried…"

On his way down the hall, Miles stopped and turned around. Dan glanced between us, and his lip curled. "You're bullshitting me. I can tell."

"I'm sure you could, since you're now an official expert on how to lie to someone's face without repercussions," I shot back. "But I'm not. Do I want Miles? Hell, yeah. He's gorgeous, smart, sexy, and fun. But he said no, and I respect that."

"You? Respect boundaries?" Dan snorted. "Fucking liar."

"People can change if they have a reason. Who the fuck are you to be so sanctimonious? Look what you did to me," I roared.

"I fell in love. You don't love anyone but yourself."

If he'd bashed me in the face a second time, I couldn't have hurt more.

"If you hadn't gone after Miles, we could've been friends again. You would've forgiven me because you never really loved Lindsey. But not now. I told you years ago, don't even *look* at Miles."

Did he honestly think I could ever trust him after everything? And seeing how he treated Miles made me want to choose violence instead of words. But Miles remained standing where he was, and I wouldn't demean myself by lowering to Dan's level. Miles said he liked the man I was when we were together, and I wanted to show him I was the person he wanted me to be.

"I like Miles. He's a good person, unlike you."

"You're only saying that because he's in front of you. You'll do anything to hurt me, and that includes sleeping with my brother if you think it'll work."

My head throbbed, and my cheek hurt, but that pain was nothing compared to what those words did to Miles. He absolutely deflated before my eyes. Dan's words crushed him. And because it hurt Miles, it hurt me.

"You selfish goddamned prick. You think everything's about you. I don't give one crap about what you think or feel.

But I do care how Miles feels. And I hope you know that Miles is a hundred times a better man than you'll ever be."

I marched away from them and into the living room, where I shoved my feet into my shoes, picked up my tie, and stomped back to the front. Dan had Miles nose to nose at the wall and was giving him an earful.

"Y-you're leaving?" Miles peered over Dan's shoulder.

Much as I wanted to stay and comfort Miles, I couldn't, because that would involve me holding him and telling him how wrong Dan was. That was private—for us to share. "Yeah. I'll see you tomorrow."

"No, you won't," Dan barked. "Get out."

"Go to hell."

I slammed out and called a car. I had just enough time to button my shirt and tuck it into my waistband before it arrived. The driver's eyes met mine, and I attempted a smile.

"You should see the other guy."

"I don't know. I don't want no fights in my car…"

But I knew how to turn him around. I slid into the back, pulled out five twenties, and tossed the folded money onto the front seat. "Please, just go."

As I was winging away from Brooklyn and over the bridge, I noticed I'd left my suit jacket at Miles's house. Hopefully he'd bring it to the Den tomorrow.

I didn't realize how bad it was until my doorman rushed to help me. "Are you okay, Lyon? Do you need to go to the hospital? What happened? Were you mugged?"

Ruefully, I touched my swollen cheek and winced. "No. Just a run-in with someone I used to know. I'll put some ice on it."

"Okay. If you want me to send your shirt to the cleaners, let me know." I glanced down and saw spots of blood dotting the white fabric.

"No. It's fine. Thanks."

Once upstairs, I stripped off my clothes and tossed them into a corner, then finally looked in the mirror. My cheek and eye were black and blue and swollen. Dried blood surrounded my nose.

"Bastard." I took a washcloth and entered my shower, gingerly cleaning my face first. By the time I'd finished and gotten dressed, my head throbbed. I went to the kitchen, swallowed some Tylenol, found an ice pack, and put it on my cheek. Strangely enough, my thoughts weren't on my battered face—that would heal. I'd never suspected how Dan had kept Miles under his thumb. How he treated him like a person who didn't have the sense to make the right decision. That kind of damage buried deep into your soul and didn't fade away. I lay on my couch and stared up at the ceiling.

I shifted the ice pack and grimaced, stretching out my legs. All the plans I'd had for the night—wild sex with Miles, him staying with me the night and us having more fun in the morning—were obviously down the drain, but that wasn't important now. I couldn't help worrying about what Dan was saying to Miles. Was he going to listen? Lately he'd seemed more independent, but old habits and feelings were hard to overcome.

After all, I still thought my parents had valid reasons for why they didn't give a damn about me. I'd spent enough of my childhood picking through my life, wondering what I'd done to make them stay away. Did I cry too much? Have too many nightmares? Did I get too many colds? I tried to be good and never cause problems whenever they did come home, but it didn't matter. Nothing did. They'd always pick up and leave, returning whenever they felt like it. Which wasn't that often. Occasionally we'd be introduced to a new mother or father. After the third or fourth, it no longer mattered.

As I grew older, I stopped caring why they left. I stopped caring about everything except what made me feel good.

Sex, I'd discovered, was a wonderful panacea, and I filled my nights with as many people as I could. It didn't cure the loneliness, but it made it easier to bear. Scott had married and had Beth's large family to take him in and make him feel wanted. I had Dan by my side.

But then he wasn't, leaving me adrift and lost, the old insecurities of being unloved and unwanted circling me like sharks smelling blood in the water. I'd even contemplated jumping in and giving them what they wanted. They might rip me to pieces, but at least I'd feel something, when I never felt anything at all.

Until Miles told me I made him laugh, and that he liked spending time with me. I could tease him, and he'd come right back at me with a fun jab of his own. It was easy with him.

I closed my eyes, wondering if this was going to be my life from now on. Sitting at the club, listening to other people's happiness. I didn't want to grow old alone. Much as I loved Uncle Harry, I didn't want to be him.

But I didn't miss the noise and crowds either. I didn't miss pretending to be interested in whatever some random man or woman had to say to get them to come home with me. I didn't miss waking up, still drunk from the night before, with a stranger I'd have to somehow extricate from my bed politely but firmly.

I missed Miles. I missed his smiles.

The bell rang, and I rubbed my damp eyes, wondering why the doorman hadn't buzzed me first. Hoping it wasn't one of my neighbors asking me for help with something, I dragged my feet answering, but when the bell rang a second time, I huffed in annoyance.

"Coming."

Miles stood outside waiting, and held up my suit jacket. "You left this at my house. I figured you might need it."

Those big eyes grew even wider with dismay when I turned on the light by the door. "Oh my God, Lyon, your face." Without asking, he reached out and touched my jaw. "Are you okay? Is anything broken? Do you think you need to go to the hospital? I can't believe Dan hit you. He's such a jerk."

My face hurt like a bitch, but his mini rant made me smile. "Come on in. I didn't think I'd see you tonight. It's pretty late." Almost two a.m. to be exact, but instead of feeling tired, I was curiously filled with sudden energy.

"I told Dan to leave."

Dying to hear the story, I pointed at the couch. "Sit. Do you want anything?"

"I should be doing that for you." He picked up the ice pack. "Sit down yourself, and I'll get you some fresh ice for this."

Deciding I liked this cozy, domesticated scene, I lowered my ass to the couch and watched him putter around my kitchen. When he returned, I held out my hand, but he sat by my side and put it to my cheek himself.

"I'm sorry. I can't believe he did that. Does it hurt bad?" His fingertips brushed my skin, then all too quickly were gone.

"It's okay. I didn't like leaving you, but I thought it was best to remove myself from his presence." I dropped my gaze to my hands and flexed my fingers. "I didn't want to resort to hitting him back."

"I'm glad you didn't. Violence never solves anything. I'm so disgusted and upset with Dan."

"What did he say about me? I'm sure he gave you an earful."

Miles nodded. "Nothing he hasn't said before. I was his target this time."

Despite their estrangement, I knew how much Miles

loved and looked up to Dan, and in his own twisted way, Dan wanted the best for Miles. On his own terms, of course.

Miles said, "Dan can be cruel, you know. He likes to dredge up people's mistakes and use them to make them feel stupid."

"Not you. You know you're not stupid. You're smarter than anyone I know."

The droop of his mouth was heartbreakingly sad. "You don't know me that well."

I ran my knuckles down his cheek. "Then tell me. Why does Dan think he can control you? Why do you let him? Talk to me. I want to learn what Miles is made of."

"I'm not that interesting."

"I disagree. I don't hang around with boring people," I teased.

Some of that sparkle lit up his eyes. "So, it's all about you, huh?"

"No, baby. Not me. You. I find you fascinating. I already know what you taste like and how you sound when we're together. But it's not enough. I want more." My thumb skated over the high point of his cheek, and his thick lashes lowered.

A smile creased Miles's cheek. "We're both on a journey of discovery. Because I might've known you all my life, yet I'm learning you aren't who I thought."

I shifted closer, and I didn't care about my aching cheek and bruises. Having him here with me made all those earlier, ugly thoughts fade away. Miles made the world a little bit brighter. He was my sunrise, breaking through the darkness of my cold night.

"So again. Why is Dan so overprotective? I'd do anything to help Scott and his family if I thought they were in danger, but I've never told him whom he could or couldn't date.

This is different. It's almost an obsession with him. Is there something you're hiding that only he knows?"

The way I knew I'd fallen in love with Lyon was that I wanted to tell him my story.

I started with college and my roommate's betrayal, and I watched his eyes flash fire. By the time I'd finished with the dates who'd stolen from me or used me, Lyon's face was dark red with anger.

"Those two fuckers in college should've been arrested. Dickson Monroe. Stupid-ass name."

"Well, it's certainly one I've never forgotten. I always thought Miles was preppy enough. Anyway, I never saw him or Clifton after freshman year. I have no idea what happened to them and don't care."

"So you got Dan to help you. That was nice of him, but it still doesn't explain his rabid overprotectiveness."

I forged on. "After the incident in college, I never let another person get close to me. And even if I dated, I kept the men at arm's length. I figured at some point, they'd use me, and it was easier to be alone than risk humiliation again."

"It's natural to protect yourself from getting hurt over and over. And you're a kind and giving person, so I'm thinking those bastards you dated seduced you with one hand and picked your pocket with the other."

I chewed on my lip. "You're right on one account. Except they didn't seduce me. Dan told me they were only after me for sex."

Lyon's brow furrowed. "What's wrong with him? There's nothing wrong with enjoying life, and sex is part of that. God knows, he sure as hell had enough fun."

Trusting Lyon with what I was about to tell him would mean exposing myself in a way I'd sworn not to. But those were different days, and I was a different person. And so was Lyon.

"I listened to him because I knew he had my best interests at heart. He said to wait until the right guy came around and that I'd know. So I didn't have sex with them." I met his gaze. "I didn't have sex with anyone. I never had. Until you."

Watching his eyes, I could pinpoint the moment Lyon picked up the meaning of what I'd said to him. "Wait. Hold up. You didn't…are you saying you were a virgin when you and I…" He swallowed, never breaking that penetrating stare.

"Yeah. It was my first time." I hesitated, then decided to hell with it. "You were that guy. The man I've always wanted."

If I'd turned up naked at his door, I didn't think Lyon could've been more surprised.

"Why did you let me believe you'd been with someone? Miles…were you all right after?" His jaw dropped. "That's why you left. You didn't want to tell me?" He let the ice pack fall. "If I'd known…I should've—"

"Done absolutely the same thing." I smiled to show him I meant every word. "It was incredible. The best night of my life."

"I can't believe it."

"Sure you can. I was Miles the Mouse."

"Shut up with that already," Lyon said, but with such affection, my heart swelled with joy. "You were never that dumb nickname, and I'm not the same person who once called you that." He brushed my lips with his. "I can't believe the man I had in my bed that night, the wild, insatiable lover who turned me inside out, was a virgin. You were incredible. And I'm not lying when I say you're the best lover I've ever had. But I still wish you'd told me."

"You would've laughed at me. Maybe Dan was right on that account, and I am stupid."

Lyon grabbed my arms. "No, he's not. He never was. *Never, ever* let anyone call you that. Dan, me…anyone. You're smart and good and so much better a person than either of us—than anyone I've ever met."

"I'm no saint, Lyon. I'm far from perfect. And I didn't tell you because I wanted to know what being with you would be like when you didn't hold back."

"Oh, I didn't. I gave you everything I had." His eyes glittered. "And I want more."

Desire surged through me, and my breath quickened.

"But your face—"

"Is fine. I don't care if it hurts. Not making love to you will hurt me much more. I don't want you to leave. I want you in my bed with me. The whole night."

I smiled as I drew up his T-shirt and tossed it aside, then

repeated the action with mine. I stood and kicked off my shoes.

"Let me." Lyon pushed aside my fingers, popped the button, and drew down the zipper. I swayed at that simple touch, and Lyon nuzzled my groin, inhaling deep. "You smell like you want me."

"I always want you." Where I got the nerve to speak those words, I had no clue, but now I stood naked and exposed. And I'd never been more free.

Without waiting for his next move, I took off the rest of my clothes and watched Lyon wriggle out of his sweats. He took hold of my hand, and through the dark apartment, we found our way to the bedroom. Not letting go, we climbed onto the bed, and I placed eager kisses on his uninjured cheek, until he rolled me under him and took my mouth in a harsh, powerful kiss.

I clung to his broad shoulders and locked my legs around his waist, bucking my hips to thrust my hard, aching dick against his. There was an emptiness inside me, and I throbbed with a desperation only he could soothe.

"Lyon, God, please. Fuck me. I can't wait."

"Slow down. I don't want to hurt you."

I was wild with the need to be taken and reached between us to grasp his hot, hard cock. "Please, I have to…I want it…"

"Shh, okay, baby." He left me only to get the condoms and lube, but I put my hand out.

"No. No condom. You're my only one."

"Okay, but just so you know, for your peace of mind, I got tested when I learned that Lindsey cheated on me. I want you to know you're safe."

"Please, Lyon. I want to feel you. My first." I wanted to say *my only* but couldn't. Not yet.

"I like that I'm your first." Eyes on fire, Lyon slicked

himself up. He slipped a finger in me, and it wasn't enough. I clenched tight, and he added a second, then a third, stretching me, all while kissing my dick and tonguing my sac. "You should see yourself…a golden god. And I'm going to worship your beautiful body."

His fingers withdrew, and were replaced by the blunt head of his cock. "Hold on, baby. Breathe deep." He pushed my legs up and nudged in past the ring, taking care to move slowly. But I wanted him to be as out of control for me as I was for him.

"Don't hold back," I writhed on his shaft, lifting my hips to force him deeper. "Give it to me hard."

He held still. "I'm trying to be gentle."

"Don't," I gasped and pulled him to me. "Fuck me hard." I clenched my inner walls to squeeze him.

"Son of a bitch." Lyon hissed, and his dick swelled in my ass. A deep groan slipped from his lips as he began to thrust. Sweat dripped from his brow, falling on my lips, and I licked it.

"Fuck, baby, that's hot."

I locked my ankles around his waist, and he bent me almost double as he pumped into me over and over. My dick was trapped between our heaving bodies, and the intense friction sent me toppling over the edge.

"Lyon," I screamed. "Lyon." I came, my come mixing with our sweat, the bed banging into the wall as he took me apart. He hit that tender spot, and while I continued to wail and thrash, Lyon moved harder and faster. This was more than sex, more than a hunger to possess. It was something necessary for our survival, like air, blood, and water.

I managed to open my eyes and was immediately captured by the intense, hungry expression on his face. Though I'd climaxed seconds before, I was still on a high, and I twitched and shivered as Lyon slammed into me one last time. His cock swelled and he filled me.

When we'd caught our breaths, I rubbed my cheek to his. "I know we should go clean up, but I'm so damn comfortable."

"You won't be if you end up sleeping on the wet spot."

I pushed at his shoulder. "Then get off me, you big lug."

Half-hard, he was still large, and he withdrew slowly. I missed the touch of his skin against mine, and maybe he felt the loss too, as he held out his hand.

"Come."

He helped me walk on my shaky legs to the bathroom, and I would never have believed that the hard, sharp-tongued Lyon could be the one murmuring sweet nothings in my ear. His hands were gentle as he cleaned me, and when he wrapped me in a heated towel and led me back to bed, I was swooning.

Once under the covers, he spooned me and nipped my shoulder. "How do you feel?" His voice rumbled in my ear, and I shifted until we were settled into place, with his arm around my waist and our legs tangled.

I sighed. "Like I died and went to heaven."

"*Mmm*, baby, you are the heaven. You chase away the hell."

About to drift off, I blinked to awareness and rolled over to face him. "What hell?" The blinds were half open, and dawn was approaching, the brightening sky illuminating the pain and fear in his poor bruised face. "Lyon, talk to me. What's wrong?"

He smiled. "Nothing. I was trying to be poetic but failed." He kissed my nose. "Thank you, by the way."

"For what?"

"For sharing your story. I know you haven't told anyone else but Dan, and I promise I won't break your trust."

My bones dissolved into a puddle. God, I might never move again. I was too caught up in him.

"I know you won't. Like I would never break yours if you wanted to tell me more."

"More about what?" His voice, like his face, grew guarded.

"About why there are two Lyons. The devil-may-care public face and the man here with me."

"There's nothing more than what you see. I've said it before. I am who I am. I don't change like the seasons. Now I'm exhausted. Let's go to sleep."

*You are a terrible liar.*

As gently as possible, I said, "I don't believe that. Please tell me."

"That's your problem, not mine." Lyon had shut down. "My face hurts. I need to rest."

"But…"

He closed his eyes, and I stared at him, but the idiot either pretended really well or he was that tired. There'd be no further talking, that was clear, and I huffed out my annoyance. I curled away from Lyon and punched my pillow, wishing I could shake some sense into him so he could see that all I wanted to do was help.

The following morning I awoke to Lyon holding me tight. "Good morning," he whispered in my ear. "You snore."

"Good morning too. You're rude."

Apparently, his strange mood was gone, and I wasn't willing to chase this Lyon away. One day he'd tell me.

"I thought you were going to sleep the whole day." His eyes danced. "It's after ten."

"What? Are you serious?" In disbelief, I sat up, and my mouth fell open. "I've never slept this late. Good thing I hired an assistant to help Gordon at the store now."

"I wore you out." His smile was smug, and I alternated between wanting to kiss him and smack him, but his face was swollen, and multicolored bruises had spread over the left cheek and under his eye.

"How does it feel?"

"Like it looks, but I'll live."

"I'm sorry."

"It is what it is. I ordered breakfast, and I already showered, so the bathroom's all yours."

"You've been up that long? I didn't even notice you'd left." I swung my legs over the side of the bed and winced. Ouch, my ass hurt.

"*Mmm*, yeah. I decided you needed the rest. Like I said. I gave you a ride yesterday, so you're probably a little sore." He hopped out of the bed and I noticed he was fully dressed.

"You're enjoying yourself way too much," I grumbled, and he snickered but surprised me by taking my hands and pulling me up to stand flush with his chest.

"I'm enjoying you. A lot. And it's not enough. I want more." He rubbed my ass and kissed me. I returned it eagerly, but the buzzer rang. "Breakfast is here," he murmured against my mouth. "But I can have you for dessert."

"Dessert with breakfast?" I panted, trying hard to catch my breath. "I was always taught it was a treat on special occasions."

"Every minute with you is special. Now go shower." He patted my ass, and I rolled my eyes but laughed and walked into the bathroom. I washed up quickly, and when I came into the bedroom, I saw that Lyon had thoughtfully laid out on the bed my clothes from the night before. I heard yelling, so I pulled on my jeans and T-shirt and ran to the living room. Dan was there, spewing his bullshit.

"You son of a bitch. You couldn't keep your hands off him, could you? Don't you have any shame?"

"Ironic, coming from you."

"Lindsey never loved you. No one gives a damn about you. Only your brother, and that's probably because he has to."

Lyon paled at the cruelty of Dan's words, and my heart hurt for him.

"Get the hell out of here."

"Not until I see Miles."

"Who said he's here?"

"He's not home, and he's not at work."

"Go away. Go take care of your wife and baby-to-be."

"So help me God, if you fucked Miles, I'll—"

"You'll what, Dan?" I strode across the living room. "What'll you do, hit him again? Where is all this hate coming from? Lyon was your best friend."

Dan grabbed me. "You stupid idiot," he screamed in my face. "Haven't you learned anything?"

"It wasn't like that, you bastard." I was elbowed aside, and Lyon shoved Dan against the wall. "And don't you ever, *ever* call Miles stupid. You know nothing about Miles and me. Nothing."

"Oh, yeah? What're you gonna tell me, that you're in love with him? That's a joke. The only person you love is yourself."

Lyon's jaw tensed, and I waited to hear his answer, but he said nothing.

So I stuck my feet into my sneakers and walked out the door.

God, I felt like shit.

Seeing Miles standing there, waiting for me to say something in response to Dan…but fucking hell to the no would I let Dan dictate when I said to Miles the words I'd never said to anyone.

Then Miles walked out the door, and my world went to shit.

"If you don't want to leave by stretcher," I told Dan, "I advise you to leave right now." If I could get rid of Dan, I'd be able to catch Miles.

"Can't lie your way out of this one, huh?" Dan sneered.

"Why not? It worked for you with Lindsey. Oh, I forgot. You just hide it better."

Dan took three long strides toward me, and I wondered

how we'd come to this place of hate and anger when all I ever did was love him as my best friend. He raised his fist to my face, but I didn't flinch.

"Leave my brother alone. He's too good for you."

He pushed me out of the way and left the apartment, slamming the door behind him.

"That might be the only correct thing you've said all morning," I muttered to myself. But I had no more time to waste on Dan. I'd had three weeks of mourning that loss, and now I saw that he never cared as much as I did. Same old story for me.

But I wasn't going to give up on Miles. Not with how he made me feel.

Wanted.

Important.

Needed.

Necessary.

Like he'd become for me.

*Shit.* I stopped running around my apartment like a beheaded chicken and had to hold on to the wall to keep the room from spinning.

Was that…love?

With my stomach in knots, I ran into the bedroom. Sweat beaded on my forehead, and my breath came in short, hard pants. I felt dizzy and light-headed. The comforter and sheets lay in a twisted mess, and I smiled, thinking of Miles and how much I liked waking up to his head on the pillow next to me. I needed to talk to someone with a level head, someone I respected and loved. The list was short.

I grabbed my phone. "Can I come by to talk? Are you busy?"

"No. I don't have any clients today. What's this about?

Everything okay?" Scott sounded puzzled, but I had little time to explain.

"See you in a few."

I put on my socks and sneakers, grabbed my keys and jacket, and ran out.

It wasn't until I received a few odd looks from the people in Scott's office that I glanced at myself in their hallway mirror. In all the commotion going on in my head, I'd forgotten about my black-and-blue face.

"Go ahead, Lyon," Scott's secretary, Gabrielle, smiled at me.

"Thanks." I rushed past her with barely a smile back.

Scott stood waiting for me, his brows raised. "What did you do, have a run-in with a wall?"

"No, Dan's fist."

His jaw dropped, and he shut the door behind me. "Get the fuck out. Do you want to press charges? There are plenty of people here to represent you. Or were you the aggressor?"

"Hardly," I scoffed. "I wouldn't waste my time on him." I told him the story, and I could see his eyes grow wide with shock and anger. I finished and folded my arms. "But that's not what I'm here to talk to you about."

"No? Because I have questions."

"I'm sure you do, but I'm probably not going to want to answer them, so let's leave it for another day."

"Then what are you here for? Not that I don't love talking to you, but has something come up you need my help with?"

Now that I was in front of Scott and had told him the

story, I realized how foolish and premature it was to rush here. It wasn't the place I needed to be. "You know what? I'm sorry. I shouldn't waste your time."

"Lyon, sit down. I always have time for you. You're my brother. I love you. And if something is going on with you, I want to know. I need to. You've always been there for me." He hitched his chair closer and put a hand on my arm. "Let me try and do it once for you."

But saying the words would make it real, and I wasn't sure I could handle that much reality. "Uh…how did…when did you know Beth was the woman you wanted to marry?"

As always when Beth's name came up, Scott's eyes turned soft. "After five years, it's hard to remember not loving her. But to answer your question, I guess it would've been when I walked into our classroom and she smiled at me, even though we'd only left each other an hour earlier. I knew that look was only for me, and I didn't ever want her to be with another man that way." He blinked and focused his attention on me. "Why?" From the gleam in his eye, I thought he already knew, but I couldn't take any more time.

"I needed clarification. Thanks."

"No, Lyon, wait. What's going on?"

But I took off, even as Scott called after me. If I'd stayed, he would've kept me there until I told him everything. And I couldn't.

I called for a car to Brooklyn.

Forty minutes later, I rang the bell to Miles's house. It took several more rings and knocks before Miles answered.

"What?"

"Is that all you have to say?"

"Okay. What the hell do you want?" His mouth drooped, and I hated that I was the cause of his sadness.

"Can we talk?"

"You didn't have anything to say earlier. Why now?"

"If you let me in, I can explain."

Miles lifted a shoulder, and I thought he'd deny me, but he opened the door and let me in.

First hurdle surpassed.

He didn't ask me all the way inside and stood in the hallway, barring entry farther into the house.

"Miles—"

"Let me save you the trouble. It was all a joke to you. I was a joke. The only thing I can't figure out is with whom you were laughing about it."

"There's no one, and it wasn't a joke. Not you, and not what happened between us. None of it."

"Really? Why couldn't you answer Dan when he asked you about what was happening between us?"

"I don't know." I searched his face, hoping he understood. "I didn't understand it then. I still don't."

"Understand what?"

"How I feel about you." I closed the space between us and backed him up against the wall. "I…I like the way you smile at me. I like seeing you in my bed and feeling you next to me when we're sleeping. I like touching you."

Blushing, Miles held his head up. "So? You could get all that from a puppy. Maybe you should adopt one."

"God, you're a pain in the ass." I placed a hand on his neck, felt his pulse beating fast beneath my fingers. "I like kissing you. I crave your taste. I want to make love to you every night and hear you call out my name when you climax." I took advantage of his frozen state and kissed his open mouth. "Most importantly, I don't want anyone else to have what you've given me. My Miles smiles. You. I want you all to myself."

"Lyon..."

"Tell me you want that too." I couldn't stop kissing him. "Tell me you want me."

"I do, but—"

"But *what*?" Frustrated, I let him go and ran my hands through my hair. "What's wrong?"

"Nothing," he said shyly, casting his gaze to the floor. "I do feel the same. But why couldn't you say it to Dan? Are you ashamed that you feel like this about me?"

"No, of course not," I burst out. "But it wasn't right to say it in front of him before I told you. I wanted you to hear it from me first."

"Hear what?" Miles's eyes glowed a brighter blue than any summer sky.

Warmth flooded me, and my lips curved. "You're going to make me say it first, aren't you?"

Those bright eyes danced, and a dimple winked in his cheek. "Say what?" He put a hand to his ear.

I grabbed it and settled my lips over his, hearing his *hum* of pleasure, knowing no song would ever sound as beautiful to my ears. "That I-I love you."

Miles's smile was tremulous. "Are you really sure?"

I smoothed the hair off his brow. "I went to Scott's office to ask him how he knew he wanted to marry Beth. And he told me how he didn't want anyone else to get the smiles she gave him. And when I thought about it, I knew I couldn't let you give my Miles smiles to anyone but me. I can't think about anyone touching you or making love to you but me. I love that of all the people you could've given your trust to, or have your first time with, you chose me."

"I wish you could do the same."

My heart tumbled. "Wh-what do you mean?"

"You're so hurt, still. But you don't want to talk about it."

My lips curled. "I don't give a damn about Dan anymore."

Miles slid his hand up my arm. "Not him. Your parents. They damaged you in a way you've carried with you throughout your life."

"I-I don't want to talk about it."

"That doesn't fly when you love someone. You tell them everything. I told you my deepest hurt that no one knows but Dan. It's affected every move I've made since then. I gave you my trust, and now I'm asking for yours."

The implication was there. If I didn't, he'd walk. And I couldn't chance that.

"Please, Lyon?" He held out his hand, and I laced my fingers with his.

"Okay. Can we sit down at least?"

Miles kissed my unbruised cheek and led me to the couch.

Once we'd settled—and still holding his hand for dear life—I licked my lips and said, "It's stupid."

"Can we please stop using that term?" Miles scowled. "It's really offensive."

Chastened, I lowered my eyes. "Sorry. It's foolish, I know, to allow your childhood to dictate your adult life, but I guess I never bothered to try and get to know anyone or get close to a lover because I always knew they'd leave me. Like my parents. It's why I only trusted the people I've known since I was little and who stayed—Scott, Uncle Harry, and Dan. Everyone else was one step away from the exit."

"You knew me."

"Did I?" I played with his fingers. "I don't think so. I don't think we knew each other. Until now."

"Yeah. Until now."

Miles smiled at me, and my heart pounded. "I thought… why should I love someone when there's something so unlovable about me that even my own parents didn't want to stay? It was simpler to just have fun and walk away."

"I'm sorry, Lyon. I hope you know they're wrong."

"I'm at peace with it now. I guess it hit me when neither showed up for my tenth birthday party."

"I remember that. Uncle Harry talked to you. What did he say?"

"Nothing earth-shattering. That one day I'd understand that the fact they weren't there had nothing to do with who I was and everything to do with them. That he loved me and I was like a son to him. The son he'd always wished he could've had. I was ten, and I didn't understand." I looked at our entwined fingers. "But I'm thirty-five now, and I still can't fathom why a parent wouldn't show up for their child."

"I'll always be here for you. I love you too, Lyon."

Miles pressed his cheek to mine and put his arms around me. I clung to him. Until then, I'd never understood needing the comfort of another person. I'd always drowned my sorrow in sex or liquor. But holding Miles was everything. I needed his lithe, strong body pressed against mine, and for the first time, I was able to stop shaking and breathe.

"Don't say it back because you feel sorry for me."

"You're such a dummy."

I held him tighter. "I love it when you whisper those sweet nothings to me."

Miles brushed the hair away from my eyes and skimmed his fingertips over my swollen cheek and black eye. "Are you going to take the night off and rest?"

I grinned and waggled my brows. "Are you offering to be my nurse? I can picture you in a sexy outfit coming to take my temperature."

"I think I saw that in a really bad porno once," he responded dryly. "But maybe you should get your face looked at."

I shook my head. "No. I'm fine. And I should get to the club, but I have to get dressed first."

Miles rubbed up against me. "What if you showed up like this, in jeans and a sweater? I like you in casual clothes."

I kissed him until I couldn't breathe. "I like you in nothing at all."

I'd successfully avoided answering questions about my face from curious members by staying in my office for the most part, but I decided, fuck it. I had nothing to hide. I passed by the library and stood off to the side, watching with satisfaction at how busy it was. A line stretched the length of the room, and Miles handled their questions with ease. I left him to it and took a seat at my usual table in the corner.

Victor immediately appeared with my drink. "What the hell happened to you?"

I smiled thinly. "Rough sex?" I sipped the Scotch and grimaced as it hit the cut on the edge of my mouth. "Ow. Bring me a water, please."

He snorted. "Nice one, Boss. Now try again. With the truth."

Victor and I might be friendly, but I wasn't about to share confidences. I also knew he'd nag at me like a mosquito bite until I gave him something. "Dan and I had a disagreement. He chose violence."

Victor whistled. "And you let him live. Damn, Lyon. I have to give you props."

I thought of Miles and how, despite everything that had happened between us and Dan, together and separately, he still loved his brother. Family was family. Then I thought of my parents and grew cold, knowing that adage didn't work for everyone.

"He's not worth it," I told Victor.

I nodded to several members who walked in, and one of them, Madden Steele, approached my table. "What happened to you?"

A year ago, Madden had joined The Lyon's Den after his somewhat scandalous relationship with a male escort had been made public. He wanted a place to relax and talk business without having to worry about paparazzi in his face and was vouched for by his brother-in-law, Victor, and his close friend, Anthony Gigante, both of whom were long-standing members.

"Nothing worth talking about. And I'm sorry to hear about your aunt. I saw the obituary in the Times."

His jaw hardened. "We weren't close."

I imagined not, after she tried to wrestle his company away from him. I admired Madden for not pretending platitudes of sorrow. If anyone understood the concept of family letting you down, it was me.

His lips pursed. "I heard about the wedding being called off. I'm sorry. I can't imagine how you feel."

I gave him a wry smile. "Actually, pretty good about the whole thing. I think I dodged a bullet." I knew I did because the two nights with Miles had wiped away all the years of emotionless, anonymous sex.

"Glad to see you're taking it so well. And I meant to tell you, I just renewed my membership, and I love the new format. I hope to see more participation with charities in the future."

"I can add the ones you're involved with, if you'd like. Let's have a meeting and talk about it. I think you'll be seeing many changes in the coming months."

I spotted Miles across the salon floor and couldn't help smiling when I caught his eye. I loved that little blush, especially now that I knew it covered him from head to toe.

Madden glanced over his shoulder. "For you especially, I'm guessing?"

I rose to my feet as Miles got closer. "Not really. People don't know me as well as they think."

Madden put his hands up. "Hey. I'm happy for you. I'm sure as hell the last person to judge anyone. I'm meeting my brother-in-law for dinner, and I see him at his table. I'll call you, and we can talk about fund-raising possibilities." He walked away, and Miles passed him, but his eyes were on me.

"Hi. I'm taking a break for half an hour. How do you feel?"

"First of all, you don't need to explain yourself to me. You're not on a schedule."

A waiter appeared with a glass of wine. "Here you are, Miles."

"Thanks, Jules. How're Marsha and Patrick doing?"

His face brightened. "Great, thanks." He sent a nervous smile my way. "I'm sorry, Mr. Elliot."

"Don't be. What happened? Who're Marsha and Patrick?"

"Uh, Marsha's my sister, and she had a baby last week, Patrick. He came a little early and was in the NICU, but he's home now and doing great. Well, I better go get my order from Victor." He hurried off, but I stared at Miles.

"What's wrong?" he asked me.

"You've been here less than a week, and you already know the life stories of my staff. I don't even know all their names."

"It's all a matter of priorities. Maybe that's another change forthcoming at The Lyon's Den?"

I draped my arm around his shoulders. "Stranger things have happened."

"Get your hands off him."

Miles and I turned to face a furious Dan and Lindsey, who couldn't take their eyes off of me.

"Why?" I smirked and held Miles tighter. "What're you going to do about it?"

I pushed Lyon's arm off me and glared at my brother. "What do you want?"

"To talk some sense into you," Dan said. "Let's go."

I looked to Lyon, who remained silent but intent, unable to keep his lips from twitching. He picked up his drink and sipped it.

"No," I told Dan. "I'm busy."

"Doing what? Being Lyon's fool?" Dan snapped, and my cheeks burned. Lyon set his drink on the table, his jaw hard, the epitome of *if looks could kill*, and I had to admire his restraint.

Lindsey put a hand on Dan's arm. "Don't speak like that to Miles, Danny. Honey," she appealed to me with her big brown eyes glowing. "I'd love to talk to you. We haven't had a chance to sit down and have a chat."

Before I could answer, Lyon spoke up. "I think that's a great idea, *Danny*," he sneered. "You and your baby mama go have a nice talk with your brother."

"What're you talking about?" I protested. "I'm not leaving the library to talk to them."

"Don't call my wife that. Come on, Miles. You don't belong here." Dan waved to me, but I held my ground firmly.

"Why not? I see lots of people I know. Why don't you think I belong here? How come you never tried to get me to become a member? I'm sure there are other gay men here I could've met. Why didn't you want me to join?"

"This place is full of guys who sit around and drink all night. They're not your kind of people."

"Maybe that's all you do, but that's not true for everyone. In the library I just set up, I was speaking to Jason Patterman. He has a rare book collection, the complete works of Dickens, and he's invited me to see it. And Marty Holmes is a mystery buff who has one of the largest private collections of Sherlock Holmes first editions and actual manuscripts. Troy Merriweather is an avid gardener. Martin Lawry is a collector of Tiffany glass. Did you know any of that?"

Shifting on his feet, Dan couldn't meet my eyes.

"I know why Dan doesn't want you here." Lyon's quiet voice rose between us.

"Shut up, Lyon. You don't know shit."

"That may be true about a lot of things, but not about you. I know exactly why you like to keep Miles in your pocket." Lyon pointed at me. "It's because you're insanely jealous of him."

I had to laugh. "I love that you have my back, but come on. Dan? Jealous of me? That's a joke."

But Lyon's attention remained on Dan. "That's it, isn't it, Dan? That's the reason you never wanted Miles to join. He's gorgeous, smart, and sweet. He's the fucking nicest person, and being around him only made you realize your shortcomings."

"Fuck you," Dan mumbled but couldn't look either of us in the face. "I love my brother."

A crafty smile curled Lyon's lips. "He never had to cheat on exams to pass or have your father donate millions to get him into college. He didn't walk right into a ready-made job because he knew he couldn't succeed on his own. Mommy and Daddy always provided for you."

"Like you're any different," Lindsey entered the fray. "You used your family money to set up The Lyon's Den."

"Yes, sweetheart. But I run it. On my own. I have a business degree and went to class, unlike your *husband*, who always slept in late and used my notes."

My head whirled. "Dan, is this true? You didn't want me to come here?"

"Come on, you know you don't like the scene. You've always said hanging out and partying isn't your thing."

A violin played a ballad from *Swan Lake*, and the pensive music added to my overall sorrow. "Is this what you consider hanging out and partying?" I swept my hand out. "I see men enjoying conversations about business deals and their families. I've been asked multiple times about my bookstore. Maybe if I'd been a member here, things could've been different, and I wouldn't have been sitting alone, night after night, wondering why the hell no one cared about me."

"You know I care."

"But it's not enough. You're married, with a baby on the way. You found your life. Everyone wants to be loved. You tucked me away in a box and decided what was best for me, but the fact is, you don't even know who I am."

"This isn't you." Dan's hands balled into fists. "It's Lyon trying to come between us because he hates me and wants you to hate me too."

"I don't hate you, Dan. You'll always be my brother, and I love you."

"Then let's go. You don't need him or this place. It's toxic."

Lyon chuckled. "That's rich, coming from you."

Interested stares from the room forced my hand. "Shut up both of you. I don't want to have this conversation in public." I appealed to Lyon. "Can we go to your office?"

"If you want."

With Lyon, Dan, and Lindsey trailing behind me, I led the way and waited for Lyon to unlock the door. When he walked away, I called after him. "Where are you going?"

"I figured you wanted this to be a family discussion."

"Yeah? And?" I rolled my eyes and pointed. "Get your ass in there and stop being ridiculous."

He grinned, retraced his steps, and murmured in my ear, "I love when you get bossy with me. Save it for later."

With everyone inside, I closed the door and sat on Lyon's desk. Lyon lounged by the door, but his expression remained alert and fixed on me. Lindsey and Dan held hands, and inwardly, I rolled my eyes. Yes, technically they were still on their honeymoon, but they could show a little humility toward Lyon and not rub their togetherness in his face.

"I don't think it's too much for me to ask why you never wanted me to join The Lyon's Den. And this bullshit about you wanting to protect me is just that. Bullshit."

"No, it's not. You're the person who always thinks the best about people and doesn't see that most of the time, there's an ulterior motive behind what they do."

"That's a sad way of living. I refuse to believe the worst of people."

"Why? You've seen it. What those bastards did to you in college—"

"What the hell?" Shame burned a hot path through my gut. "Please tell me you didn't repeat the story to Lindsey."

"I mean, yeah. She's my wife. I trust her with everything."

Hot tears of humiliation burned my eyes, and I didn't trust myself not to cry. I shook my head and stared at the floor.

"I don't fucking believe the shit that comes out of your mouth," Lyon muttered, and in three long strides, came to my side and put his arm around me. "You okay?"

"Yeah. I am now." Grateful for his comfort, I drew a deep breath. "You had no right to say anything. That was my story to tell, *if and only if* I wanted to."

Lindsey smiled at me. "It's okay. It wasn't your fault."

"No shit," Lyon spat at her. "That's not the point."

"You told him?" Dan pointed at Lyon.

"This conversation is veering off course," I shouted. "This isn't about who told what to whom, although we *will* discuss boundaries later. This is about the fact that you need to leave me to live my own life and make my own choices. Just because I've made some bad ones in the past doesn't mean I don't deserve to try again. And if I fail, I fail."

"But *him*?" Dan let go of Lindsey's hand and hitched his chair closer.

Lyon stiffened, and I knew he was hurt. I jumped to his defense.

"And? How are you any better? Neither of you is an angel."

Lindsey flushed and hung her head but said nothing.

"Exactly, but I'm married to Lindsey now."

With a defiant stare, I picked up Lyon's hand and held it for both Dan and Lindsey to see. "And I'm with Lyon. I love him."

Dan turned white, then beet red. "No. No way."

"Yes." Lyon squeezed my hand. "It's true. I love Miles, and there's nothing you can do to keep me from being with him."

"If I beat your ass and put you in traction, you won't be able to," Dan growled, and Lyon dropped my hand.

"Go ahead, big shot. Miles isn't a little kid anymore. He's a grown man. All man. And he doesn't need your help for anything. Trust me." At Lyon's cocky grin and insinuation, Dan rose to his feet, and my heart plummeted.

"I already messed up that pretty face once," Dan snarled, and I was anticipating ambulances and blood. I stepped in between them.

"Stop it, you two. You're like wild animals waiting to piss on each other to mark your territory." I put my hands out. "I don't belong to either of you. I make my own choices. Now sit down and stop talking. Both of you." I glared at Lyon, who cast his eyes to the floor but did as I said. Dan, however, remained standing, his jaw thrust out, until Lindsey tugged at his shirt. Only then did he return to his chair. "Listen to me, Dan. I need you to step back from my life and let me live it how I choose, the way you have, consequences be damned. And you." I faced Lyon, whose wicked half grin never failed to send me into a tailspin of desire. "I love that you defend me, but please stop with the innuendos."

That smile broadened, but he dipped his head in acquiescence. "Whatever you want, baby."

"Oh, for fuck's sake," Dan muttered.

"Dan…" Lindsey grabbed his hand.

"What, honey? I'm gonna do what Miles wants even if I think he's wrong."

"No, Dan. Something's happening. I don't feel right. I think it's the baby." She started crying. "It hurts." Helpless, I turned to Lyon, who'd already grabbed the phone.

Panicked, Dan yelled, "Call a doctor. Lindsey, baby. It'll be okay."

"On it." Lyon spoke quickly and hung up. "They'll be here in a few minutes. I'll tell Anton at the front to let them in."

Dan whirled to face Lyon. "This is all your fault. If you'd left Miles alone, she wouldn't have been so stressed. If anything happens, Lyon, I swear I'll kill you."

Lyon paled but said nothing, although I could see the whites of his knuckles as he gripped the desk. I was caught between my brother and the man I loved, and I wanted to comfort both. Dan massaged Lindsey's back, giving her words of encouragement as she cried, and Lyon retreated behind his desk and sat stone-faced and as untouchable and remote as I'd ever seen him.

EMS came and took Lindsey out. Dan went with her, but before he left the room to ride with her, he yelled out, "Don't you fucking dare come to the hospital, Lyon. You're not wanted there. Or anywhere." He ran out.

Devastated, Lyon rested his head in his hands. "It's not true," he whispered. "I never wanted her to lose the baby. I'd never wish that on anyone."

I spun his chair around and took his face between my hands, forcing his eyes to mine. "I know. Dan is scared and being irrational. I'd better go stay with him, you know? He shouldn't be by himself." Feeling torn, I hated leaving Lyon, but I knew my place was with my brother.

He kissed me. "I understand. And don't worry, I won't come and cause any commotion. Can you just call and let me know what happens?"

"Yeah, of course. And Lyon?"

"Yeah."

"I love you."

That disarming soft smile, which I knew belonged only to me, returned. "I know. And I love you too."

One final kiss and I ran out.

# Chapter TWENTY-ONE

It was after seven by the time I got word that Lindsey and the baby would be okay. She was on bed rest, but the cramping and bleeding had stopped.

"Go home and rest, Miles. You must be exhausted. I'll see you later." I'd been on the phone with him for the past half hour and didn't like how hollow he sounded.

"I'm okay. I'm going to stay a little longer with Dan. With both sets of parents away, I don't want him to be alone."

*What about me? I'm alone.*

But I kept my mouth shut, knowing Miles was under stress and I didn't need to add to it.

"You do what you think is right. Just let me know where you are and if I can do anything for you."

"Are you sure this is Lyon Elliot? Because whomever

I'm speaking to sounds like a devoted boyfriend." His voice dropped, soft and low. "I like this Lyon, in case you didn't know."

"Me too. I like you. And I miss my Miles smiles."

Uncle Harry walked in with Scott, and I knew there'd be no avoiding this conversation. They stopped at a table of older men with whom my uncle often sat and whiled away the hours.

"Uh-oh. Double trouble just walked in."

Miles chuckled. "Let me guess—your uncle and brother."

"You're so intuitive. You know what I'm thinking without me having to say it."

"It doesn't take much. I usually just assume your brain defaults to sex."

"I resemble that remark. And only with you, baby. Like right now, I wish you were naked and I was eat—"

"Stop that. Didn't you say your uncle was there with your brother?" Miles's outraged squeak had me laughing out loud, which drew stares my way. Jesus, you'd think they'd never seen me laugh.

Then again, I hadn't really been happy until Miles, so maybe they were correct.

"They stopped to talk to some people."

"Thank God," he said faintly. "I'll let you go. Speak to you later."

"Bye."

Uncle Harry finished his conversation with his cronies, and he and Scott headed across the salon. I stood. "Pull up a chair. I assume you've heard the news."

Uncle Harry removed his cap before sitting. "Well, now, which news is that? The news that Lindsey is in the hospital, or that you seem to have had a run-in with Dan's fist over your relationship with Miles?" He frowned. "And to that effect, when are you going to tell me about you and Miles? He's a very nice man, and I like him."

"Why does everyone assume I'm going to be the bad guy?" I retorted with a sulky frown, and Uncle Harry raised a brow.

"Your track record speaks volumes."

I lifted a shoulder, loath to discuss anything about what happened between Miles and me. It was too personal to talk about over a table where food and drink were being consumed. "We're friends."

"Good friends."

Since when had Uncle Harry become such a buttinski? Lucky for me, Scott jumped in to save me. "Uncle Harry, maybe Lyon just needs a little space? He's had a rough few days."

"As I see by his bruises. Tell me what happened."

"Dan showed up when I was at Miles's house. He proceeded to make his unhappiness with me known by connecting his fist to my face. I left, but in the morning he showed up at my apartment, and he and Miles got into an argument."

"I…see. So you and Miles…?"

"Spent the night together. Yes. Is that what you want me to say?"

"Don't get your back up with me. Do you know why I'm pressing you?"

I bit my tongue because I wanted to blurt out, *Because you're nosy*, but I respected my uncle too much to ever be so rude, so I held off and shook my head. Uncle Harry took off his glasses and rubbed his eyes, then replaced them.

"I don't want you to become me. Alone, and still too wary to take a step that some might not approve of."

Scott and I shared a glance, and I gentled my tone. "Are you talking about you and Maxwell?"

He nodded. "I think it's time I shared my story with you. Maxwell and I have known each other since childhood, and as we grew older, realized we cared for each other. In those days there were no rainbow flags or places we could go in public or even in private where we could be safe. To keep up appearances, we'd date women, but there was never any question where our true devotion lay. With each other."

My heart broke in pieces listening to Uncle Harry, and from Scott's devastated eyes, he was similarly affected.

Uncle Harry's gaze was solemn. "Later on, we tried places in Greenwich Village we'd heard were welcoming, but I was always afraid." His smile was sad but sweet. "Maxwell was always the brave one."

Scott moved his chair closer, and I took Uncle Harry's hand. A server approached, but I held up a finger, and he backed away.

"I think you were both very brave."

Uncle Harry shook his head. "I'd keep my hat pulled low, and Maxwell and I would slip in later in the evening to Julius's. I was too scared of a police raid and ending up in jail to stay long or ever feel comfortable. I frustrated Maxwell because he loved the social scene. I was always happier at home with a book." He wet his lips. "And my father wouldn't have been happy to have to come and bail his son out of jail for being arrested as a homosexual."

When he said out loud what we'd always suspected, a chill ran down my spine. Uncle Harry had lived through the worst of times, and I couldn't fault him his emotions or judge him for his choices. All I could do was love and support him as he'd always done for me.

"It was a different era, Uncle Harry." I squeezed his fingers slightly. "Although even now some people don't approve, those of us who are part of the community have more freedom. Sure, there will always be people who disapprove, but I personally don't give them any real estate in my head. And neither should you."

"I try." He sighed. "But old habits die hard. Over the years, Maxwell would grow angry at my fear and leave me, but it never lasted long. We always found our way home to each other. When AIDS began its devastation in our community in the 1980s, we made a promise to be there only for each other. I knew I couldn't live without him, and from that time on, we've been together, although we're still discreet."

My eyes burned, and Scott wiped his with the back of his hand. "Dammit, Uncle Harry. I didn't expect to cry today."

"I'm telling you both this because all I've ever wanted for you since you were young boys was your happiness. When you told me you were marrying Lindsey, I wasn't filled with the same joy as when Scott brought Beth to meet me. I instantly knew they were right for each other. Lyon, I don't want you to end up like your parents—unhappy and searching for something they're not ever going to find."

My heart hurt, not only for him, but for all of us who were lost. "I think you're right. In a way, Dan saved me from hating myself. I guess you could call him the worst best friend. And I'm very glad you and Maxwell found your way."

"We've known each other our whole lives. He's another piece of my soul. That's how I want you to feel about the person you love. It took a long and winding road in my case, but it eventually brought me to where I always belonged."

He cleared his throat, and I caught Victor's eye. In less than two minutes, our drinks were served.

I raised a glass. "To you, Uncle Harry." Scott joined me, and Uncle Harry beamed at us.

"I couldn't love you two more if you were my own, and in a way you are. You're part of my blood and a legacy I hope to leave, even if you aren't my own children. And I agree with you, Lyon. Dan did you the biggest favor of your life."

"Strangely enough, I'm still worried about Lindsey. Miles said she'd be okay and so would the baby, but of course they're all still concerned."

Uncle Harry set his glass down. "You've grown up, Lyon. The man I knew a few months ago would never speak like this. He'd carry a grudge and would've pretended not to care if Lindsey lost the baby or how anyone else felt. So whether it's your relationship with Miles or some other steps you've taken, I applaud it and hope it continues."

A waiter brought over Uncle Harry's favorite dinner of grilled salmon, and Scott and I both had the steak *frites*. Scott lifted his glass again.

"I wanted you to be the first to know that Beth and I are having another baby. We want the kids to be close in age so they can have the relationship Lyon and I had." He tipped his drink to me. "I love you, Lyon. You've always been there for me, and if I haven't told you before or enough, I'm sorry, because you were and are the best brother. You always watched out for me and put yourself second to make up for our parents' lack of interest. I realized it when I was older, and I can only hope my kids grow up to be good friends."

I stood and hugged him tight. "I love you too. You're a superstar father and husband and baby brother."

Scott huffed. "Baby, huh? I can whip your ass in a race any day."

Once seated, I checked my phone, hoping to hear from Miles, but my messages were empty. I caught Uncle Harry and Scott watching me and set my phone facedown on the table.

"No news?" Uncle Harry asked kindly.

"No."

Halfway through our dinner, Miles came rushing into

the salon. I forgot everyone and met him in the center of the room and kissed him, uncaring that my brother and Uncle Harry—along with everyone else—were watching.

"I didn't know you were coming here." I held his hand and squeezed it tight. "Why didn't you tell me?"

"I'm sorry. I should've let you know, but Lindsey went in for some tests and Dan said to go home. I thought about it but decided I didn't want to." Those dark-gold lashes swept against his cheeks, then lifted. "I wanted to be where you were."

"Who said you don't know how to make the best choices? Come with me."

I seated him, and a glass of red wine immediately appeared. He sipped it and sighed. "I could get used to this."

"I would hope so," I murmured. Deciding to hell with what people might think, I took Miles's hand and set it on top of the table. "Since everyone is baring their secrets and souls today, I'll go next. Miles and I are a couple. We're together. I love him, and for whatever reason I'm not questioning, he loves me too."

A wash of red spread over Miles's cheeks. "What brought this on?"

I met Uncle Harry's eyes, and he nodded with approval.

"I just didn't want to wait until it was too late."

I dragged him into my office, shut and locked the door, and proceeded to kiss the breath out of him.

"Wha—what's going on?" Miles asked, his voice hoarse with need. His lips clung to mine, and I was shaking, I wanted him so bad.

"I love you. Completely and totally. I don't ever want you to doubt it, and I couldn't sit another minute without touching you now that Uncle Harry and Scott left." I popped the button of his jeans and yanked them down, along with his briefs. With my hands cupping his perfect ass, I dipped my head and took his mouth in a hot kiss that left no doubt what I wanted.

Miles undid my trousers, and they fell to the floor. He teased his long fingers along the bulge of my erection, and I sucked his tongue as he peeled my briefs past my hips.

"Mine," I growled and thrust into his palm as he took our shafts in hand and we humped each other. I flicked the buds of his nipples, and he wailed. My stomach turned sticky from his precome.

"Two can play that game. Mine." He nipped at my ear, then nibbled on my neck. "All mine."

"More," I grunted and pinned him against the door. "Mark me."

I ran my fingers along the crack of his ass to tease the sensitive rim. "Lyon," he moaned, but I continued to play, dipping my fingers in and out of him, loving how he twitched and cried out. His eyes rolled back in his head and he came, sticky come shooting over my stomach.

"Fuck, baby, oh fuck." Seeing Miles fall apart was the sexiest thing I'd ever witnessed, and my orgasm exploded from my toes to my chest, my vision whiting out from the indescribable pleasure he gave me.

When I lifted my head from his shoulder, I let him go and looked down at the mess we'd made of our stomachs. "I guess I got a little carried away."

"A little? You guess? You were like your namesake—a ravaging beast." He touched my cheek.

I remembered the last time I kissed him in the library and he'd gotten angry with me. I didn't want that to happen again.

"I'm sorry. I should've asked you if—"

"Shh." He placed his fingers over my mouth. "A storm doesn't ask permission. It just barrels in and takes over, consuming everything in its path. You're my storm, Lyon. And you own me."

"I don't want you to think I was taking advantage of you."

"Be quiet and kiss me." Eyes dancing, Miles held me close. "You can take advantage of me like this anytime you want. I loved every second of it."

# Chapter TWENTY-TWO

Lyon rolled on top of me, and I groaned. "Again? How many times already?" But I met his lips eagerly and lifted my hips to him. Who was I kidding? I loved that he couldn't keep his hands off me.

"Who knows? Or cares? I've lost count. I'm insatiable when you're near." He bit my ear and pushed inside me with little resistance. I sighed as he filled me and began to move.

"You're killing me."

"*Mmm*, baby, but what a way to go." He pushed my legs over his shoulders and dragged his shaft out, then drove back in hard and heavy. Heat seared through my blood, and I tingled all over. I writhed on his thick cock, aching for him to fuck me into the bed until I couldn't move.

"I love you," I whispered. At least I thought I did, because my lips were so swollen from our kisses, I couldn't be sure they moved.

"I love you too. I know what you want, baby. And I'm going to give it to you." He pinned my hands overhead, and as if he'd read my mind, thrust hard and fast, each movement drilling me into the mattress. My head thrashed on the pillow, and I screamed with the scorching-hot pleasure pouring through my veins. With my dick trapped between us, I came, and Lyon followed a moment later, burying himself so deep, I didn't think he'd ever leave me completely.

Our chests were plastered together, our hearts pounded in tandem, and every muscle in my body ached. When Lyon withdrew, I glimpsed my naked body and smiled. Finger-shaped splotches on my hips marked where Lyon gripped me tight when I climbed on top of him and rode him like a racehorse. I'd given as good as I got—Lyon's back was covered with scratches, and several large purplish spots covered his neck.

"Damn. You're going to have a little work to hide those marks on your neck. I hope your back doesn't hurt too bad."

"I drove you wild." He smirked, and I rolled my eyes.

"Rein in that ego. I look like I've been mauled by an actual lion."

He swooped in for a kiss and murmured, "That's because you drive me wild too. *Rawr*." He cackled and kissed me again before leaving me to shower.

My heart swelled with joy, and I cuddled the pillow closer. It was only eight a.m., and I decided to be a little lazy and lie in bed a little longer. I reached for my phone to check my messages and sat up when I saw a string of texts from Dan. Fearing the worst, my heart pounded.

*Lindsey's okay. She's coming home this morning.*

*Thanks for being there with me. I really needed you.*

*But I can't think of you with Lyon. I'm warning you*

*because I have to give all my attention to Lindsey now. If you don't listen to me, I'm not going to help you anymore. You're on your own.*

I'd never experienced this sense of isolation and loss. Dan had always been my rock, and to not have him there was such a gigantic loss, I wasn't sure how to move on. The phone fell from my fingers, and I cried. Great big, ugly, snotty tears that left me shaking in the bed. I wasn't even aware that Lyon had climbed in with me and held me as I wept.

"Baby, what's wrong? Is it Lindsey? Did she lose the baby?"

I coughed and wiped my face with the sheet. "N-no. She's okay. B-but Dan said that if I continue seeing you, he won't be there for me anymore."

"You're kidding."

"No, look." I showed him my phone and watched his face morph from worried to enraged.

"And why are you crying?"

"Because I'm going to lose him."

"Listen. I don't want you to have to make a choice. Dan is your brother and—"

"And what?" I wriggled out of his grasp. "That automatically means I give in to him? Even if what he says is ridiculous?"

Lyon's eyes twinkled. "Like I said, it is Dan. All I'm saying is, he's stressed and needs to worry about his wife. If it'll make him feel better to think you and I aren't together, then tell him anything you want. I don't give a shit when I know the truth. Consider it part of my revenge." His kiss was warm and soft. "No matter what he says, you belong with me. To me. And I belong with you."

My insides turned soft. "And to me."

"You know it. Now move that lazy ass and get to work. You have a library to run."

Laughing, I scrambled out of bed. "Who knew you were so devious?" He arched a dark brow, and I snickered. "Oh, yeah right. How silly of me. It's you we're talking about. Now you're bending me to your evil ways."

"I'll bend you every way I can." He winked. "And you love it."

I blew him a kiss as I went to shower. "Every single second."

I stopped off at Dan's apartment to see him and Lindsey before going to the Den. She was ensconced on the large sectional, and Dan introduced me to Bernice, a nurse he'd hired to be with Lindsey. The doctor said that the minor bleeding and cramping she'd experienced were common in the first trimester but he said he didn't want to take any chances.

His eyes lit up when he saw me at the door. "I knew you'd come. I knew you were smart enough to see I was right. *Fuck Lyon.* Blood is thicker than water." He hugged me tight. "You want to meet someone, I'll introduce you to some of the guys I think will be good for you. Who needs Grindr when you have your own personal dating service?"

Did he really believe the shit he said, or was he simply that oblivious?

"I'm not sure I'm ready just yet."

"Yeah. I'm sure Lyon did a number on your head. Take as much time as you need. Meanwhile, you can hang out and be a guncle to your niece or nephew."

"Yeah, sure. I can't wait."

Lindsey waved to me from the couch. "Can you tell your brother I'm not made of glass? I have a business to run. The tequila opening is next week, and I intend to be there." She glared at Dan, who scowled.

"We'll see."

"I don't recall asking for permission. I'm simply telling you I'm going to do it. Now, Miles, what's going on with you? Did Dan just say that you and Lyon were done?"

Lyon and I had agreed to keep Dan in the dark, but I hated lying. It wasn't in my nature, not even when it was in my best interests.

"I'll always be there for my brother. Nothing can change that. But we're going to have to talk about boundaries."

Dan sat on the end of the sectional. "What're you talking about?"

"You can't keep telling me who I should date or what I should do. If I want to have sex with whomever, I will. If I don't, I won't. It's my choice, not yours."

Dan's frown deepened. "You're acting like I'm in the wrong here. You know I was only trying to keep you from getting hurt again."

"And I appreciate it. But with everything that happened, I realized I was letting you do it by running to you every time I had a problem. I was as much in the wrong by dumping all my problems on you as you were enabling me by accepting them."

"I didn't mind."

"I know. And I love you for it. But it's high time I broke free, and I need you to let go."

As I spoke, Dan's gaze grew harsh. "Is this Lyon forcing you? You're not seeing him, right?"

"No, of course not," I answered, leaving it purposefully ambiguous.

"Good."

Lyon and Dan had been as close as two men could be without being related, yet here they were now, the deadliest of enemies. And I wanted to know whether there was a glimmer of hope that something of that friendship could be revived.

"Can I ask you a question?"

"Sure. Linds, you okay? You need anything?"

"Yeah. For you to stop hovering. Go away and talk to your brother. Let me breathe my own air." She made shooing motions, and I ducked my head and smiled to myself. Funny enough, I could see her and Lyon being friends. They had the same humor.

Dan didn't take it to heart and kissed her cheek. "Love you, babe. Come on, Miles. We can go to the terrace."

He slid the glass door open, and we plopped ourselves on the lounge chairs. The skyline broke through the clouds.

"Why did you really do it, Dan?" He huffed and scowled, but I wasn't going to let him off the hook. "You knew they were getting married. He was your best friend, goddammit. Lyon was more of a brother to you than me, and don't give me that look, because it's true."

"I love you."

"I never said you didn't. I love you too. But you also loved Lyon, and nothing you say will convince me otherwise."

He rested his arms over his knees and stared out to the sky. "Yeah, well…what I said initially was the truth. Lindsey and I did get drunk, and she was lonely, and I dunno…I always thought she was hot, and I let my libido get the better of me." He scratched his neck. "I remember putting my arm around her, to comfort her, and she smelled so good, and her skin was so soft…I kissed her, and the next thing I knew she was kissing me back and our clothes were off."

"I'm not blaming only you. She had equal responsibility. But even the next day, when you weren't drunk? Why would you keep seeing her, knowing she and Lyon were getting married?"

"We'd stay away from each other, but a few days would pass and I'd miss her and call, or she'd show up at my apartment…" Guilt was written all over his face and he shrugged. "I'm weak. What can I say?"

"How about no?" I grew furious with how little Dan seemed to care. "I can't believe you."

"She kept saying she was going to tell him, but she didn't want anything to jeopardize the tequila deal. Lyon could've canceled the contract. It was within the time period."

"So she waited until it was too late for Lyon to do anything? You've got to be fucking kidding me."

Red-faced, Dan couldn't look at me and hung his head.

"You're as cold and heartless as she is."

"You don't know how hard it is to say no to a naked, beautiful woman telling you how much she wants you."

"I can only imagine. But where did Lyon fit into all this?"

He threw his hands up in the air. "He didn't. Dude, you don't understand what it's like to be in love. No one and nothing else matters but the two of you."

If you were two extremely selfish people, perhaps that was true.

"Stop. At least take *some* responsibility for your actions. This wasn't some guy you barely knew or a friend of a few years. This was your best friend since you could walk. You two did everything together. Don't you feel even one tiny ounce of remorse for your actions?"

"Why do you care so much? Lyon was never nice to you.

He called you Miles the Mouse. If you're not with him any longer, why defend him?"

I was ready with my answer. "Because it's just not right. And I know exactly what Lyon called me." I shrugged. "Maybe he wasn't wrong. I did hide away. But stop turning the tables. This isn't about Lyon or me. It's about you and your actions. I'm incredibly disappointed in you, Dan. Not only did you sleep with your best friend's fiancée, but you refuse to take any accountability."

"But Lindsey told me it would be all right."

The entire situation was ugly, and I decided to give up because I was never going to get the answer I wanted. Dan couldn't admit he was wrong.

"Dan…you're my brother, and I'll always be there for you, like you've been there for me, but it's going to take me some time to feel comfortable with you two."

"It's fine. You'll come around eventually. I mean, even I'm going to have to deal with Lyon, since he and Lindsey are business partners. Starting with the tequila launch next week."

Dan's confidence in my forgiveness annoyed me, and I was tired, not only of this conversation, but because I'd been up half the night with Lyon. Yawning, I stretched. "I have to go, but I'll call you later to check on Lindsey."

"Thanks."

He walked me out, and I stopped to kiss Lindsey on the cheek. True to what I'd heard about her, she was on the computer, checking spreadsheets, and I wondered if Dan was up to being married to such a go-getter. I knew my brother, and he wasn't exactly from the school of hard workers.

I called for a car, thinking about everything my brother said, knowing he was wrong about Lyon's motives. Waking up with Lyon, seeing the light in his eyes, thrilling to his touch, I knew what we had between us was as real as it got.

# Chapter TWENTY-THREE

It was harder than I'd thought to keep my personal and professional distance from Miles. For the past week, I'd see him working in the library, always with a crowd around chatting him up, and Miles of course responding with his natural warmth. I itched to be with him, but we'd agreed for the time being to keep our hands to ourselves in public, in case Lindsey had another reoccurrence.

That afternoon I stomped through the Den, annoyed and grumpy. While getting ready for bed the evening before, Miles had shown me a string of texts from Dan praising him for making the right decision in dumping my ass and telling him to be strong. I hated that he believed he'd bullied Miles into submission once again. Revenge might be sweet, but it wasn't always palatable.

I stopped in the hallway outside the library and caught

a glimpse of Miles listening to some bullshit from Taylor Dumbrowski, who was leaning in way too close and smiling into Miles's eyes. He might be a hedge-fund billionaire, but he needed to step the fuck away.

I only held back because I knew if I clocked him in the jaw like I really itched to do, Miles would be upset and there'd be a ruckus and probably a lawsuit.

So messy.

I'd never given a damn when another man would flirt with Lindsey. I'd shrug it off and go on my merry way, but it wasn't so easy with Miles. A red rage descended over me as I watched Dumbrowski slip his business card into Miles's hand when Miles handed him the book he'd asked for. I knew what that fucker wanted. But my fury faded in the next moment when, after he walked out, Miles tossed the card into the wastebasket and went on to help the next person in line.

Light replaced the darkness in front of my eyes, and I laughed at my jealousy. Before Miles, I'd never reached the level of having another person be truly significant to me.

Proud for showing remarkable restraint, I returned to my office to go over the launch of Lindsey's tequila. Miles had recounted their conversation and Dan's confession that she'd continued with the wedding plans until the date passed that I could cancel the tequila deal. I didn't fly into a rage and call Scott to find a loophole so I could void the contract. It all came down to a simple fact: I no longer cared about anything she did or said. If she disappeared tomorrow, I wouldn't notice. That only highlighted the differences between my relationship with her and the one I was building with Miles, because I knew if Miles left me, I'd scorch the earth to find him and do anything to bring him home to me.

"Whatever you're thinking must be pretty good."

I glanced up to see Miles at my door. I'd taken to keeping

it open now while inside. I had nothing and no one to hide from anymore.

"Fucking fantastic. I was thinking of you."

"You were? That's nice to hear."

"I always think of you."

At my words, his face lit up like the sun. "Me too." His eyes sparkled. "Who knew you were such a romantic? I thought you were a tough guy."

"Not when it concerns you. I was just thinking about what would happen if you ever left me."

His smile dimmed. "That's not going to happen, so you can stop thinking it."

"Mine or yours tonight?" I was already anticipating.

This past week, we'd taken to alternating where we'd stay after I closed up the Den. Miles would leave first, and if we were heading to my place, I'd given him a key so he could let himself in. I was debating if it was too soon to talk about moving in together and where we would live. I knew Miles loved his house, and I had no personal ties to my apartment, but I didn't want to push him if he wasn't ready.

"How about mine? It's chilly enough to have a fire, and I can have a hot toddy ready for you when you come."

"A hot toddy and a hot boyfriend. Sounds like a perfect evening."

He blushed. "Silly. What're you up to for the rest of the day?"

"I'm finishing the plans for the tequila launch. Lindsey's assistant has been by every day to make sure it goes off without a hitch. Which, knowing Lindsey, it had better, or someone's ass will be in a sling."

"I'll leave you to it. I'm going to order some more books. Seems we have some war buffs here, and they were asking if I could get some World War Two books in."

"Good. Whatever you need."

"I need you."

Hearing those words and knowing he meant them was everything.

"You've got me."

He left me with a silly smile on my face.

My phone rang. "Elliot," I answered.

"It's Lindsey."

I tensed, my hand growing sweaty. It was our first conversation not in Dan's presence, and inexplicably, my heart pounded.

"Hi. How're you feeling?"

"I'm fine." Strangely enough, her brusque manner was comforting. It was expected, and I appreciated that she didn't try and pretend we'd be friends or even friendly. "I'm calling about the launch party tomorrow. I intend to be there."

"Okay. I expected that. You're the owner of the tequila company. That's normally how it works."

"I didn't want you to think I'd be staying away out of some weird belief that I was ashamed and couldn't face you."

I chuckled. "The last thing I'd ever imagine is you feeling shame for anything you do. In the long run, it's the best thing that could've happened. For both of us."

"I'm glad you're being adult about it. And I agree."

But I wasn't going to let her off that easily. "I'm qualifying my remark to mean only that we never should've gotten engaged. You sneaking around behind my back and sleeping with my best friend is still a goddamned shitty thing to do to anyone, and that is something I won't forget. Especially since it was always only about the tequila contract." I wanted her to hear that I knew about her sneaky little plan.

"I think we've gone over this enough. I apologized, and there's nothing left for me to say."

In Lindsey-speak that meant she knew she was wrong, refused to admit it, and had no intention of talking about it anymore. As far as she was concerned, it was resolved. Truly a sign of a selfish person who didn't care about the carnage she left in her wake.

"Was there anything else?" I had little desire to be on the phone with her.

"Dan will be with me." Her voice was edged with caution.

"You've mentioned before."

"Just making sure you remember and don't try and ban him from the club because of your disagreement."

"His personal membership is revoked, but he can come for business purposes only. If he even understands what that means." I sneered. "And you two should live in California because you're really in la-la land. Disagreement? He *assaulted* me. Dan's lucky I didn't press charges. His ass would be in jail."

"Oh, please. It was a simple fight, and Dan had every right to be worried. We all know you were after Miles only because you knew how enraged Dan would get. Miles is way above your level."

"That may be the only true thing you've said to me in years. Now I'm busy. I'll see you tomorrow."

Without waiting for a response, I ended the call but sat staring at the wall instead of tackling the hundred things on my desk. I didn't need Lindsey or anyone to tell me Miles was too good for me. I knew it from the start.

I just had to do everything I could to keep him from seeing it as well.

Did I mention how much I loved staying at Miles's house? He greeted me at the door in a black T-shirt and gray sweats that clung to his fabulous ass. I kissed him in the doorway, hungry for his mouth.

"Wow. That was a nice greeting."

"I missed being able to do it all day, so you're the beneficiary of all my pent-up desire."

Those blue eyes blazed. "I can't wait. Come with me."

I shed my coat and suit jacket, and he took my hand and led me to the family room where, as promised earlier, a fire crackled behind the grate. A plate with cheese, crackers, and fruit sat on the coffee table, and he brought me a mug. The tantalizing aroma of sugar and cinnamon greeted me when I brought it to my lips, along with the powerful punch of Scotch.

"Irish coffee." Miles sipped his. "It's the only way I can drink hard liquor, but it's perfect on a windswept night like this."

"*Mmm*. You're perfect."

"Silly." But he kissed my cheek. "Sit with me."

I nibbled on the cheese and sipped my drink until it was finished. "That was delicious. Thank you."

He smiled and put his head on my shoulder. We stared into the dancing flames as the wind picked up and rain pattered against the windows. In the past, on nights like this, I'd be out in a club, drinking and looking for a person to spend the night with. My mornings would be spent making excuses why I couldn't stay.

Now I sat here with a man I couldn't bear to leave.

"Lyon?"

"Hmm? What is it?"

"I think after everything's settled, you should move in here with me."

Warmth, from neither the fire nor the drink, filled my heart. "You do?"

"Yeah. I do. I like having you here with me."

"Damn, you're bossy." My lips twitched, and I played with his fingers. "I like being here with you too."

"But?" Miles sat up. "I feel like there's something you're not saying."

"Dan is coming to the tequila event tomorrow. How do you feel about that?"

A cloud darkened his bright-blue eyes. "He can't hold on to me forever. He's going to be a father, and he'll have to think of his wife and child before messing in my life."

"I also spoke with Lindsey today."

"Aren't you filled with surprises? How did that go?"

"She's in her CEO mode. Which means she'll steamroll over anything and everything in her way that she doesn't feel is important. Meaning me."

"Business as usual for her, as you've described her."

"Yeah. She was quick to tell me that she's moved on and I should too, and that Dan will be coming."

"Will you ever be able to forgive Dan?"

I gazed into the leaping flames. "If it had just been the cheating and marriage, it would've taken some time, but I think we could've co-existed. Eventually. But to hear all the vicious things he's said about me, how he always felt about me…" The loss was less excruciating now because I had Miles in my life. "No. There's no coming back from how bad he hurt me. He made me doubt myself. I still do."

"In what way?"

"Every way. With you, most important of all."

"Me? You know I love you."

"And yet I still wonder why. Because I don't know that I'm not the person Dan accused me of being."

"I do."

"How?"

"Simply by the fact that you're here and we're talking about this. The Lyon I used to know wouldn't give a damn what other people think. Let me rephrase that. The Lyon I *thought* I knew."

"I still don't care what anyone else thinks." I picked up his hand and kissed the palm. "Only you."

"Case in point." The flames played off his face. "You care about me."

"I do. I love you. And I've never said that to anyone before. I'm not even sure I know what it means, but when I think of where I'd be without you, it's an ugly, dark place. Here with you, it's happy and bright."

"I feel the same. You took my life filled with clouds and rain and turned it into rainbows for me." He put his arms around me. "Don't doubt what we have. It's real."

But all I could hear were Dan and Lindsey's words. "I want to be good enough for you."

"You're better than good. You've given me the courage to come into my own as a man and stand up for myself."

"Don't leave me." I kissed him, the heat from the fire adding to the always explosive chemistry simmering between us. "That's all I ask." I pushed him under me on the couch, straddled his hips, and pulled his sweats past his hips. His erect cock thrust up, and I took him to the back of my throat, moaning with pleasure as his taste filled my mouth.

"Lyon, *Lyon*," he gasped.

I licked up and down the velvety-steel shaft, holding his thighs steady. His groans filled the room, and I knew from the way his hands curled into fists and his hips bucked wilder that he was close. Increasing my pace, I swirled my tongue over the smooth crown and was rewarded with bursts of salty cream.

"I love when you come in my mouth." I licked him clean and sat back. Miles cupped me through my suit pants and unzipped them to trace my bulge. I panted, and when Miles slipped his hand inside my briefs to squeeze me, I came swift and blindingly hard all over his hand and my pants.

Miles licked his fingers. "Sorry about your pants." He grinned, looking supremely pleased with himself.

"No, you're not." I stripped them off. "And to answer your question, I'd love to move in with you. I have a feeling I'll be changing my clothes more often than usual. Especially if you're going to take advantage of me in my hour of need." I leaned down to kiss him. "Except when I'm with you, I need you every minute."

He threw his arms around me. "I'll always need you."

# Chapter TWENTY-FOUR

I kissed Lyon. “Don’t worry. You’ll look great, and the launch will be a success.” He had to leave my house early and go home to change, since his suit wasn’t fit to wear after our little fun on the couch.

*Sorry, not sorry.*

His smile was grim. “I don’t care about the launch. At all.”

My heart hurt for him. I knew the real issue was seeing Dan again.

“It’s going to be painful, but you’ll be okay. I don’t predict there will be any trouble because Dan wants Lindsey to be safe and successful, so he’ll stay out of your way.”

“Thanks, but it’s not even that for the most part. When

I cut someone out of my life, it's like they were never there. He's gone."

I cocked my head. "Then why?"

His breathing quickened. "Because I hate this. I hate having to pretend there's nothing between us. He doesn't deserve to feel peace when it makes us upset. I know we're doing it so Lindsey doesn't have another scare, but it's not right for us to put our lives on hold for two people who didn't give a damn about ours."

"It's kind of ironic, isn't it?"

"What do you mean?" Lyon asked as he called for his car.

"We started this whole fake relationship to screw Dan over. Now that we're together, you're unhappy about having to fake that we *aren't* together."

His lips twitched. "I hate it when you're rational and make sense."

"Get used to it." I snickered. "Go to work, honey. I'll see you later."

His kiss was warm and sweet. "I'll be looking even if I can't touch."

After Lyon left, I puttered about the house a bit, thinking how nice it would be to come home and have Lyon with me every night.

I decided to go to The Book Nook to see how Gordon was doing. Even though he said everything was fine, I didn't want to lose track of my business. When I pushed open the door, Gordon was ringing up a sale, and his eyes lit up.

"Miles. I didn't know you were coming."

I unwrapped the scarf from around my neck. "I decided to stop by before going to The Lyon's Den to see how you're doing. Looks like smooth sailing."

He nodded eagerly. "It's great. Brittany has been a real

help, and sales are steady, and I was thinking about some new ideas. Now that you're here, maybe we can talk?"

"Sure." I joined him behind the counter. "Tell me what you're thinking."

"Well, what if we host readings for LGBTQ authors? It's hard for them to get space in the mainstream bookstores, especially if they're not with a publisher. We could do nonfiction, poetry, and autobiographical readings as well as fiction."

"I like it. I'm gathering you have some authors in mind?"

Eyes bright, he nodded. "Yeah. Tom—my boyfriend—is in a theater group, and he knows a lot of authors of plays and short stories."

"Sounds good. Start the ball rolling, and when you have a lineup, we'll discuss."

"And…"

"And?" I laughed. "You *have* been busy thinking."

"Yeah. I think we should have drag queen story hour. It's a great way to get kids into the store. We carry children's books but don't do much to promote them."

"Another good idea. Gordon, I love it. I'm glad I decided to make you the manager here."

He beamed at me. "Thanks, Miles. How's everything going with you? Are you and Lyon…you know…" He waggled his brows, and I couldn't help my face burning.

"We're finding our way."

Gordon snorted. "I've been to your house. Only one way to the bedroom. Up the steps."

"Ha! Okay, okay. Enough."

"How's the library going over at the club? Are the members using it?"

"Yep. We're busy as hell, and I'm already ordering more books."

"Great. Looks like we're both doing what we love." He snickered. "And whom."

"Wiseass. I'll talk to you tomorrow. Keep up the great work, and we'll meet next week about your ideas."

"Thanks, Miles. I really appreciate it."

On the car ride to the city, I thought about the future—having Lyon move in with me, facing Dan with that decision, and giving Gordon increasing responsibility in The Book Nook…I had the chance to reach my ultimate joy—a family—and it had me wondering about something I never dared to before.

*Take it easy. One step at a time with Lyon.*

I entered the Den and noted the festive atmosphere. Pretty young women were strolling around, wearing sparkling shorts and bikini tops and carrying trays filled with shot glasses, lime wedges, and salt shakers. Banners with the picture of the tequila bottle draped the walls. Men waited in line to take pictures with smiling Dorado girls.

I spotted Lindsey at a table with a laptop in front of her. In true CEO mode, she was issuing directives to her assistants, with Dan at her side. When he saw me, he waved.

"Miles. I didn't know you were coming."

"Yeah. Have to show support for my family." God, I hated faking it, but Lindsey was too busy to care and Dan didn't even notice.

Lindsey huffed. "It's a struggle to get some of these men to try tequila. Most are die-hard Scotch drinkers. Crystal," she called out to one of her staff. "Make sure all the shot glasses are filled and have the bartender display the full bottles."

Dan frowned. "Linds, they're on it."

"No, they're not. There's only one bottle on the bar. I want four or five, labels out. And the bartender should be making margaritas."

"My members aren't margarita drinkers, Lindsey. I told you that initially when you proposed this idea," Lyon's voice rumbled, and heat rushed through me. "Hello, Miles."

"H-hi."

Outrageously handsome in a gray suit, violet-and-white shirt, and a deep-purple tie, Lyon arched a brow. "How have you been?" His wicked smile sent a delicious thrill through me.

*You know exactly how I've been. You were inside me not four hours ago, making me scream.*

"Fine."

"Miles, come sit next to me." Frowning, Dan pulled out a chair.

"Yes, Miles. Go sit by your brother." Lyon smirked.

I scowled but took the chair and sat. A waiter brought me a glass of red wine, and I gave him a faint smile. "Thanks."

"You're welcome. Do you want your turkey sandwich?"

*Shit.* I'd forgotten the waiter would know what my preferred lunch was.

"Uh, no thanks. I'm fine."

"How do they know what you like?" Dan asked me, clearly confused.

I shrugged. "Lucky guess? I don't know. How's the launch going? The crowd looks into it."

"They are," Dan said. "Despite Lindsey's complaints, the reception is good. We're hoping to see a spike in store sales after this."

I sipped my wine, watching Lyon from beneath my lashes as he worked the room, joking with members and lightly flirting with the women, who were more than happy to hang on his words and cling to his arm, most likely playing up to his ego. I smiled to myself. I wasn't worried. I knew who'd be in my bed that night and every night after.

An elbow poked me.

"Earth to Miles."

I jumped to see Dan frowning at me.

"What? Why're you looking at me like that?"

Why did I feel so damn guilty for being in love?

"What's going on with you?"

"Why? Because I'm not your little puppy rolling over to do what you want? I'm here to support your wife. Why are you starting shit?"

Uncle Harry and Scott arrived, heading directly to Lyon's side. There was a huddle for a few minutes, and then all three approached us. Uncle Harry removed his cap.

"Congratulations, Lindsey, on the launch. It seems to be a success."

She dipped her head. "Thank you. I-I know this is awkward—"

"Not for me, dear girl." To some, Uncle Harry might appear to be a silly old man, but I knew how wise he truly was, and he showed it right at that moment. "In truth, I was happy you and Lyon didn't marry. I never thought the two of you were good for each other, and I know you didn't love each other. Lyon deserves better."

I noticed he left out that Lindsey deserved better as well, and from her deep blush, she hadn't missed the subtle dig.

Red-faced, Dan shifted in his chair. "I'm sorry, Uncle Harry."

"Save your apologies, Dan. I didn't say I was accepting any, and even if I was, it certainly would not be from you. Lindsey, while Lyon's ex-fiancée, didn't know him as well as you—which is not to say I'm excusing her behavior, but I don't have long-running ties to her. She and I can be cordial." He coughed, and Lyon waved toward the bar. Immediately, a waiter brought a glass of water, which Harry accepted and took a long drink. He handed it to Lyon and fixed Dan with a frown.

"But you? I'm ashamed of you and disappointed, not only by your actions before the day of the wedding, but how you've handled yourself after everything came to light."

I buried my face in the glass of wine I held, but inwardly I cheered Uncle Harry on. I was sure Dan was seething. A side-eye check of him confirmed my suspicion.

"I-I guess I could've handled it better."

"You guess? You used your fists on someone."

"Maybe we can hold off on this until after the launch?" Lindsey said, looking frustrated and increasingly annoyed.

Uncle Harry remained unperturbed. "I don't see why. One thing has nothing to do with the other."

"Because I'm trying to concentrate on my business."

"Which is admirable for you, but as you are no longer a potential family member, your wishes don't affect me. Nor do Dan's. I'm here solely for Lyon."

Lyon stooped and placed a kiss to Uncle Harry's cheek. "You're my hero. And because I have zero desire to stand here and have this conversation, I'm going to remove myself. If you'll excuse me, Uncle Harry. Lindsey, per our contract, my sole purpose here is as the distributor for your product. I'm not required to, nor will I do anything to help promote your tequila. If it all goes down in flames, so be it. I'm going to have lunch with my brother and uncle."

With his hand holding Uncle Harry's arm, Lyon gave us all his back, and the three of them walked away. Lindsey said nothing, continuing to study her numbers and talk to her assistants via her headset. Once the three men were out of earshot, Dan snorted.

"Who gives a shit what he has to say? Harry's just an old fool."

I winced at his nasty tone, and it hit me then: Why, at my age, was I chasing Dan's approval? Why was I the one who had to give up even a moment's worth of happiness and joy for him, when he was so unconcerned about me? Dan was a married man and a father-to-be. If his wife's health and unborn child's safety weren't enough to keep him in line, nothing ever would. Not me, certainly.

"I have to go."

Lindsey paid me no mind, but Dan's brows drew together.

"Why? I thought you'd hang out and we could have lunch."

"I have a lunch date." I rose to my feet. "With Lyon." The storm clouds brewed in Dan's eyes, and he opened his mouth, but I put my hands on the table and leaned in close. "Don't. Don't make me choose, because I swear you won't like the outcome. I'm done. I've been your obedient puppy for way too long. I'm living my life now, like you are, other people's opinions be damned."

"But he—"

"Loves me. And I love him. He was willing to wait until Lindsey had the baby, out of respect for her health, but it's not fair to us. And if you're so concerned with your wife's pregnancy, you're the one who should keep quiet and not upset her. Not me."

"The first chance he gets, he's going to cheat on you."

A wide smile broke across my face. "Yeah? I guess you're the expert on that, aren't you?" I turned on my heel and walked to Lyon's table, where I stopped between his and Uncle Harry's chairs. "Is this seat taken?"

Lyon gazed up at me, then over my shoulder. "I thought you were going to stay with Dan and Lindsey?"

I sat with a contented huff. "Revenge may be sweet, but it's ultimately unsatisfying."

"Explain, please."

A glass of red wine appeared before me, and I cradled it in my hands. "I don't want to hide anymore. It's not fair to me…to us. I told Dan that if he couldn't behave for the sake of his wife and child's health, I shouldn't be held to a different standard and have to change my life for him."

Still, Lyon protested. "I know how important your relationship with your brother is. I don't want to come between you."

"The only one coming between Dan and myself is Dan. It's his choice."

I sipped my wine and listened to Scott talk about the new baby. Lyon remained quiet until Scott left for his office and Uncle Harry's friend Maxwell appeared and they moved to their own table to sit together and have tea.

"They're very close, aren't they?"

"Extremely."

I could guess what Lyon wasn't saying and respected him keeping quiet. It wasn't his story to tell. "They've been together for so long. I don't think I remember Uncle Harry not being with Maxwell."

I set my glass on the table. "I decided I'm not willing to play this game, hoping Dan comes to his senses about us. I want to be free to be with you in the sunshine as well as the shadows. Lindsey will have her baby, and I'll still be in love with you. Nothing's going to change that. I've wanted you my whole life. I won't hide for Dan or anyone."

Eyes shining, Lyon took my hand, rubbing his thumb over mine. "I just want you to be happy."

"With you, finally I am."

# *Epilogue*

*Six months later*

*Lyon*

I stood under the flowered arch, nervous but excited. As I'd been doing all afternoon, I put my hand in my pocket to touch the rings and make sure they were there. The minister gave me a nod.

"Ready?"

"I believe so."

First Beth, holding Lilah, walked down the aisle. The little girl scattered rose petals at their feet. Maxwell walked with his great-niece, followed by Uncle Harry with Scott. After fifty-plus years together, they'd decided to get married, and

Uncle Harry had confessed he'd still had a spate of nerves when Maxwell presented him with a ring.

From Uncle Harry's brilliant smile, I gathered those nerves had been replaced by happiness. We were in the backyard of Miles's house, which Beth had decorated with pots of flowers and fairy lights strung in the trees, giving it a magical feel. Twilight had begun to fall, and for after the ceremony, a banquet table had been set up to hold the intimate wedding dinner celebration.

I listened as they recited their vows, awed and overcome with emotion at the courage it took to live their lives. When they kissed, the sun was setting over the horizon, painting the sky with brilliant strokes of orange, lavender, and red, as if the world was also celebrating and expressing its joy through the glorious color.

There weren't many at the wedding dinner, but present were the people who mattered most to both of them. I'd never met Maxwell's family, and Miles and I enjoyed talking to his great-niece and nephews, who were as thrilled as us that the two men had made their lifelong partnership official.

A tall, gray-haired man accompanied by a young woman walked into the yard from the side entrance. I frowned.

"Who the hell just opens a gate and walks into a private party? Assholes need to leave." I stood and strode across the grass to confront them, Miles and Scott following a step behind. None of us would allow anything to spoil Uncle Harry and Maxwell's special day. It wasn't until I was close enough to see the man's face under the backyard lights that I stopped short.

"The fucking hell."

"Lyon."

My father put out his hand, but I didn't return the gesture, and neither did Scott.

"Dad." Scott's brows drew together. "What're you doing here?"

"Harry invited me. I figured since Shauna and I were in the States, we would stop by." He directed a beaming smile at the woman clinging to his arm, who didn't say a word to us. She couldn't have been over thirty. And I didn't miss the enormous diamond on her hand.

"Number five or six?" I mused. "Or is it seven?" I tapped my chin. "I've lost track."

My father's smile faded. "Don't be disrespectful. Shauna and I got engaged two months ago. She's in town for her final wedding-dress fitting. We're getting married in Maui next month."

"How sweet."

Uncle Harry interrupted us. "Charles. I didn't think you'd make it."

"We wouldn't miss it. Our flight was delayed, or we would've been here earlier."

I couldn't remember the last time I'd seen my father, and begrudgingly, I had to admit he looked well. Selfishness must be good for the skin.

"How come you didn't tell us you'd invited him?" I asked Uncle Harry. "It would've been nice to get a heads-up."

"Because I didn't know if he would come. Your father and you two boys are the only family I have left. I always hold out hope, however feeble, that some reconciliation can be had. Scott has children. Perhaps he wants them to know their grandfather. As you know, life is short."

"Well, I'm fine as is, thanks. I've done just peachy without him, and I hardly think I need a stepmother who is probably ten years younger than me." Miles's hand crept into mine, and I held on to it like the lifeline he was. My father immediately homed in on us.

"You're with him? I thought by now you'd be married maybe and have children. Like your brother."

Scott scowled. "Don't try and pit Lyon and me against each other. We're both very happy with our lives."

Only because I loved Uncle Harry did I not tell my father to go to hell.

"First of all, *he* has a name. It's Miles. I'm sure you remember him, considering how close the families were. Oh, wait. That's right. You were never there." I huffed out a breath that hurt deep in my heart. "And yes. We're together. And one day we'll get married too." I didn't know why I blurted that out. Miles and I hadn't yet gotten to the point of marriage talk.

"I haven't seen Miles in ages. As I recall, his brother is your best friend."

I didn't bother to correct him. It didn't matter. He didn't need to know I had neither seen nor spoken to Dan in months. Not since Lindsey's tequila launch at The Lyon's Den.

"Uncle Harry, I'll leave you to your host duties. I'm going to finish my dinner." Still hanging on to Miles's hand, I walked away, but of course, my father couldn't let it go and called out after me.

"I thought maybe you'd matured enough that we could have a conversation and try to work on our relationship."

Letting go of Miles's hand, I stalked over to him. "Relationship? There is no relationship. You're my father by blood, but that's the only connection we have. You chose a life of partying and sleeping around, over your children."

"I should've never married your mother. We were wrong for each other."

My laughter was broken, with little humor. "You think so? What about all the others after her?" My gaze fell on Shauna. "Good luck. You'll need it."

"Charlie loves me, and I love him." She pouted and tossed her flowing mane of red hair. "He's everything I ever wanted."

*I'll bet he and his bank account are.*

I didn't voice my thoughts. With the number of ex-wives he had, I was sure my father had an ironclad prenup, ready for his lawyers to pull up when he replaced one wife with the next.

"People make mistakes, Lyon. I'm sure you've made many in your life."

"Business-wise yes, but not when it comes to family. I stick by my own. Always. You said I should be mature enough? I had to be like a father to Scott since we were kids. I took him to his first baseball game and taught him how to drive. Me. Not you." By then, I was breathing heavily, but I didn't care. A lifetime of hurt spilled out. "Because you were never there. Not for me or for him. Not for our birthdays or graduations, none of it. Only Uncle Harry was. He was a better parent than either of you ever was."

"I think we should go to the table." Miles had come over and now tugged at my hand, and I let him lead me away. By the time we found our seats, I'd calmed down. After wiping my face with a napkin, I shook my head, grimacing.

"Dammit. I didn't mean to lose control like that. I'll have to apologize to Uncle Harry." I picked up my Scotch, hating how my hand trembled.

"Your father is a lot like Dan. Sees only what he wants to and doesn't think how his actions affect others." Miles chewed on a breadstick.

I knew how their separation hurt Miles. From the time Miles told Dan we were together, Dan had basically shut him out, and though Miles claimed he was okay with it, I knew better.

"Has Lindsey had the baby yet? She must be due by now."

Teardrops glittered on his long lashes. "Yeah. Three weeks ago. I spoke to my mom. I didn't want to say anything to you."

*Bastard.*

"I'm sorry, baby. One day he'll wake up and get it through that thick head of his that family is more important than being right."

Miles wiped his eyes. "Shouldn't you practice what you preach? Your father's here, and from all appearances wants to make an effort to reconcile."

"There's a difference," I said grimly. "You and Dan had a falling out because he loved you too much. My father is the opposite. He didn't love us enough."

Miles pressed a kiss to my cheek. "Then I'll have to make it up to you and love you so much, it'll wash away the hurt."

"You can never love me too much, because it'll never be enough. I'll always want more from you." I didn't know what I'd done to deserve a man like Miles, but I was a greedy son of a bitch. I recognized I had the perfect diamond and wasn't about to fuck up the best thing in my life. I planned to hold on to him with both hands and never let him go.

"And what was that you said to your father? Do you really want to get married one day?" His eyes sparkled like the twinkle lights hanging above us, and I loved him so much, it hurt to breathe.

"I want to prove I can be faithful. Loving. And deserving of a man like you."

"You don't have to prove anything to me." Miles touched my cheek. "I'm not perfect. Far from it. But I'd love to marry you one day."

I patted his cheek. "I know. And it wasn't a question." I grinned. "You're mine."

"Now who's being bossy?"

The following morning, I didn't tell Miles where I was going. He assumed the club, but I had other plans. Living together for almost six months now, I knew him as well as myself, and though we'd laugh and tease each other, the brightness had dimmed in those special smiles he gave me, all because of his estrangement from Dan.

Last night, after the wedding was over, Miles had been checking out Dan and Lindsey's social media, and it broke my heart to witness his distress as he scrolled through pictures of her family and his parents with the baby. Then earlier that morning, he'd spent an hour on the phone with his mother, who said she'd tried to talk to Dan to get him to change his mind but he steadfastly refused.

It was time for me to get involved. I didn't want my guy hurting, and I intended to do something about it. Nobody made Miles cry and got away with it.

That was why, at eleven in the morning, I was at the corporate offices of Halloran's, where Dan had his token job. When I appeared at the front desk, the secretary recognized me from all the prior years of my friendship with Dan and shook her head.

"Sorry, Lyon. He's home today. The baby had a doctor's appointment, and he went with Lindsey."

"Thanks."

I hustled out and into midtown traffic to hail a cab. Half

an hour later, I was chatting up Dan's doorman, who knew me well.

"Christos, how goes it?" I leaned on the front desk, all chummy-chummy, with a grin like butter wouldn't melt in my mouth. "Long time no see."

"Lyon. How's it going? Can you believe your buddy is a father?"

"I know. Crazy times. She's so cute, though, right?"

"Yeah. Lindsey's got her all dressed up like a little doll."

"Are they back from the doctor's? I have a special gift for them I want to drop off."

"Yeah, sure. Go on up."

I gave him a wink, and we bumped fists. "Thanks. Catch you later." I rode up the elevator, uncertain what I was going to say. I made my way down the familiar hall to his corner apartment and rang the bell. When Dan answered it, his face grew tight and he started to slam the door, but I put my foot in the way and my shoulder to it and pushed my way inside.

"What the fuck are you doing here?" he hissed at me. "My daughter is asleep, and I swear if you do anything to upset her…"

"If she's asleep, how can I upset her? I came to talk about Miles."

In an instant his face turned from rage to fear. "What's wrong? Is he sick? Did something happen to him?"

"Physically he's fine. But he's heartsick and heartbroken. And I can't stand seeing him so sad. I want to talk to you."

Mistrust filled Dan's eyes, but after a moment, he jerked his head. "Come in and sit down. Lindsey's in with Maddy."

I settled on the couch, and he took the love seat facing me. I rested my elbows on my knees and stared at him. A stranger I'd known all my life.

"Miles and I are still together after all these months."

His jaw thrust out, but he said nothing.

"I love him." When Dan snorted, I questioned, "Why is that so hard for you to believe?"

"Because I know you."

"No, you don't. Not anymore. Just like I don't know the man you are now. You say I'm still the same man going through lovers, but what makes you different? Because you married Lindsey? I'd marry Miles in a second, but I want him completely happy." I ran my hands through my hair. "And he won't be until the two of you make up."

Lindsey had come into the room during my speech and sat next to Dan. "I know you'll get mad at me for saying it, Danny, but Lyon's right. You miss Miles, and I think it's time for you to put this silliness behind you and make up. Maddy should know her uncle."

"But Lyon's going to hurt him."

"Goddammit. People change. Look at you—married with a baby daughter I know you'd kill to protect. I'll tell you the whole unfiltered truth. I'll admit that when I first started seeing Miles, it was for revenge, but your brother is way too smart—smarter than the two of us, for sure—and knew what I was doing. But he was so pissed at you for warning me away from him that he agreed to play my game of revenge as well."

"Both of you played me?"

"Yes." I smiled to myself. "But somewhere along the way, it stopped being a game, and I fell in love with him. How could I not? He's the most caring, kind, decent, loving person I've ever met. And crazy enough, he loves me too. He saw something in me worthy of being loved, even when I didn't think it existed. I'd never cheat on him because I'd rather cut off my arm than hurt him. Say whatever you want about me, I don't care, but you know I don't cheat. I'd rather walk away.

I'd never, ever do either to Miles. He means everything to me. He is everything."

Lindsey stared at me and nodded. "I know Lyon well enough to be able to tell if he's lying." She bit her lip. "He's not. He really loves Miles."

Dan balled his hands into fists. "I miss him. So damn much. I know how much he loves kids, and he'd love being Maddy's uncle."

"Then let him. Scott and Beth are going to have a baby next month, and I know he's thrilled, but I've caught him looking at the pictures you've put up of your daughter on social media." When Dan brushed at his eyes, I went in for the kill. "Let him go, Dan. You can't shield him from all of life's hurts. Who among us hasn't made some dumb mistakes? And while we're at it, let's be real." I fixed him with a hard gaze. "You slept with your best friend's fiancée. That was a deliberate choice you made. What happened to Miles in college was beyond his control, and it's unfair to keep him shackled to that. And by constantly reminding him of it and the other mistakes he's made, you won't let him move on and grow."

Dan lowered his eyes but wouldn't answer, and my heart sank. I couldn't grovel anymore. A cry sounded from the bedroom, and a minute later, a woman dressed in a uniform walked out with a swaddled bundle in her arms.

"She's hungry, Mrs. Halloran."

Lindsey took the baby and left us without a word. I knew my time was up.

"I'm going, but I hope you think about what I said."

Leaving Dan where he sat, I let myself out of the apartment. In the cab to the Den, I tapped on the window. "Can you make a stop, please, and wait?"

"It'll cost you waiting time, buddy."

"Not a problem."

When we hit midtown, I had the cab pull over, and I ran out. Once I had what I wanted, we were on our way again. I had a busy day ahead, as it was end of the month when I did reconciliation of numbers. We'd had several benefits at the Den and raised money for hospitals and children's charities. I was damn proud of our accomplishments and was already planning how to exceed them. That afternoon, I interviewed ex-baseball player Walker "Walk Off" Scanlon for membership, and when he mentioned he was a spokesperson for several children's charities, we set up a meeting to discuss how the Den could help. Miles was at The Book Nook, organizing the signings Gordon had arranged. At six, I came out of my office for a break to stretch my legs and get a drink. Victor brought me a glass of water and sat.

"Join me, why don't you?"

Victor's grin was cocky. "Thanks. Just checking to see how the wedding went. Harry and Maxwell get off all right?"

"Yep. They flew out an hour ago. Wedding was great." I drummed my fingers on the table. "My father showed up with his new flavor of the week. Had a diamond on her finger as big as an egg."

Victor's eyes went wide as saucers. "Damn. Did you speak with him?"

"Yeah. Long enough to tell him I didn't want to end up being a man like him."

"Sorry, Boss. That had to be rough."

I finished my water. "Actually, it was a good thing. It put things in perspective and gave me a kick in the ass as to what I needed to do."

"Which is?" Victor leaned back and crossed his arms.

"Nothing I'm going to tell you yet." I checked my watch. "Matter of fact, I'm leaving early. I have stuff to do." I rose to my feet. "I'll be in late tomorrow."

"You know that already?" Victor's brows rose. "Got a hot night planned?"

"Maybe. See ya."

Anticipation rising, I left the Den for home.

*Miles*

I'd been considering this proposal for a while, and with six months of solid, climbing profits, I knew the time was right.

"Gordon?"

His brow was furrowed as he peered at the iPad, arranging the calendar. "Hmm?" He met my eyes over the screen.

"Put that aside for a sec. I want to talk to you."

"Uh, sure." He set the iPad down and clasped his hands. "Is something wrong? Did I make a mistake somewhere?"

I smiled. "Just the opposite. You're doing an incredible job. So much so that I want you to take over The Book Nook full-time. I'm going to let you build up equity, and then you and I will own it fifty-fifty."

Gordon's eyes widened. "Me? You want me to be a partner with you?"

I was enjoying his reaction. "Yeah. What do you say?"

"I mean…I love working here, but I'm not sure I'm ready to own it. Plus, that takes lots of money, which I don't have."

"I can respect that. But I want you to know that the opportunity is here when you are."

Shiny-eyed, Gordon blinked rapidly. "Thank you for having faith in me. No one else ever has, so it really means everything."

Gordon's parents had turned their backs on him when he'd come out, and I felt like an older brother to him. Which was ironic, considering my situation with my brother.

"You'll always have a place with us. I'm going home now, but we'll talk tomorrow, okay? And anytime you want to revisit this, you let me know."

Gordon swiped at his eyes and nodded.

Feeling lighter at heart, I left for the quick walk around the corner.

"Miles?"

I stopped short. Dan stood in front of me, but it wasn't him I stared at. A bundle swaddled in blankets lay cuddled in his arms.

"Is that Madeline?"

"Yeah." A proud smile on his face, Dan peeled away the blankets from her face, and my heart melted. Big eyes held mine, and a little hand waved in the air.

"She's gorgeous." I wanted to laugh and cry, hug him and her, but I remained frozen with shock that after all these months of silence, he'd shown up. "Thanks for bringing her to see me."

"I'll walk home with you."

He kept pace with me as we turned the corner and walked up the steps. I slid the key into the lock and asked him, "Do you want to come in?"

"Yeah. If that's okay. I'd like to talk."

Overcome, I nodded and walked into the house.

"Why are you here?" I had a sneaking suspicion but wanted confirmation.

"Uh…Lyon came over. We talked, but he didn't know I'd be coming by."

As I'd suspected. I washed my hands and held out my arms. "Can I…can I hold her?"

He nodded and carefully placed her in my arms. I gazed at her tiny, perfect features. "Hi, Maddy. I'm your uncle Miles." I tipped my chin. "Want to sit? Let's go to the living room."

We sat on the couch, and I waited. I figured since he'd come to me, he had something important to say.

"I—I'm sorry, Miles." He hung his head. "I was wrong." He played with the handle of the diaper bag he'd placed on the floor at his feet.

"About?" I needed to hear him say it.

"Everything. I shouldn't have tried to control your life because of what happened in your past. I…uh…I've made my share of mistakes, and it wasn't fair to hold you to a different standard." His pleading eyes met mine. "But I didn't do it for any other reason than I love you and didn't want to see you taken advantage of and hurt again."

I allowed myself a tiny smile. How could I stay angry while holding such a delicious bundle of life? But Dan couldn't simply walk in after six months of silence and expect absolution. I needed more.

"I understand, but love doesn't give you the right to control my life to the point where you deliberately make me unhappy."

"I couldn't see past Lyon and his behavior."

"What about your behavior? I don't recall you being a saint." His face flamed, but I refused to let him dump everything on Lyon and not take responsibility.

"I know, I know." He glanced around the room, his eyes

settling on a photo of Lyon and me laughing as we danced under the stars at a party at Scott and Beth's house. I'd never been as in love with him as I was that night. "You're really happy with him."

"I love him. With every piece of my soul. And I know he loves me too."

Maddy began to whimper and squirm, and I handed her over to Dan, who laid her on the sofa and put a pad under her, then expertly changed her diaper. He put a pacifier in her mouth and laid her over his shoulder.

"I guess I can stop being so overprotective. I'll always have your best interests at heart, but I won't butt into your life like I have been." He rubbed Maddy's back. "I have someone else to watch over now, and you have Lyon."

"So you're okay with Lyon and me being together? Seems like a pretty shocking turnabout."

"Sometimes it takes a loss to get you to see what you really need. And I need my little brother."

"I need you too, but I also need Lyon. Can those two things coexist?"

He wrapped the sleeping baby in her blanket and slipped the diaper bag over his shoulder. "I guess we'll have to see."

I let him out and stood for a moment, thinking.

"Did you two have a nice talk?"

I jumped almost a foot when Lyon spoke behind me.

"Were you here the whole time?"

He chucked and slid an arm around my waist. "Yep."

"Did you hear Dan and me?"

"I did."

"And?" I poked him. "What do you think? And why do I have to drag this out of you?"

"Because it has nothing to do with me. You and Dan are

brothers and have to work it out. It's your decision alone to make."

"But I love you."

He held me close. "And I love you. Which is why no matter what, I'll be behind you."

"Never behind me," I whispered. "I want you at my side."

"Hey." He kissed my ear. "Do me a favor."

"Mm, what?" I had visions of him asking me to get naked.

"Reach into my pocket."

"Is that another way of asking me to tickle your pickle?" I teased at his groin, but to my surprise, he didn't laugh and pushed my hand away.

"Do it," he murmured. "Please?" I reached into the pocket of his slacks and felt a small box. My heart slammed. "That's it." Lyon's hand closed over mine, and together we pulled out the little box.

"Lyon." I licked my lips. "What is this?"

"I think you should open it and see."

"I can't. My hands are shaking. Open it for me?"

His eyes sparking indigo light, Lyon flipped the box open so it faced me. A gold ring sat in black velvet, and he picked it up. "Marry me?"

"Are you sure?" But I couldn't stop myself from holding out my hand, and Lyon's wicked, thrilling grin as he slid the band on my finger ignited the flame flickering between us to a full-blown conflagration.

"You're the one. The man to whom I willingly gave a heart I didn't know I had. The one I can't sleep without anymore, even if you do steal my covers. The one I don't want to live without. And can't. Please say yes. I love you."

I thought about being the kid always on the outside, watching, never fitting in, making the wrong choices. That young Miles would have never imagined a night like this was possible, with a man like Lyon asking him the question of forever.

"Yes." I kissed him. "Yes. Yes."

"Good." Lyon nibbled on my lips. "Now let's go upstairs. This might've started as a game of sweet revenge, but now I'm playing for keeps."

I hope you enjoyed reading Lyon and Miles's story and consider leaving a review. Reviews make such a difference to an indie author and enable me to keep doing what I love—bringing you happily ever afters for people who were denied happiness for so long.

Were you wondering about Victor the bartender?
I have a steamy short.
He definitely surprised me—the little devil.
**https://claims.prolificworks.com/free/zPGKB5vF**

# ABOUT FELICE STEVENS

Felice Stevens has always been a romantic at heart. She believes that while life is tough, there is always a happy ending around the corner. Her characters have to work for it, because just like life in NYC, nothing comes easy and that includes love.

Felice is the 2021 Lambda Literary Award-winning author for best Gay Romance. She lives in New York City and has way too much black in her wardrobe. If she's not writing, you'll probably find her watching reality TV or procrastinating on FB in her reader group, Felice's Breakfast Club.

## CONNECT WITH FELICE

**BOOKBUB**
https://www.bookbub.com/profile/felice-stevens

**NEWSLETTER**
https://tinyurl.com/y85e69ab

**READER GROUP**
https://www.facebook.com/groups/FelicesBreakfastClub/

**FACEBOOK AUTHOR PAGE**
https://www.facebook.com/felicestevensauthor/

**INSTAGRAM**
https://www.instagram.com/felicestevens

**TWITTER**
https://twitter.com/FeliceStevens1

**WEBSITE**
felicestevens.com